Hey P.

Happy Birthday,
my favorite Tiefling
Paladin

Fate Favor You.

XO

i

DEDICATION

This book is the product of the effort of many years and uncountable
hours.
Throughout the process, my deepest inspiration came
from the person who said yes.

Thank you, Angel.

CONTENTS

ACKNOWLEDGMENTS

Faced with trying to figure out who to thank for helping me with this work has proven a worthy challenge. Thank you is insufficient a term for the contributions made, but I will try.

My brother Stephen is probably the first person to have ever known these stories, as it was he and I that played in these marvelous worlds as young children. He helped me crystalize my vast nebulous ideas into something that other people would be able to understand, and not just us.

I cannot say thank you enough to my wife Kristen, whose absolute command of the written word helped me see the little things that I was missing during the steeper parts of my learning curve.

Throughout the process, I was more than a little bit lucky to have kids who were able to share their energy and perspective and support.

Music has been part of my life for as long as I can remember. It has been a curse, a blessing, a path, a goal and the prize at the end too. I found that I was able to draw on the raw emotional imagery in many of the songs in my eclectic listening mixes. To that end, I would send out a big thanks to: Owl City, Cry of the Afflicted, Godsmack, Evanesance, Taio Cruz, Madonna-Timberlake, Jon Bonjovi, Ricky Martin, Jon McLaughlin, Eminem, Billy Joel, Quincy Jones, Kansas, Glass Tiger, Katy Perry, Guns'n'Roses, Johnny Clegg and Savuka, AC DC, Disturbed, Collective Soul, Klaus Badelt, Katrina and the Waves, Tyler Bates, Riverdance, Rihanna, Lorenna McKennitt, Tom Cochrane, Joni Mitchell and many others. They all helped me see the Twelve Realms with startling clarity.

When all is gone,
Despair's work, done.
The final note, in the dark,
You will hear with your heart.

> Part of *"Lament for a Lost World"*
> From the Academy Archives, Central Library.

Prologue, Part one - A Little Hope

"This is it? An empty room with four benches in it?" one of the brothers said, slightly louder than he had intended to. The others looked over at him from their tasks ruefully. He shrugged back to them, knowing he had voiced the question that most were thinking. The baby was awake now, and enjoying a fun game of "Dinner" with his mother. The baby's father was busy setting up a small apparatus with the short poles and components that they had each been carrying in their packs.

"Yes, this is a Communing Room. Only the Nexus on the Allgem Plains is a stronger focus point for the Core. And when we're done, he'll be safe," the old woman finished, sitting on a bench near to where her sons were setting up the device. The poles made a geometric shape resembling both a cube and a pyramid. The screen and tiny controls attached to it were dormant, waiting.

"All we need now," she continued, "is this." The matriarch pulled off her amulet, and opened the front cover. A glittering blue-and-green gem shone from inside. It caught the light of the torches and played it back in many colors. It also glowed, ever so faintly. She rose and placed it on the floor, in the middle of the now finished structure. She backed up a few paces then went over to where she had laid her staff down, against the bench. Her daughter and grandson were sitting there. The wide-awake infant suffered his mother's attempts to clean his face with impatience. His baby-blue eyes were sparkling with curiosity, and his pudgy hands waved about. He saw his grandma and reached out to her, ba-ba'ing happily.

"He'll not be harmed?" the young woman asked again, setting aside the feeding spoon and the last jar of food they had for him. She held him close to her face, drinking in his scent, his sound. The grandmother came forward and moved her finger close to his grasping fingers. He caught it gently and pulled it towards himself. She smiled warmly.

"No, love," she said. "This is absolutely the safest way to get him out of this Realm." She bent over and looked into the little one's eyes as he tried to chomp down on her finger.

"He'll have his chance there," she murmured.

"Then best it was done quickly, then," said his father, turning the little monitor on. The assembled components started warming up, humming gently. The Councilwoman nodded, kissed the baby on both cheeks, and rose to her feet. She took up position in front of the apparatus, and gripped her staff firmly. The hidden crystalline badge on her left shoulder started to glow, as well as the tip of her staff. Instead of trying to conceal her powers, she now called on them all as strongly as she could. She struck the floor with her staff twice, and a panel on the far wall opened, revealing a huge blue-green gem whose colors swirled about its surface. The jewel on her staff

2

flared brilliantly in resonance with the native stone, and an aura of swirling multicolored light enveloped her. She sent forth a bright beam from her eyes, aimed at the amulet on the floor. In the next moments, the Talisman lit up, and started to grow.

*

"Yes, we're picking up a power surge from the old Council building!" yelled the black-armored soldier into the com-unit in his helmet. "It's getting stronger by the second: Full-bore Gem-based power in use! Level's high enough to be seen from orbit." His unit was running double time march down the road leading into the city, weapons drawn, and the enormous, four-legged tracking beasts released from their leashes. They were growling and baying into the night, following the distinctive scent that energy had.

"Find that woman, soldier, and take her down. She has to be the last of the ruling Council for that accursed planet. Once she's gone, this planet will be done, and we can get on with the next phase." The neutral voice almost sounded satisfied.

"Yes sir!" the soldier shouted. He turned off the com-unit, and followed the sounds of the hunt. Maybe she would resist; maybe she had an escort, bodyguards even. He almost felt . . . excitement.

*

The pyramid shone with a swirling, milky, multicolored light, as energy gathered there. There was the faintest sound of rushing wind coming from it, as well as the loud crackle of power flowing. From the maelstrom, a strong clear voice emerged.

"You're alive, after all!" The words came from the coalescing image of an older man, dressed in a yellow and orange ceremonial robe, akin to the old woman's. He also

3

held a staff similar to hers, but the gem glowing at its tip was a brilliant yellow, instead of multicolored swirls.

"Yes, I'm alive, as well as what's left of my family," the old woman said, effort clearly showing in her voice and on her face. "It's time. Are you going to be able to help us?"

"You mean you're ready to send him, already?" he replied, startled. He looked around himself then peered closely at her. "There has been no news for weeks now. It's gotten that bad, then, has it?"

"I believe that we are possibly the last living souls left here. Our world has been destroyed." She let the importance of those words sink in for a second. Changing the subject, she nodded toward her grandson.

"He's only a baby, but also our last, best hope. You must see him safely hidden."

"He's truly Gifted," the boy's mother piped up. "He should be able to adapt to wherever he grows up. And he'll always see things differently than the children in your Realm." She moved to stand directly beside her mother. "Please, sir, help him. I beg you."

The man on the other side of the portal stepped forward, to the very boundary that separated them, his eyes set and glowing bright yellow with intensity.

"Dear girl," he said gently. "I have been your Realm's staunchest ally on my world's Council. Your mother will attest to that. I swear, by the Heart of Light, that I will care for him as if he were my own." He paused, the light in his eyes growing darker orange-red. "The Necromancers and their spies will NEVER find him, this I also swear!"

"Mother!" the baby's father shouted, staring more closely at the little screen on the apparatus. "We have a squad of hunters in the building: ten soldiers, three or four beasts. We have three minutes before they get here, at best." He tossed aside his traveling gear, and donned a battered, bright

4

red, light-armor vest. His vast Ruby strength was unfettered now. He drew his long sword from its sheath, pressing a button on the hilt, setting it shimmering with destructive scarlet power, then moved closer to the door. The brothers, who had been battle-ready from the start of their trip, retrieved their weapons and took up a triangular placement around the women and the portal.

"We have no more time," the matriarch said, drawing even more Power into herself from the Core of their world. "Bring him to the portal. When Saul reaches across the threshold, pass him over." The crackle of energy was rising in intensity again, reaching its highest point. "I'm very old. . . I will only be able to hold it open for a few seconds. Be ready, both of you."

The baby watched the lights of the portal mutely, absently stroking his mother's arm around his belly. The young woman burst into tears, sobbing once, then moved toward the nimbus of power. The image of the man became suddenly sharper, more in focus. The man on the other side braced himself, and then reached through the barrier, grimacing slightly as jags of power licked up and down his arms.

"Now! Give him to me now!" he grunted loudly, voice nearly concealed by the sound of power holding this doorway between worlds open.

Drawing the baby close, one last time, she said to him "Fate favor you, dear heart." Kissing him one more time, she quickly placed the baby into the man's arms. Trembling with effort, they enfolded the child protectively, and brought him through into another Realm. The old woman whipped the amulet that was the focus of this portal through after the baby, and it landed at the man's feet.

Holding the infant to his shoulder with practiced ease, the old man hooked the amulet with the end of his staff and flipped it lightly into the air. He caught it with the glowing topaz at the top then lifted his staff high, declaring in a voice strong enough for both worlds to hear: "It is done! He is safe across. Be at peace. You have done your part. I will take care of things now." A brilliant aura of yellow and white light came from the man's staff. It blinded them all for just a second, then, in an instant, it faded. Man and baby were gone.

Mother and grandmother cried openly, both relieved and agonized at the same time. Through a curtain of tears, the old woman let her face relax. Without the amulet for focus, the flow of power started to diminish, the mad swirling of colors slowing and fading. She let go of her staff with one hand and let it fall against her shoulder. Only her indomitable willpower kept her standing. She felt her daughter put an arm around her waist in thanks and sympathy. The giant gem slowly returned to its hiding place in the wall.

Then, with a deafening crash, something hit the wall from behind. Another crash occurred, and a blast of energy punched through from the other side, destroying the Gem and sending clouds of dust into the air. The Hunters had finally found their sanctuary. The soldiers paused only long enough for the dust to settle; the tall, four-legged, black and grey beasts did not, leaping through the jagged and crumbling hole with their red claws clattering on the stone and leaving scratches as they moved, baying wildly in triumph. They had found their prey.

The three men backed up to make a defensive circle. The women hugged each other for a moment, and then turned themselves toward the soldiers as well. The younger woman drew a smaller, scintillating sword, a rapier, no less dangerous than her husband's weapon, and activated a small shield on her forearm. The old woman, eyes wild and furious, took her staff in both hands. She blinked once then struck the ground hard with the end of her staff. The round gem at its tip turned from blue-green to a sharp sided, red crystal that had what looked like flames boiling inside of it. A haze of fire seemed to envelop her.

As one, they started humming the note A - one pure note. The same note that the very Heart of their world sang. It filled the room with more than simply sound; it seemed to raise the dust around them in shimmering little whirlwinds. It quickly got louder, and stronger, as a very old type of power responded to their call. The soldiers waited for a moment, not sure what to make of this. Finally, the single note got louder and louder until it shattered into an enraged scream, and with the dust and the very air helping them, the family leaped to attack. Fear, anger, sorrow . . . everything that had been lost, the nightmares that they had endured, all of it lent them strength and focus. Finally, they had a clear and visible enemy to fight. They held nothing back as they clashed weapons with their destroyers, all blind with berserker rage, with a determination comparable to Garnets and a fury that would have daunted Rubies.

*

When it was over, beasts leashed and weapons holstered, the lieutenant commanding this strike force noted in his voice-log that five opal refugees had not escaped, noting the date and time. As a personal note, he added that they had lasted longer than anyone his team has hunted to this point, and that he had to admit that he respected that. No survivors . . . of course.

*

Another Opening: (Beyond . . .)

<Is it beginning? >
<Yes. >
<Again? >
<Yes. You knew it would. It always does. >
<Well, maybe this time will be different. >
<Possible, but not likely. You know why. >
<Of course. >
<Well, then? >
<It's all such a waste. >
<And from the ashes will come the next spin of the Wheel. >
<There are other Wheels too. >
<Yes, of course. Sometimes they influence each other, sometimes not. There's no way to predict that, even for us. >
<I don't know. Something feels different this time. >
<What? >
<Can't say, exactly? I get the feeling that the Darkness will try to make use of the Wheel of Fate this time. >
Pause
<I hadn't considered that. They never needed to, previously. Hrmmm. >
<And if they use Fate . . . >
< . . . then there is the possibility . . . >
< . . . of Hope. >
<If Hope survives, then this Cycle might proceed differently. >
<Is there anything we can do? >
<You mean, beyond observing? >
<Anything. It doesn't have to be big. Something to help Hope survive this time . . . survive long enough to . . . >
<If the Wheel of Fate is spinning, then your answer might very well find us. All we can do is wait, and be ready. >

<The Cycle doesn't seem like such a long time anymore. >

<True. Anything different is good. >

*

Part 1

Early Days

Notable events in History for this day:
- *Sapphire and Ruby armies declared a cessation of hostilities, ending their four-year conflict.*
- *The Council acknowledged the current Energy Crisis in the Topaz Realm*
- *The first round of deportations began, forcing many people with Blue or Brown topaz powers back to their home regions.*

Kalpa City News Service

Chapter 1 - Sorting Day
(Topaz Realm, 11 years ago)

The Large Sun had set and the breeze coming off the fields carried the scent of yellow aster flowers. Saul breathed it in deeply. It brought to mind a time long ago when he had gathered those blooms to try to impress a young girl from Brumen Cala. He grinned to himself. It did bring him hope that he could find a little bit of the natural world speaking to him in such a densely populated urban area. It took your mind off the more unpleasant realities, sometimes. He would have to recommend a walk like this to some of his more irascible peers on the Council. With the Shadows beginning to loom on the horizon, everyone would need some connection to the Realm.

Thinking like this made seeing the rows and rows of black solar collectors on all the windows and rooftops in the city a little more bearable. Those clever machine-makers on Sapphire had invented them at the request of the topaz

Council, to help supplement the native powers here. They had no connection to the Heart of Light at all, having been constructed off-world, but they did gather the sunlight well enough, something like glowstones, only they did not release the light, they only stored it. That aspect of the technology never sat right with him.

He had never stooped to using them for any of his Light-constructs himself, but he knew that there were experienced Adepts of the Light these days who did, as disturbing a thought as that was. For the average citizen, though, being able to capture and release E.M. radiation of any kind was a step closer to having powers themselves, and that helped morale generally. That is what he kept telling himself, and he could almost believe himself now. Sighing once, he put those concerns to the side for what he had to do. The function he was attending deserved his brightest thoughts and outlook, and so it would be. He entered gates of the park, using his Staff of Office as a walking stick, and made his way down the manicured pathway to the central yard.

There, surrounded by old trees and statues, dozens of young children played on the large, brightly colored playground, all of them around two to three years old. Dressed in their best outfits, their parents and guardians labored to keep them as tidy as they could, despite dirt and dust. Running, climbing and sliding, they played in a celebration of motion that they would lose as they got older. Their own little universe was a world of discovery for them. All bright eyes and shining faces, several of them waved to Saul as he approached. That brought a smile to his lips. Their parents had trained them to acknowledge those with Light powers and not to fear them. If only all the children he had seen over the years had learned the customs and traditions. He had to stop himself from following that train of thought too far. Instead, he watched the children here.

He sat on a bench off to one side of the playground and once again marveled at what he saw. Tiny dramas, victories of friendship, territorial conquests and acts of great compassion were playing out before him. One boy threw a hand full of white sand in the air, thinking it funny, and it got into the eyes of one of his playmates who cried. The group of little girls all wearing the same little style of shoes telling the little one in new sneakers that she could not play with them; then the miffed looks on their faces as another little girl wearing sneakers come up and ask the first one to play. All the emotions and passions of the adult world, he noted, but none of the filters or subtlety. It was so straightforward and honest that it was very refreshing. The glossing over of their true natures would occur the older they got and that was always somewhat sad for Saul.

He had been a Selector for the Council for ten years now. He knew a few of his superiors thought this to be a dead-end job, a place to assign troublemakers. Saul knew better. He always enjoyed this first visit with the newest children of the Light and treated it seriously. These little ones were the future of the Realm. Caring for them was caring for the world to come. Hope and possibility mingled and distilled into beautiful young souls, that is what this group was.

A raspy high-pitched man's voice from behind him rent his moment of reverie. "So, what's the crop like this year? Any of these *null-born* brats showing signs of sparkle yet?"

Saul's expression darkened for a moment then became a mask of neutrality. He did not turn to face the speaker as he answered.

"Representative Pazos," Saul mused aloud. "Well-spoken as ever, I see. Knew you'd *brighten* my day here eventually. The children seem to be just that - twenty children, aged two to four, all of them fresh from their

Communing, innocent and pure as sunbeams. And aside from the odd argument over whose turn it is on the swing or the like, I don't think we'll have to worry too much about crowd control."

Pazos stepped forward, crunching the stones around the bench under his boots. Saul turned his head slightly; caught a glimpse of the man then immediately closed his eyes and shook his head, sighing. Pazos had chosen to wear the uniform that he wore when he attended sessions of the Council . . . immaculate yellow jacket, indicating his affiliation with the photic class of topaz powers, and his official Representative's sash and badge. He was entitled to wear this, but only off-worlders would have been impressed. Fortunately for everyone, at no time had Pazos ever had the ability or affinity to be chosen as an Apprentice of the Light. Saul could imagine the damage he would have done by now if he had become an Apprentice. The only thing that he could do with Light powers was change the color of his left eye for a few moments at a time. This detail did not keep him from making sure everyone treated him with the respect due someone much more powerful than him. The city of Kalpa - Saul could remember why he had stayed away so long from here. Coming here meant having to deal with this insufferable little man.

"Pazos," Saul sighed. "You were told not to dress formally for this. Every time I see you, you're treating everyone around you the same way you would deal with hooligans from Ruby or malcontent Emeralds hanging from the ceiling. The posturing and show are not necessary here."

"Just because you choose not to remind the *nulls* living here of who you are, or why they should be showing you the proper respect at all times, doesn't mean that I won't." Pazos made sure to straighten the medallion on his chest one more time. In doing so, Saul could see a personal hard-light projector strapped to his wrist, projecting the image of a fanciful watch around itself. How this servant-to-ambition ever got into public office with negligible Light powers was still a mystery to him.

"Well, I can't speak for everyone here, of course, but I know from experience that the citizens of Kalpa shouldn't be called *nulls*, because it is simply not true. Nobody here is completely devoid of any powers. All of them have some measure of potential to use the Spectrum in some way. It's why I'm here, after all. That means that they all deserve OUR respect. You haven't forgotten that, have you?" Saul turned a casual glance into a pointed stare for a second, before picking up his staff of office. With a gentle tap of his finger, the golden yellow crystal at its' top started glowing brightly. "Parents come from all over the Realm for this. They are nervous enough. We're going to help them as much as we can by following the time-honored, traditional method."

"Traditional? You mean you want to use the Arch? Really? Councillor Saul, that's one of the most outdated methods of testing imaginable, inefficient too! The Potentiometer in my pocket takes minutes to get results, with an acceptable margin of error. Using the Arch, we're going to have to spend at least an hour here. Humph." Then, he remembered who he was talking to and modulated his tone considerably. "But, of course, it's your call...sir." Pazos muttered quietly, with a show of respect that belied the insolence underneath. Saul gave him a withering glare, which caused Pazos to blink then bow his head, knowing that he had almost crossed a line there. He got out a small notepad and a stylus and started jotting things down quickly.

The glowing staff had gotten the attention of the parents, who descended upon the playground and claimed their little ones. Two little stragglers remained focused on their digging in the sand under the slide. A young couple came forward, took both little boys by the hand then led them away from the play area. Once the area was clear, Saul raised his staff and the glowing crystal blinked a couple of times, with the sound of gentle crystal chimes. The playground structure itself faded from view; a brightly colored, *solid-light* construct that had been hiding in plain view. All the parents and children made sounds of surprise, and applauded. It was not often that the average citizen got a chance to see a really sophisticated and well-built light construct like this. Saul grinned and waved his staff where the structure had been. With another crystalline chiming sound, rows of chairs appeared, both adult and child sized. The people applauded again then moved forward to take their seats.

"This is such a waste of time," whispered Pazos via a tight-beam message from the wristband that he wore, which mimicked an Apprentice's ability to communicate using only a pulsed beam of light. Saul needed no such apparatus to understand what the little man had to say. "We could have been on our way back by now."

<*As you said, this is my call. They deserve the same introduction to our culture as everyone else.*> Saul sent his responding tight-beam from his eyes back to Pazos' device. It would take a moment for him to read it, of course. That suited Saul just fine.

Saul stepped forward and a podium of simple light rays assembled in front of him. He waited for the last of the children to settle then cleared his voice.

"Welcome, ladies and gentlemen. My name is Saul, and I speak for Light." He set his staff into a holder behind him, and looked over the little ones, all glancing about, some focused on him, some noticing everything else. He grinned. "I'm so glad you've come today. I know that you have had to take time from your busy lives to be here. This ceremony is almost as old as the Realm itself, and for many years it has

16

been my honour to preside over it. Since you have all performed the traditional Communing when your children were born, they all have the touch of the Heart of Light upon them. Our task today is to begin helping them learn about what that touch means to them, whether it just means that they have a photic yellow's *skin-sight,* galvan blue's *zap-touch,* thermal brown's *convection will* or even the rare clear's *ultra-sight.* We should be able to guess at what their eventual power-level will be. Every child here has great potential. All will show the rudiment levels, and thus join our society. Some will show the potential to use the Spectrum more actively, which could mean that the Core might choose them as Apprentices when they graduate. Out of that group, a very select few will get the chance to attend the Academy, to hone skills to their own personal highest potential, and thus come back to us as our shining champions: Adepts of the Spectrum Light."

He paused a moment, knowing that all the adults were hearing the words and dreaming of what their little ones would accomplish. Even Saul had a vision or two in his mind, but he suspected that his were a bit different from everyone else's. He returned to his introduction: "We are here to celebrate new life, and hope, represented by these children. They are our future, and it is our duty to guide their steps in the Ways of the Spectrum to the best of our ability, so that they can realize their potential. To that end, I come before you, to help you choose the starting path best suited for them."

Pazos, grumbling about time wasted, had stepped to the side of the podium and was pulling out a series of non-descript metal rods from his dull grey briefcase. He worked with precise motions and in less than a minute, he had assembled a child-sized archway. Still grumbling under his breath, his face almost petulant, he picked up the constructed arch and moved forward until he was in front of the podium.

He set it down in the sand, and tapped the apex of arch once with the flat of his hand. The rods glowed with a milky light that flashed yellow, blue, smoky brown before turning completely clear. It settled back to the sheen of dull metal after this.

"This device is able to sense the hidden gifts - the potential, if you will - within each child. Each Realm has something similar for its children." Saul continued over the chatter of excited parents. "It will glow with the type of topaz power your child resonates with the most. Sometimes it is the same as your own, which is most often the case, but sometimes the Heart of Light chooses different topaz colors for them. It is impossible for us to know why, but we must trust the Core to have made the right choice. It is the best way that we can help your little ones learn to their full potential. When you are ready, have your children step through the arch, one at a time. We will record the results. Afterwards, I will remain here to answer any questions you have." Saul stepped back and to the side of the podium, beckoning to the listeners to approach.

Gingerly at first, then with growing confidence, the parents brought their children to the arch. Some little ones went through easily enough; some needed a little coaxing. Each time a child passed it, the rods would all glow one of the colors of the topaz Spectrum, and the parents would cheer and clap. The children had no idea, and just clapped along, or cried, or looked bewildered. Pazos noted the results of each test, and scribbled notes on his pad as to how brightly the arch glowed, how quickly, which colors appeared. The children were not different from their parents thus far, and none of the rarer topaz colors showed themselves, only the primary four.

Finally, the last couple brought two children forward - the boys from under the slide. The parents turned to grin and nod to Saul, who returned the grin, and nodded back. The first little boy, his bright red hair a tangle of sand and playtime, walked confidently up to the device. It started to glow a bright yellow even before he actually entered it. Pazos raised an eyebrow then scribbled even more furiously. As the boy passed through, the arch sent up a tiny flash of yellow light into the air, which floated down and hovered over the child for a moment before fading to nothing. His mother was there to greet him on the other side of the arch, hugging him warmly and kissing him many times.

"Still think the old ways are a waste of time, Pazos?" Saul mumbled to his aide, a hint of pride in his voice. "That sapphire-built junk wouldn't recognize this boy at all. They're set too low, and would have shorted out measuring him. We might have missed a potential Apprentice."

"Humph." Pazos grumbled in response, but less acrimoniously than before.

The mother of the red-haired boy brought the last little boy forward, his dark brown hair just as tangled as his playmate. She was reassuring him that everything would be all right. He nodded, looking up at Saul hopefully. Saul nodded, and gestured for him to walk through the arch.

With tentative steps, clutching a rectangular pendant on a colorful lanyard around his neck, the brown-haired toddler walked through the device. At first, the arch did not glow at all, which made everyone pause. Pazos stopped scribbling, Saul leaned his head to one side slightly. No one made a sound for a moment.

Then, the arch rattled audibly. It started glowing, slowly at first, then brighter and brighter. Then all four primary colors of the topaz spectrum started playing across its surface in a random seeming pattern. Then, like when his little friend had passed it, the arch sent up a flash of blinding visible light, in all four colors. It came back down, hovering in front of the child. Instead of fading, it exploded with a pop into a starburst firework. The little boy blinked, and stepped back a few paces. His eyes were wide and wet; the corners of his mouth were turning down and his lower lip starting to quiver. He started sniffing nervously, as frightened tears came to him. Saul moved instantly, walking over to him. The little boy reached his arms up, and his uncle swept him up into a comforting embrace. He buried his sad face into Saul's tunic, and hugged him around the neck. Saul wrapped him in his arms and whispered reassurances to him.

"You did a good job. That was wonderful. Did you see all the pretty colors?" Saul was murmuring to him as he returned to the podium. The boy nodded, nervous tears still spilling down his rosy cheeks. The red-haired boy and his parents came up and offered their reassurances. Saul hugged him once more then let the young mother take the boy back to her seat, where he sat on her lap, hugging her. Saul caught the parents' eyes and mouthed 'thank you' to them. They nodded in answer, and proceeded to entertain their charges.

Pazos was dumbfounded, his stylus forgotten. Then he started scribbling faster than he had yet. He did not stop until Saul had fielded numerous questions from the assembled parents. He slithered up to Saul's side.

"I did not know you had any children, Saul," Pazos drawled, savoring new information. "How could we not have known about him, eh?"

"Not son, nephew," Saul answered, picking up his staff which caused the podium to dissipate. "His parents perished in an accident, just after he was born. I was his only relative, so he came to live with me."

"This is still a surprise, Saul. Moreover, what was that display? He clearly has vast powers within him, but in all four disciplines?"

"Yes, I noticed that too."

"There has never been a child of the topaz Realm who was not one of the primary four spectra specifically. It has never happened before."

"So . . . the Heart of Light has made a different sort of choice for him. We don't have any say about that. All we can do is help him learn what he is able."

"But the test showed that he would have aptitudes . . . in all the areas of focus. All four areas!"

"Yes, it did."

"That thing said that he'll be able to learn any of the Disciplines, he might even be able to learn more than one. We're going to have to try and teach him ALL of them!"

"True."

"True? True?! No one can learn more than one set of disciplines! It is not done! He'll never realize his potential if he doesn't focus on one of them."

"Maybe he will be more skilled in one area as he gets older."

"Maybe, but he might simply stay at the Rudimentary level for his entire life."

Saul started walking toward the Council transport that was waiting for them outside of the park. He opened the door with a wave of his hand, and motioned for Pazos to precede him in.

"Then being MY nephew is the best thing for him. My duties bring me all over, into all four territories. He'll get his chance to learn the Rudiments of wherever he's living at the time."

"It's never been done, Saul. There will be talk about this, you know there will be." Pazos' voice was taking on almost a whining tone here. "The Council will want to be kept fully appraised of how he develops."

Saul sat down opposite Pazos in the comfortable seats of the large transport, and waved his hand at the door again, closing it. Then he turned and faced Pazos directly, and spoke in a low, even tone.

"They may ask me about my family life, if they wish to. I have many friends that I have known far longer than I have known you who will certainly be very interested in his welfare. But . . ." he leaned forward slightly, his tone becoming slightly darker. "I will not tolerate anyone, Council or otherwise, interfering in my personal affairs, nor that of my family. I would be most . . . displeased."

Pazos' eyes widened slightly, and a bead of sweat appeared on his forehead. He nodded, gulping, and chose not to say anything more. Saul leaned his head back, and closed his eyes as the smooth air vehicle whisked him back to the local Council chambers. There was work to do now.

"No, Pazos, you little shade-ghoul. You will not have any contact with, nor influence over my nephew. He will be free of you and those you answer to." Saul thought to himself. He knew that he would definitely have to pay very close attention now, since Toivo's potential had shown itself just a tiny bit. He had enough influence to keep this result from becoming public knowledge, but Pazos was right. There would be talk. He and his nephew would have to travel frequently as the boy grew. Saul would have to find all the corners of the Realm where they could hide in plain sight.

They *had* to hide…to keep Toivo safe. After the test of the Arch, this was much more than clear to him.

*

How many colors do you see?
One and two and more than three.
How many powers will there be?
All to share with you and me.
    Nursery Rhyme from the ruins of Opal

Chapter 2 - Home and Away
(Topaz Realm, 10 years ago, first day of preschool)

"Be good, Toivo," Saul was saying as his nephew hopped out of the hover-car. "Remember what we talked about."

"Iwilllloveyoubye!" the little boy babbled excitedly, jamming his words together almost too quickly. He waved to Saul then caught up to his friend Pho. The boys linked arms and marched in step through the tall metal doors of the Kalpa City Preschool Center. Pho's parents, Filamina and Rhyol, came over to Saul and greeted him.

"They seem to be set," Rhyol commented, looking to his wife, who was composing herself after having released her 'baby' into someone else's direct care for a couple of hours. Whether Pho was feeling any separation anxiety or not was entirely moot: she felt it strongly enough for all of them.

"Indeed. Toivo was so excited that he did not even notice that he skipped breakfast entirely."

"Best pre-school in the city," Filamina murmured. "Our boys are special. This place will be a good place for them to start out."

*

The boys certainly had fun, in those first days of school. Many silent little tests were happening with and around them, like a tiny dot of white light that flashed against their hands when they touched something they should not. Most of the children flinched away from it, which made the teachers nod and enter notes into their light-pads. Toivo reacted too, but only if he saw the dot with his eyes. The teachers were less enthusiastic about their notes for him.

Different children enjoyed different parts of the day. Pho, for example, joined any running and jumping game. He loved playing with the shiny reflecting shapes and glowstones. There was no light too bright for him; he would stare deeply at the suns themselves, just for fun.

Toivo liked running and jumping, but also hiding and exploring. He would play with the different things than Pho did, but he would lose interest after a very short time. Of all the children, he was most and least sensitive to the light at the same time: he tried to stare at the suns, like Pho, but only for a moment before he looked away with his eyes watering. On the other hand, he was virtually incapable of distinguishing the standard light intensities that made up some of the topaz Realm's primary technologies.

One part of the day held his undivided attention, though: story time.

When the chime sounded for the children to gather on the carpet, Toivo would appear at the front of the carpet, almost on top of the teacher's feet, eyes bright and eager. He would babble excitedly about any physical book the teacher had in her hands, guessing at the titles, the characters, what was going to happen. Even if it were a tale that the class had already heard before, Toivo would pay rapt attention, then be able to repeat the story word for word later. It got to the point where other students would gauge when to stop their activities by how quickly Toivo was getting ready to make his dash. A number of the other children started finding this funny, and giggled at Toivo when he ran. Toivo never noticed.

That day, the teacher had assembled the children on the carpet, as usual. Toivo had saved the spot beside him for Pho, who had come forward to wedge himself into the front row beside his friend. The teacher signaled for the children to back up a little bit, using a small glow-stone in his hand. All the children nodded, having understood the flashed message as easily as speech, started making room at the front of the carpet for whatever the teacher was about to show. Only Toivo remained there, sitting alone at the teacher's feet, oblivious to the silent, photic-language instruction. The teacher aimed the stone right at Toivo, and flashed the signal again. Toivo did not even blink, as any other child would have. Sighing, the teacher pocketed the stone, and resorted to speech.

"Toivo, move back," the teacher said, in a pseudo-patient voice. "You have to pay attention when I give instructions in Photic. You'll need to understand it if you want to succeed in school."

Toivo blinked, blushed then moved back to where Pho was waiting for him. His face stayed bright red. He made an effort to say nothing all the while holding back embarrassed tears. Was there any way for him to explain that he simply did not recognize that the blinking lights in the teacher's hand as anything more than pretty lights? He did not know. Right then, and there, he started feeling as if he were dumb. Fortunately, the teacher started projecting something into the space in the middle of the carpet. This distracted him from his feelings.

Starting as a small bright spot of light hovering above the carpet, a richly detailed hologram started to expand. It spread out to reveal a model of a cluster of stars. At a glance, Toivo could see twelve stars there, each of them different from each other.

"Today, we are going to learn about the Twelve," the teacher started saying, sitting forward in her chair slightly. In her hand, she held the 'jector's remote, which she fiddled with just a little bit. The hologram shifted, the stars moving into a large circle in the air. "We live in the Topaz Realm, which is one of the twelve planets that make up the Dodecal." Using a small red dot of laser light, she pointed to each of them in turn, naming them as she went: "Garnet, Amethyst, Aquamarine, Diamond, Emerald, Pearl, Ruby, Peridot, Sapphire, Opal, Topaz . . . " The children interrupted her to clap briefly, hearing their own home's name. ". . . and Turquoise. These are the names of the twelve different Realms. Let's recite them together."

The teacher led the children in a chanting repetition of the names of the Twelve. By the second time through, Toivo had them firmly in his mind. He raised his hand, asking if he could say them backwards, then did so without waiting for permission. The other children - those who were paying attention to him - were both puzzled and dazzled by his recall. A few of the others started trying to say them backwards like him, getting the names all confused in the process. The teacher had to flash the STOP signal several times to get the children to stop talking and refocus on her. She glared angrily at Toivo, flashing several sentences at him. He did not understand what she was saying, but was very clear about the feeling behind them. The teacher had the children chant the names of the Twelve in the right order once again then continued with her lesson.

Each of the Realms has a different climate, a different native language and a different type of Power." The children all looked puzzled by this. People who were *not* users of the Light? The concept was alien to them.

"Some of you might travel to different Realms with your parents, someday, so we have to learn about how to recognize the different gem types when we see them." A small box of simple text appeared under each star in the hologram. Standing, the teacher tapped on the first star, and it expanded. A small red-brown world was orbiting the larger, reddish star. The teacher expanded the text under the star, and read it out to the class:

> *Garnet Force, through gem or stone,*
> *Barriers smash, skills to hone.*

The children repeated the teacher's words, with varying levels of accuracy. Toivo repeated them, verbatim, with exactly the same inflection that the teacher had used. Despite her frustration with him, she smiled at this for just a second. She pulled the star in turn, into focus, reading each stanza of the poem as she went:

> *Amethyst Influence, in silent ways,*
> *Mind and Soul to serve or save.*
>
> *Aquamarine's Change, never staying*
> *Matter always Rearranging.*
>
> *Diamond Shield, pure and bright,*
> *Channel all Twelve with equal might.*
>
> *Emerald Genesis, Life's belief,*
> *Friend to paw or wing or leaf.*

Pearl Ascend to Realms unseen
Know yourselves, and be the Dream.

Ruby's Fire, Passion's Heart,
Renew your strength of Arm and Heart.

Peridot's Power, know the Way
Plan, Prepare and Win the day

Sapphire Endurance, watchful Eye
Keeps Sea in balance with the Sky.

Opal Sight, find the way,
See that Truth and Hope hold sway.

Topaz clear and golden Light,
Blazing in the Dark of night

Turquoise Knowing how and when
Done at Starting, Begins at End

The children recited the words after the teacher spoke them. It was a bit much for them, most of them losing interest after about the fourth stanza. The teacher doggedly continued to present them, ignoring the yawns and wandering eyes.

"Can we go play?"

"Can we have snack?"

"Can we go home?" came the myriad questions as the presentation wrapped up. The teacher nodded, sighing herself in relief, and signaled for them to disperse and play. They all cheered and jumped to their feet, returning to every other activity in the room.

Toivo got up too, but he came up to the teacher and, using the best manners he had, asked if he could look at the holo' again. The teacher looked down at the untidy little boy; his mop of brown hair pushed aside and his eyes pleading and did not know what to say for a moment. The Council mandated the presentation of the memory-aid poem, but it was deadly dull. Even she did not see the point of it. She refused weakly once, getting a whole series of pleas from Toivo, beseeching her to let him play with the holo'. She pondered a moment longer, and then acquiesced, pulling the small, transparent crystal from the projector's armature and placed it in his little hands. It was an old record, the edges of the crystal itself showing chips and wear marks from repeated use over the years. If he dropped it, or it cracked through misuse, she would not have minded. She could obtain a newer copy from Pazos, the district Council representative, easily enough. He had made the offer only last week, after all.

Toivo acted as if this were the most precious object in the universe, and, holding it with both hands, walked gingerly over to the private holo'jectors at the side of the room. They were all busy, but he waited his turn with atypical patience. When the other child was finished her picture story, Toivo took his place at the reader, inserted the crystal in the slot, and the image of the Twelve materialized in front of him, on the table. Toivo's eyes went wide again, his little tongue working as he carefully and methodically pulled up each image, one after the other. The teacher had never seen this much focus out of him, and made a small note on her light-pad about it. He was even reciting the poem by rote as the associated image flashed in front of him.

*

By the time Saul came to pick him up, Toivo had already drawn a dozen pictures on paper using color-sticks, all of them of the different Realms. Some were scribbles of color; others were more detailed than a four-year-old should have been able to draw. Saul gathered them all up, placing them in his briefcase. The teacher let Toivo draw another one as she spoke with Saul about how he was not showing signs of understanding even rudimentary photic, and that this was going to be a serious problem. She suggested that Saul take him to the Med-Center for Skin-Blindness treatments. Saul nodded, his face grave, after all, S.B. was a serious matter, and those with such a disability needed special care. He assured the teacher that he would look into it. The teacher nodded, her mandated duty dispensed with, and went to retrieve Toivo from the Craft table. He grabbed his almost finished drawing up and ran over to his uncle. After a hello-hug and several reminders for him to pick up his carryall, they moved to the hover-car that waited for them. Toivo climbed in and buckled up right away, planting his nose against the window to watch the world going by as he always did.

Saul did not get a chance to look at the last drawing until he was storing the lot of them in a secure-lock box. It made him stop dead, and stare incredulously. Staring back at him, from the page, drawn in rough strokes and many overlapping lines, was the Crest of the Topaz Realm itself: a doubled hexagon with the vertexes joined, and a pattern of rays spreading out behind it. However, surrounding the Crest was a different pattern: wavy, swirling lines of every color coming from the outer edge of the circle, which themselves ended at the edges of a large, twelve-pointed star shape that took up the entire page. Saul actually had to sit down, breathe for a moment or so, his heart racing, and sweat beading on his forehead. He hastily placed it in with the other sketches, and then closed the lock-box up tight. He encoded the lock to accept his retina pattern only, no exceptions, and then sent it back to the Council's private Vault via a transit tube.

He climbed back up the stairs to the basement of his house then closed the hidden door behind him. His mind was whirling with the planning that his nephew's drawing now

30

required of him. He would have to make sure that the Preschool's video-logs did not show any representations of Toivo's work, now or ever. He would also have to sidetrack this particular teacher before she contacted the Education Department with his results. He would need to get Edsol and Amberyl on this right away, before anyone else could recognize what his nephew had drawn and how it stridently shouted out his true nature.

He had a lot of work to do now.

*

I don't know why unca Saul wants me to make a journal, but I'll do it. The 'corder is a nice bracelet. Sorta looks like m'pendant a little bit. I'll have to show it to Pho when I see him in school. He'll think it's shiny. Hope I don't lose it.

From Toivo's private memory-filing system, diary file.

Chapter 3 - Light and Shadow
(Topaz Realm; 10 years ago,)

The large sun was getting a deeper orange as it rolled slowly toward the horizon. This made it only an hour or so before the little sun set. It was only half as bright outside as it usually was, and thus a little cooler. With the scorch of full daylight diminished, children would come out and play in this half-light time, and that is exactly what little Toivo intended to do. After all, he was all of five years old now. He was practically a grown-up.

He had gathered his favorite pocket toys, including his newest prize: a tiny model of a Diamond glider that shimmered in all the shades of the rainbow as it turned in his hand. He was sure that Pho would love it. It was so . . . interesting, especially when it flew on the wind. None of his other toys could fly.

He made sure to check his comm-band on one wrist, his glow-band on the other, and his lucky pendant around his neck as he walked down the block. It was not so far - only four houses away - but his uncle made him promise to bring all of this, just to be safe. Toivo knew what the call button looked like. He had not ever needed to use it.

He waved to a passing security patrol in their hover-car. The officers, in their yellow and white trimmed uniforms, waved back to him, smiling. Toivo even caught a glimpse of a shoulder crystal badge. That lady was an Adept. Teacher had told his preschool class that they all had a duty to show respect to the Apprentices and Adepts. Therefore, he did. His uncle had been an Adept too and that made him proud.

He walked to the smaller, slightly unkempt house on the corner of his street and opened the rusty chain-link fence gate at the front of the yard. He closed it behind him, looking for Pho. Well, he was not in the front yard. That was for sure. The holo-'jector for the play-climber had been turned off, and no little toy cars were on the porch. He tucked his lucky pendant under his shirt as he walked toward the back yard.

"Hi," called out Pho from the edge of the back porch. Toivo waved, and walked along the footpath to join his friend. When he got near, he tried to figure out what his friend was doing. Very methodically, Pho would hit fist-sized white rocks together to create sparks then he would quickly drop the rocks to catch the pinpricks of light in his hand. Afterwards, he would gently pour them into an ornate ceramic bowl beside him. He had already gathered enough to have halfway-filled the little vessel. The light they put out merged together, making a little island of illumination all around Pho.

"Hi Pho," Toivo said, plopping himself down in front of his friend. "Whatcha doin?"

"Catching light-spots. See," Pho said, holding up his bowl for Toivo to see. "I've got a whole bunch" He leaned close to Toivo and whispered "There's inside the rocks, so I'm trying to get'em out."

He smacked the rocks together again and caught another couple of sparks in his pudgy little hand. Toivo noticed that they were sputtering in the dark right up until they touched the skin of Pho's hand. When they did, they settled down into bright little marbles that shimmered ever so slightly. He gently put them into the bowl too. "Mama says that if you gather little lights together, they can make big lights."

"*Sparkly*, Pho. Can I help?"

"Sure! You can hit the rocks together."

So Toivo picked up the whitish rocks and hit them together too, being careful not to smash his thumbs. A few sparks flew off into the air. Both he and Pho giggled and chased after them. Pho came back with his cupped hands glowing faintly.

"You're good at this, Toivo. We could get lots of light this way!" Pho said, excitedly. "Let's fill the bowl right to the top!"

Therefore, they did. The two little boys continued their game until the glowstones along the sidewalk started to light up. By then, Pho had a bowl full of light that glowed brighter than the moons.

"Toivo, you wanna turn? Your uncle might like getting some light-dots too." Pho asked, trying not to spill any of them out of his bowl. "You have rocks at your house. You could ask your uncle to let you hit them together."

"I can't catch them like you," Toivo mumbled, embarrassment filling his little cheeks with red. "Remember? They go out when I touch them. Dunno why." Then his eyes brightened a little. "Maybe I could hit them together like I did for you, and then Uncle Saul could catch them!"

Pho's face lit up excitedly, having not really heard his friend all that clearly. "If . . . if . . . if we get enough sparkles together . . . maybe we . . . we could have a picnic in the Dark! A Night Party, and play star games!"

Toivo shuddered at the mention of star games.

"Pho," he moaned. "Not again. I don't like night-games. It's scary when it's dark outside."

"No, it's not." Pho replied disdainfully.

"Yes it is." Toivo persisted. "The Dark is all around you and you have to make your own light and you can't leave the pools of light that you make or . . . or . . . or you . . . might . . . might get lost." Toivo stammered a little, trying to get the words out. The tone of his voice started to rise a little bit as he looked around and noticed that it was getting quite dark now. He scooted a little closer to Pho and his glowing bowl.

"Toivo, there's nothing in the dark that isn't there in the light. You know that."

"Yeah, but you can't see it, in the dark. The shadows cover everything."

"Oh." Pho could see that his friend really did not like the idea, so he let it drop. They walked to the back door of the house then opened it together. Only a couple of pinpoints fell out, sinking into the ground quickly.

"Pho, is that you?" his mother's voice called from the living room.

"Yes mama. Toivo is here too. He's helping me. I made a bowl of light, and we can add it to the house, so that we use less power."

"You did what?" she replied, walking in from the living room. She saw her son and his best friend standing in the doorway, holding a glowing bowl between them. She drew in a surprised breath, approached the boys with her eyebrows knitted together in apprehension.

"Oh, Pho! Look at what you did. That's . . . that's wonderful," she finally said, trying to smile. "Here, let me get a glowstone for that." She went into the kitchen and brought out an old, depleted one. The crystal facets inside the dull metal were dark and grey. Any light that it might have had stored within it had escaped or been used up long ago. She opened the hatch on the top that usually gathered sunlight, and held it down low enough for Pho and Toivo to pour the sparks into it. The light-beads fell like sand into the crystal, and it stared to lighten and glow more and more. By the time Pho's bowl was empty, the glowstone was shining as brightly as if it had been in direct sunlight for hours. His mother closed the hatch on the top, and looked wonderingly at the replenished glowstone.

"Mama, I can refill the glowstones now! We won't have to buy as much light from the power guys."

"Pho, darling, that's . . . that's amazing." She picked up her son and kissed him soundly on the cheeks. "Toivo, dear, I'll call your uncle and let him know you're here."

"I already asked him, and he said it was ok, ma'am," Toivo replied politely.

"I'll call him anyway. He might like to join us for dinner, too."

"Can we go play now?" both boys asked together, putting on their sweetest beseeching faces. Pho's mother had to laugh. She nodded. Both boys looked at each other excitedly, and jumped up and down, cheering happily. They scampered off at full speed to Pho's room and closed the door. The sounds of happy play ensued.

Pho's mother picked up the glowstone again, examining it closely. It shined like new. She closed the shutters over the crystal, and placed it back in the storage closet. She strode over to the com-panel and pressed a sequence of keys. Councillor Saul's image appeared there.

"Ah, hello there, Filamina."

"Hello, Saul. Toivo made it to our house safely. The two of them off playing in Pho's room. Since he's already here, we might as well keep him for dinner. Would you like to join us?"

"I'd love to, Mina m'dear. What can I bring?"

"Normally I'd ask if you could recharge our reserve glowstones, but not this time."

"Oh?"

"No, Pho did that for me, tonight. If you wanted to bring a salad or something - that would be nice."

"Allllll-right, I'll do that. I'll bring some wine too."

"Oh, thanks. That would be lovely." She looked down at the glowstone again and with the barest hint of a shudder, said: "Saul, I really do think you want to come over tonight."

"I can see that. I understand. Be right over."

*

The meal was a simple affair of stew and vegetables, with bread cooked in the solar oven and sweetened sun-tea. Saul ate with gusto, and told funny stories and tales from his days as captain of the Radiant Knights. Everyone oo'ed and ah'ed in all the right places.

Toivo ate quietly having heard them all before, but Pho hung on every word. His parents had to remind him a couple of times to swallow the bite he was working on. Saul's fine clothes and his powerful Staff of Office leaning against the far wall were at odds with the humble surroundings of the small house, but it was a comfortable time for all.

"So, Pho m'boy," Saul started out, after finishing the last scrap of stew from his bowl. "Your mother tells me that you and Toivo recharged an empty glowstone. That's an interesting trick. Can I see it?"

"Sure. I'll get it." Pho glanced at his mother, who nodded, hopped off his chair and scampered over to the utility room, adjacent to the kitchen. "Toiiiii-vo. Come help me," he called out. Toivo looked to his uncle, who also nodded. He went over to join his friend in carrying an older-style, wall-mount glowstone. It was almost as tall as the boys themselves, but they managed to carry-drag it into the middle of the kitchen floor. They stood it up, and uncovered the shutters. The crystal inside was glowing warmly, with light the color of sunrise in summer. It hummed gently in its mounting, as if the very crystal itself was happy to be so bright.

"See what I mean?" Mina said to Saul. "That stone has been in the closet for years. I haven't been able to charge it past halfway for even longer, even if I were to have left it open from dawn to dusk on the brightest day of the year. Now, it's shining like new."

Saul came over and examined it. He tapped the crystal itself a couple of times, and noted the movement of the light patterns within it. His eyebrows rose slowly as he examined it further.

"Yes, this old thing has been renewed, all right. Revitalized, more like." Saul lifted it and placed it on the wall hanger that was meant for it. The light inside the stone hummed again, and then it and the lights inside the whole house brightened slightly. The holograms that made up the furniture became a little crisper. The images in the vid-screens became clearer.

"Wow." Pho's father said under his breath. "I doing temp work with the Power Grid, and there hasn't been this kind of photic energy flowing through this old house since the power shortage began. My son did this?"

"If he truly did this, then he's showing signs of having considerable gifts from the Core already." Saul said. "May I explore this a wee bit with him?" Both parents nodded vigorously, relieved to have a family friend who knew how to help them.

"Pho, Toivo, I think you did a fantastic job." Saul said, as he sat cross-legged on the floor. "How did you manage this kind of trick?"

"Pho hit rocks together then caught the sparks." Toivo piped up right away. "When I came, I got to hit the rocks together. The sparks were nice and big. Pho caught almost every one, and put them in his bowl."

Pho held up his special bowl, for Saul to see. The older man took the bowl and examined it, recognition flickering across his features. He glanced at the parents, who nodded at him, confirming what he thought. It was a senior student's training bowl, used to help those with Light-gifts to hone particular skills.

"Then I poured them into the 'stone. Mama says that it's glowing really _shiny_ now." Pho finished. Saul nodded sagely, and returned the bowl to him. Pho went and put it on the counter, by the sink.

"Well, boys, I've got to say, I'm impressed." Saul said, bringing his open hands together. When he separated them, a large ball of glowing light hung there, between them. Both boys' eyes went wide as they saw the scintillating sphere hanging there. "I'm so impressed that I'd like to figure out how you did that, Pho, if I can. Most of the time, only an Apprentice or an Adept could restore a glowstone like that." He moved his hands about the sphere, separating it into three smaller ones as he spoke: "These days, we use sunlight for everything, of course. It's a yellow color when it comes out. But that's not the kind of light you poured into your stone, I can tell. It's all different sorts of shades of white and yellow, all mixed together, isn't it? You said that you hit rocks together and caught the sparks."

The boys nodded. Saul nodded back, rolling the globes of light around his hands like a juggler. He even made each globe into a hologram of himself. They giggled, eyes glued firmly on the display.

"If you were gathering sparks from the stones, then that could mean that you have the power to manipulate

Spectrum Light." Saul glanced over at Pho's parents, who both wore stunned - happy expressions. Neither dared believe what they were hearing. Rhyol held his wife around the shoulders to keep her from bouncing excitedly.

"That's the same kind of energy that the Apprentices and Adepts use. It's from the Core of our world, the Heart of Light. The rocks absorb it because the Core always shines, deep under the ground." He grinned at the puzzled looks on their faces then changed directions: "And every time I meet a little boy or girl who can do things like gather sparks of light in their hands, I get to play one of my favorite games with them." He gently pushed one of light-globes in Pho's direction. It moved lazily through the air, like a shining soap bubble. "Very gently, catch this globe, if you can."

Pho nodded and raised his hands. The globe of light drifted his way. He caught it gently and looked at it, wonderingly. It shimmered and shifted in his little hands. His parents were silently jubilant, holding onto each other even more tightly. Pho turned the ball of light around, and squeezed it gently. It elongated into a long rod then slowly started pulling back into a sphere again.

"Ha! Very good, Pho. You go and play with that for as long as you can." Saul clapped the little boy on the shoulder. He turned to Toivo. "Would you like a turn too, son?"

"Yes, please!" Toivo piped up, happily. Saul sent another globe floating toward his nephew, and watched closely. Unlike when Pho caught it, the globe reacted differently when it reached Toivo. As soon as his little hands came together to catch it, the globe started changing colors. It became a swirling rainbow then it melted into streams of color that flowed around Toivo like happy caterpillars. They faded after a few moments, after each one had seemed to caress Toivo's cheek.

Saul watched, fascinated, then clapped. "Oh, Toivo, that was marvelous. Different, to be sure, but definitely special!" He wrapped his nephew up in a big hug, and traced tickling fingers along the pathways that the colors had taken. The little boy giggled, and batted at his uncle's hands. Then he squirmed free and scampered off to join his friend, who was shaping the globe into all sorts of interesting things.

"He handled that construct as if it's clay in his hands," Mina said, walking up to Saul, who nodded. "What will this mean for us then?" she asked.

"We can't send him to the regular schools anymore, can we?" Rhyol asked. "He'd outshine everyone before the first week was done. I'm a blue, and I can't even begin to control E.M. energy like that. Mina's from Peridot, with no Light powers whatsoever. How could Pho have gained this kind of power so young?"

Saul reached over and patted Mina on the shoulder reassuringly.

"Well, it's fairly certain that you'll need to move away from Estan now, probably closer to Luminus City, or even the Capital. There are branches of the Photonic Disciplines Collegiate in both locations." Saul nodded to himself. "Yessir, your little man will need specialized training to harness those raw gifts of his. I'm certain that once he's there, he'll be able to learn everything that he could possibly need to harness the enormous photic potential in him."

"But we can't afford to send him to the P.D.C. anywhere, let alone move to Capital or L.C." Mina interjected. "We barely make enough now to maintain this magnificent palace we call home."

"Not to worry, Mina," Saul said, reassuringly. "Remember: I'm still on the Council. Being the head of the Selector Committee grants me some . . . prerogatives. After all, the Council always needs talented children like Pho to get proper training in the ways of the Spectrum." He sat back down at the table in the kitchen, and pulled out a light-pad and stylus. "My job entitles me to allocate resources where we need them, to help with that. So . . . since your son needs the specialized instruction that can only be found at the P.D.C., I need to make it possible for his family to move to the capital. Hrmm . . . oh, I have it! I'm putting in an order for the Energy Committee to hire a new blue-topaz power technician in the Central Council building complex. Seems we have a problem with . . . with . . ."

"Faulty conduit routing?" Rhyol chimed in, eyebrows raised as he started to get the drift of what Saul was saying.

"That's right. Faulty . . . conduits . . . routing. Very urgent. And I just happen to know a qualified technician who is ready for a new job." Saul scribbled a few more notes with the stylus on his light-pad then tapped the pad a couple of times. The messages were flashing across the screen there, to the heads of the appropriate departments. "As soon as you are ready to move, contact me. I'll have my friend Lumens find you an apartment to start. Her work with the Music Conservatory has her traveling between those two places a fair bit."

"What about Toivo?" Mina asked. "We all know that he showed all sorts of Gifts too. Would the boys be able to go to the same school?"

Saul shook his head, and his face became just a little bit tired as he answered.

"No, dear, that's not likely to happen. With his limitations, I'm going to have to pull some strings to get him registered with the Schools for the Rudiments of the Spectrum. They have branches in every major city, all over the Realm. They cater to children of visiting diplomats or anyone else who was born off-world. We'll just have to create a category for Toivo there. I'm sure we'll figure it out. Besides that, I'm

just about to move to the Calorian Plains Offices of the
Council, for an assignment there. Toivo will have to move
with me, for the time being. We'll visit, of course. We're
only a holo-call away. I'm sure the boys will be able to keep
in touch."

The adults sat back down at the table and discussed
details of how very much all of their lives were going to be
changing. The sounds of little boys playing games brought
smiles to their faces now and again. Saul was not sure but he
was almost certain that the color in that old glowstone on the
wall got a hint brighter again as Pho's parents got more and
more excited. Seeing this, Saul chuckled as that tiny little
detail showed him a little shred of Hope on another level
entirely.

*

"G'bye Toivo. See you soon," Pho waved as his
friend finished putting his shoes on at the front door. "I'll see
you tomorrow."

Toivo waved, then clamped onto his arm firmly. His
glow-band was on at full-bright, and his eyes scanned the
darkness around them continuously. Saul stroked the boy's
hair gently, then lit the gem on his staff so that it cast a warm
bright glow around them as they walked. Toivo relaxed a
little, then, and they made their way home. Pho and his
parents waved as they left, then closed the door, and shut off
their outside lights.

*

As the door closed, one of the shadows around the
house blinked silently. It pulled itself free of the outline of the
trees laid out by the glowstones on the street and flowed to the
middle of the sidewalk, like a drop of ink in the water. First it
oriented itself towards Saul and Toivo walking away, then it
oriented on Pho's house. Back and forth it turned, as if unable
to decide something. When Saul and Toivo were finally out of

43

sight, it faced Pho's house, then melted back into the larger shadows in the streets.

*

If Understanding's Spark
Sets a child's mind alight,
Then a future that is stark
Will glow with Truth and Light.

Inscription set above the entrance to every Rudiments of the Spectrum Academy.

Chapter 4 - School Daze
(Topaz Realm; 8 years ago)

"TOPAZ! Sit down!" the haggard-looking teacher said firmly from behind her large antique, wooden desk. "It is not time for you to leave yet."

"But, miss, you said that . . ." the eight-year-old boy started to say, stammering with his anxiety of feeling trapped by the teacher's merciless gaze, again. ". . . that . . . that we could go when we were . . . finished our picture." His voice tapered off into uncertainty as he held up the free drawing task that he had just completed - a city scene, with huge black birds flying over it and blue and purple rain clouds that were dropping little red raindrops.

"I most certainly did not!" she replied hotly. "I said that you were to finish the picture, nothing more."

The little boy in the purple jump suit in the desk next to Topaz snickered and turned to whisper to a girl in a pale blue dress. She grinned, covering her mouth. Both of them then closed their eyes, in concentration. Despite the trouble he was in, Topaz glanced at the two of them, and noticed them.

He knew people talked about him. He had moved so many times that it was somewhat normal for him. He would always hear the hubbub around him, as the local kids tried to figure out how to talk with him. His uncle always said that he just needed to help the other kids learn how to talk to him, and that he needed to learn how to talk to them. When he was younger, it had been easier. He had had many playmates as a toddler, in the little community he had lived in then. It was easier then. No one had learned any control over light yet, and so he was just another kid. In his earliest years at school, he was eager and friendly, and always tried. Then he started seeing how the other kids were starting to be able to play with light: bend beam of sunlight, create glows around objects, and cause flashes of the topaz Spectrum when they wished. One would figure it out, cause a light-effect of some sort, and everyone would giggle and applaud them. Eventually, everyone showed the beginnings of control over the power that was native to the topaz Realm . . . everyone but him. Every time one of his little friends learned a trick, he would try to emulate them. Each time, he would mimic their hand motions exactly; each time, he failed. The others were playing with light beams streaming in through the curtains like beads and string, or building blocks. It was the most natural thing in the world for them. They would play rambunctious games of flash-tag, where if you were "it", then the only way you could pass that along was to touch someone with a flash of light or a spark when you touched them. The game would continue, right up until they touched him, then everyone would moan and complain that the game was over. They knew that he could not pass on the "it", and so they would exclude and tease him. His uncle started moving around then, and the cycle would start all over again.

He saw his two classmates and recognized now what he was seeing. For the first time, he was finally aware of those giggles; he understood that they were snickering *at* him, and that this was what it felt like being mocked for making a fool of himself. There had always been laughter around him - he had thought that he was just naturally funny, and that they were sharing a joke together even if he did not get it. Today, he was aware of the difference. Hot icicles of embarrassment stabbed deeply into his chest.

"Well, what do you have to say?" the teacher chided, in a loud voice, clearly wanting everyone to hear, again. He knew what to say now. He had learned it as a survival and appeasement technique for when the teacher was determined to make an "example" of him.

"Sorry, miss," he said quietly, fiddling with his lucky pendant. "I wanted to go, and I thought you said that we could. I'm sorry. I was wrong." The crushed feeling showed on his little face, though no tears came.

He did not understand that he actually HAD heard the teacher's thoughts, thanks to boy in purple who was just beginning to learn how to use his Amethyst mind-reading powers. That young classmate had learned just enough to make Topaz see and hear things that were not there, or thoughts that other people wanted to keep private. He was sure that he heard the voices, but that was just what he was being made to hear. This was only the latest in a whole series of little pranks of this nature, where his perception of things was altered in little ways. It had escalated to the point where he had to wait a few seconds before answering a question to make sure that 1) he was the one that the teacher had spoken to, and 2) that he could answer the question. Even with his fiercely creative and alert mind, it was taking more and more time to see past illusion now, thanks to the seemingly *teacher-proof* interference that this Amethyst boy produced. All this meant that the teachers were beginning to treat him with less and less enthusiasm, thinking him slow-witted. He had already failed two oral tests because of this.

The teacher collected his picture with a puzzled glance at it, not understanding what he had drawn nor why he had drawn it. With a shrug, she collected the other students' work as well, and then she dismissed them from their noontime meal. The class began to put away their things and head out the door to gather their lunches from cubbies or lockers, or head down to the cafeteria to purchase a meal. As Topaz started to do the same, he tried to stand, and then blinked, catching something out of the corner of his eye. It was not so much that he saw something happen, more like he could "feel" a flash of color. Given how his day was going, he was on alert now. He looked around, trying to find where the illusion was this time. He could not see any, even when he concentrated, so he put his hands on his desktop, starting to rise to his feet.

He did not get very far. It started with his hand; it tingled a little bit. It resembled when he tried to use light powers, tried to make the energies of the topaz Realm follow his command; only he knew he was not the source. It grew, until he saw a shimmering below him. The next events happened in a split second. Somehow, the whole top of his desk, and the feet of his chair, became extremely slippery. He did not have time to compensate for this, and lost his balance. His hand slipped forward, and he knocked his papers and coloring sticks across the floor. His chair flew back and banged into the desk behind him. Essentially, it looked as if he had done this on purpose, acting out of frustration. Truthfully, he did feel that way, but not to the point of exploding like that. The raucous, mocking laughter of the entire class wrapped him in a cold blanket of helplessness. He had had no control of this; he was just the one doing it. He spotted the Amethyst boy and the Aquamarine girl just leaving the room, both giggling behind their hands. The helplessness he felt became the simmering heat of frustration.

It had never been his nature to be angry with his classmates before. They all could do things with the topaz spectrum and he could not, even the kids from other Realms, like Turquoise or Emerald. Topaz had figured that he deserved the teasing, for being clumsy and made light of it most of the time. He had never seen the teasing as vindictive. He had always figured it was a big game. He saw with different eyes now, and was more than ready to believe that these pranks were just plain mean! The teacher watched the objects go flying from his desk, and rolled her eyes. She pointed to the mess once, causing the fallen objects to glow for a second with topaz light as left the room in a frustrated huff. Her message of "Clean that up" was clear to him.

As the sound of her low-heeled shoes against the tiles of the floor faded down the corridor, he pulled his chair back under him, sat flopping his head down heavily. He noted that the desk surface was no longer as slippery - small mercy. He slowly pulled himself up, and started to gather his scattered things and stuff them back into his desk. He did not hurry. He had no reason to. He knew that there were no less than three different groups of bullies out there, in the lunchroom and the play yard, just waiting for him to come out and be their victim again. He tried to stay away from them. He tried talking to them, reasoning with them, but nothing seemed to work. They always seemed to be smarter, stronger, or more organized. In addition, they all could use their native gem powers better than he could. He never stood a chance, and he knew it.

Everyone at this special school was from one of the twelve Realms and each had the powers of those respective worlds. They were sons and daughters of visiting diplomats and important officials who were visiting the topaz Realm. They learned their fundamental education, as well as the rudiments of the topaz Realm's powers over light and the electromagnetic spectrum. He was called "Topaz" here, because at this school, the tradition was to call you by your planet of origin. Topaz lived here, but unlike any other "gifted" citizen of this Realm; he could not control his powers. His uncle Saul had made sure that instead of being farmed off to a *Center for the Un-Gifted* in the middle of nowhere, a spot had been arranged for him here. *Rudiments of the Spectrum* schools were located around the world, and so wherever they moved, Topaz always had the opportunity to learn his basics, again. Wherever he was, he was called by the name of his home world. He was the only person on the planet called "Topaz." He now understood that when everyone called him that, they were - in fact - mocking him.

*

Once back from lunch, the students in their seats, a work page was handed out. This was the part of the day that Topaz feared the most; even more than the bullies who had given him two new bruises to nurse, not 10 minutes ago: this was when they practiced their Light skills. He looked down at the page, and sighed inwardly again. With the barest hint of a purple after-image, it read: *"Only a goof would read this."* He squinted and concentrated for a moment, trying to see through the illusion. After a few moments, the actual words became clear: *"How to summon a ball of light in the palm of your hand."* Topaz looked over to see Amethyst studying his page very attentively. He sighed again, and then started reading the instructions.

He knew that he would be able to recite the words by heart almost instantly, but after twenty futile minutes, the best that he was able to do for this exercise was to make a little tracery of light play around on his fingertips. He balled his fists, and tried to find the happy state of mind that let him cope with the frustration. He raised his hand. The teacher looked over at him, from her desk.

"May I go to the washroom, please?" Topaz asked, wanting any escape from the impossible task in front of him. The teacher nodded blankly, turning her attention back to the personal display on her desk, doing some teacher-task, as always.

The boy rose, then started to move toward the door. He found, however, that his hand was stuck to his desktop. He froze when he felt it. He looked down at his hand, and could almost see the barest hint of a light blue glow around his hand on the desktop. He turned to see the Aquamarine girl in the light-blue dress staring at him, concentrating not on her light-ball exercise, but on the prank she was playing on him. Not only could he see a hint of her powers making his desk sticky, he could almost hear it coming from her, like the sound of tiny marbles rolling or maybe gentle splashing of water or maybe both together. Topaz realized that he could recognize when she was using Aquamarine energy now and a flash of understanding happened inside of him.

A burst of anger surged from him too, and he could feel a corresponding rush of energy flow from him with the sound of a quiet crystalline ping ringing in his ears. Suddenly, a series of bright sparks flashed directly in front of the girl's eyes. They were examples of the small sphere of light that the handout page had been showing him how to make; only they were about ten times brighter than anyone else's. They flashed brilliantly a couple of times, like a strobe or a beacon, and then vanished. Startled, she blinked, covering her eyes with a little squeak of fright. The marble/water sound of her power vanished, and his hand became unstuck. Topaz's anger seethed a moment longer, then subsided a little bit as he realized what he and just done. Yes. Him. He had called on the Spectrum, and formed Light Globes, better than anyone else. More important, he had defended himself, power for power. The girl rubbed her eyes then stared at him, blinking, not quite sure what had happened here. Topaz, his cheeks flushed bright red and not saying a word, left the room. He pondered these events all the way to the washroom and back.

When he got into his seat again, he found himself in a much better frame of mind. It's amazing what a little success can do for one's self-confidence, and this held very true for him. His uncle had said that he had Powers, and that he just needed to learn how to use them. He was just about to turn to the work-page again, when he "heard" another sound. This time, it was like a sub-sonic rumble mixed with a whisper. It was not with his ears that he heard this, but he interpreted it as sound, regardless. He looked about the room, to see who or what might be the source of it. The Aquamarine girl was very focused on her assigned work now, so it could not be her. He turned his gaze to her friend, the Amethyst boy. His eyes were closed, and he was concentrating. The sound intensified, and then Topaz could feel a little tickly feeling inside of his head accompanied by a slight purple tinge to his eyesight for just a second. Ah ha! It was him, and he was just starting to summon his mind-powers for another prank.

Now that he was aware of it, Topaz closed his own eyes, concentrating. He imagined himself shouting at the top of his voice, the word: *NO!* He could feel energy inside him again, moving at his command, again. He put all the force of his frustration and anger into this mental answer. Again, the new sound stopped, and the Amethyst boy jumped, eyes flying open and rubbing his temples. He looked at Topaz with a mixture of shock and confusion on his face.

"So, Topaz, show us the exercise," the teacher declared. "Summon a globe of light for the class." This caught

Topaz off-guard. Had she not seen how he had summoned three or four of them, just a few minutes ago? Clearly, she had not. All eyes turned on him. He started the exercise, did the prescribed hand motions, and tried to make another globe appear, flush with the success He had just experienced. All that happened was that his fingerprints shimmered, again, just like before. To their credit, the class had stopped actively laughing at him for this level of achievement long ago, not expecting anything else from him. He sat back down crestfallen and folded his hands politely. He watched as his other classmates showed what they had learned. The white-haired girl from Diamond girl was the best, showing control as fine as any topaz citizen. A boy in light green from Peridot was next best, then his old enemy Amethyst. Topaz sighed at that.

Deep down, Topaz was not sure if he was supposed to feel good or bad about the events in class. He had learned a couple of things, though: he could tell when others were using their powers now, by the sound their powers made and by the haze of color that he saw coming from them. The other thing he had learned was that he had been able to prevent two bullies from playing pranks on him for the first time. He had stopped them outright, without calling on Teacher. That was not a bad thing. When he thought about that, he realized that it had been necessary for him to become very angry for his Light Powers to appear, even accidentally. This made him uncomfortable. It did not feel right to him and he could not explain why. Did anyone else with Powers feel like this? He put his head down on his desk, to cover the frustrated tears in his eyes.

The little girl in light green sitting right in front of him turned, blue eyes were wide with concern. She put her little hand on his shoulder as he quietly trembled. He did not look up, but his breathing slowed a little. The Amethyst boy also turned towards Topaz, but a solid glare from the new girl made him face forward again, slightly worried expression on his face.

"Thank you," Topaz whispered into his desk. The girl smiled, leaving her hand on his shoulder. She tucked a light red curl behind her ear and continued reading her light tablet.

*

<Command, this is Pazos. Stage two mental blocking confirmed.>

<Acknowledged. What about stage one? Both boys in your area were targeted for the nyctophobia effect.>

<The primary is almost completely unaffected, but secondary seems to have absorbed both doses. He's showing interesting secondary effects, therefore our agent in the same class has planted seeds of self-doubt.>

<Good. Maintain, and congratulate the operative. His mind-powers were more than enough for this.>

*

Everything grows
If you know how to nourish it.
       Saying from the Emerald Realm

Chapter 5 - *Music* Class
(Topaz Realm; 7 years ago)

Even for the students at the *Rudiments* school, there were times when school districts had workshop-style classes with children from the other school. His classmates had taken advantage of the presence of so many topaz Realm children to make nine-year-old Topaz feel even smaller and less competent than he already thought he was. To their credit, though, the topaz children were quite well behaved, and made a point of speaking to him with turns of phrase and expressions that he had grown up with. They always included him in their conversations, even if he could not add much, himself, except for how children from other Realms would feel about this vid-performer, or that new Austerity measures in place to help with the power crisis. Funny thing about topaz children: they tended to be the center of their own little universe sometimes, the star of the conversation and everyone else should know it. Topaz had status in their eyes, but not any credit, so he found himself dragged around as entourage by various photic topaz children throughout the day.

As nice a change as this was to the bullying, he made a point of not saying much when he was with them. He may have known the same words, but it was very painful for him to be with them. When they talked with each other, they punctuated their sentences with little unconscious displays of light to indicate their feelings about what they were saying, or to show a sub-text. Occasionally, they would just look at each other, and narrow beams of light would pass between their eyes – the photic equivalent of whispering - then they would laugh at the private joke.

The shared classes they had this time were the Arts. Once they were divided into four different teams, the combined classes started their classwork. Topaz had started in the Visual Arts rotation. He found the Arts easy, so he walked in confidently on the first day. He had forgotten that there were topaz Realm students here now. When they started learning about line and form, texture and tint, they applied their lessons to holograms that they generated with their powers. Topaz could feel the burning in his cheeks as he used clay, pigments, paintbrushes or carving tools to create his projects. His work was certainly more colorful than that of his usual classmates; that at least gave him some comfort. He even invented a way to mix phosphorescence into his paints, so that when the light was just right, his two-dimensional paintings looked like holograms. (His uncle was bursting proud of any project he brought home too.) All of the bullies could say nothing, of course, but they definitely made sure to take note of all the little displays the visitors created. He was sure that they would ask him at some later date why he wasn't using a light-brush like them.

*

This term, they were starting a survey of Instrumental Music. Their new teacher greeted them in the playground, stating that this course would depend on what they could do with their fingers and lungs, as opposed to their Powers. That made Topaz smile in earnest. This would be one of those times when he might be able to succeed. He was almost giddy as the teacher guided them into a classroom that had semi-circular levels rising toward the back. It was almost like an amphitheater. With a flick of a switch, the holographic chairs appeared and the doors to instrument storage rooms at the very back of the room opened wide.

"Go, explore, find a case that looks interesting, then come back to the front of the room," the teacher called out.

Topaz did not hesitate. He zipped up the levels until he was walking past the different open doors. Each led to a long, narrow storage room lined with actual wooden shelves, not holographic ones. Cases of every imaginable shape and size rested there, each with an i.d. number. Suddenly, Topaz did not have a clue as to what to do. Every case looked just as interesting as every other case. None of them jumped out at him. He kept going back and forth, even after all the other students were finding seats with their choices. In a desperate move, he closed his eyes and reached forward. His hand hit a medium-sized carbon-fiber box, with a handle and latches. He picked it up, noting that it was deceptively light then took a seat at the very back of the room, beside the percussion instruments.

"Perfect," the teacher said, moving up to sit on a stool behind a tall conductor's music stand that was nearly bursting with scores and different parts. "Attached to the inside of each case is an instructional holo-pad. Use that to figure out how to make your instrument sound. By the time you're making noise, we'll be ready for the first lesson. Now, open 'em up, and explore."

The students in the front of the room had smaller cases. They opened to reveal various smaller wind instruments. All of them were acoustic, with no electronic parts anywhere, just shiny metal keys that covered many different holes with soft felt pads. The next row had larger versions of the same kind of instruments, and some electric versions of them too. One girl had a bowed instrument that plugged into a tiny amplifier in the case. Third row was filled with longer, more awkward instruments, each one different from the next. Topaz guessed that some of these were from other Realms.

The last row consisted of him, and the percussionists who were busy hitting various objects with various other objects. The Ruby and Garnet boys that had chosen them were having great fun with that.

When Topaz opened his case, his was the only instrument that was entirely electronic. The holo-pad said that it was called a *chroma-chord*. It sat curled in the box, a tangle of straps and topaz Realm-built devices. He pulled it out of the case and started unwinding it. The holo-pad said that the first step in setting this instrument up was to find the central box and to strap it to your chest. The only thing that could have been a box did indeed have strap, which he attached around his shoulders and waist. It held the small box in the middle of his chest fairly comfortably. He followed the steps in putting the rest of it together.

By the time he was done, Topaz wore a short vest across the back of his shoulders which housed small fiber-optic cables that led to and from the central box. The leads wound down along his arms, straps at the elbow and wrist keeping them from hampering his movements, to fingerless gloves that were festooned with different buttons and micro-glowstones. He checked the various straps and connections one last time then flipped a tiny switch on the underside of the box. The little glowstones in the gloves and at the elbows came to life. He had no idea how to make sound with this thing, so he raised his hand, to get the teacher's attention. When he did this, a rising chromatic scale with sounded clearly from the box on his chest. The glowstones projected a spray of colors that matched the notes. It was just slightly louder than the other instruments in the room, and everyone paused, turning to look at him.

The teacher heard the sound too, and turned to look as well. He saw Topaz's hand now frozen in the air, and a slightly horrified look on his face. With a chuckle, he came over to Topaz, and checked all of the connections and straps. A raised eyebrow on the teacher's face was the only sign of surprise that showed when he found that the boy had correctly put on and activated the instrument.

"Well, you've certainly gotten sound out of it. Let's see if we can make it fit even better." The teacher moved behind him and fiddled with the buckles and straps slightly. Suddenly, Topaz could not feel it anymore, it fit so well. He looked up at the teacher, slightly puzzled expression on his face. When he lowered his arm slowly, a gentle blue light shone from his hand, and a descending major chord quietly sounded.

"Heh! Well, I'd say that despite any shortcoming in Light powers you have, young man, that you have a talent for this. We'll see. Read your instructions, and as soon as you can, set it to a private playback instead of broadcast. That way, you can explore how to use it at your own speed."

Topaz nodded, feeling slightly proud now. Compliments were rare from the teachers, when it came to him. There was no denying, though, that this contraption felt comfortable to him . . . natural almost. From the light-tablet on the stand in front of him, he read how to change its settings as his teacher had asked. It involved tiny control buttons in the gloves. There were a few odd-sounding musical squeaks and rumbles as he moved his hands and fingers to make the adjustments. After a moment of fiddling, he found the sequence that set the playback so that only he could hear it, and then it was as if a bubble went up around him. All the lights and sounds could be heard by him, alone. To anyone looking in, it was like he was inside of a glass sphere.

By the end of class, thirty minutes later, Topaz had decided that he really liked this instrument, and had worked very hard, trying to learn how it worked. He moved his hands this way, and played chords, punctuated with bursts of solid color. He played individual notes together, letting their colors merge by themselves. He was noodling around, playing little melodies with one hand while painting with different colors of light with the other. The more he played around, the more he found he could do. He did not notice that the class was over until he looked up, and saw the rest of his classmates looking at him. Their instruments were all in their cases, their books gathered up, but strangely enough, they were not in any hurry to leave. They all had puzzled and curious expressions on their faces.

Topaz stopped playing, and looked around, blushing furiously from all the scrutiny. He shut down the sound-box and the bubble around him disappeared. No one made a sound for a few moments, until the teacher piped up: "Topaz, please, don't stop. I think your classmates would like to hear what you've been practicing." His classmates all nodded, mutely, stunned expressions fused in place.

"Er . . . well . . . ok,"

Topaz's face was bright red, and he could feel a cold sweat begin in the small of his back. "I'll try a few things out loud."

He set the sound box to broadcast out loud this time. He closed his eyes, and pictured in his mind a rainbow pattern of different colored swirls in the air. He mapped them out in his mind then opened his eyes. He brought his hands up, in front of his chest, triggering the sound with his thumb-switches. A gentle note started sounding, and the back of the room became a deep red color. He started drawing the swirls that he had seen in his mind with hands and fingers. The hand movements were interpreted as patterns of notes that rolled liquidly out from him. Each new swirl started on a different note, and thus they were a different color when projected on the back wall. Through the sequence of movements, the color on the back wall went through a rainbow of colors, ending in a deep violet. Using both hands, the last swirls he drew caused the whole range of notes and colors that he had used, to come out at once. Topaz felt absolutely at ease by then, letting the sound and light wash over and around him. When he stopped, brought his arms down, and switched off the device.

"There. I don't know if that was ok or not, but it was fun." Topaz said, face flushed with exertion this time.

His classmates waited all of two seconds before they broke into spontaneous applause. The athletic ones were cheering and pumping their arms in the air, and a few of the girls had the beginnings of tears in their eyes. Every topaz child was slack-jawed as they applauded. The teacher joined them, putting down his portable image recorder.

"Topaz . . . that was . . . that was . . ." the teacher was almost at a total loss of words. "That little display was more advanced than the final test for this class. I think we need to talk here." Then with a wave of his hand, he dismissed the rest of the class. He went over to his desk, and sat down, his face still a mask of amazement. Topaz undid the straps and settled the *chroma-chord* back into its case. He placed it on the storage shelf, then came over to the teacher's desk.

*

The next few classes were very different for Topaz. After a quick discussion with his uncle and the school's principal, a teacher's aide lead the class through its rudiments. The music teacher himself brought Topaz to the back of the room, and presented a new family of instruments to him, one instrument at a time. Each new instrument took a few moments to figure out, but after a startlingly short time, Topaz was playing scales and simple melodies on any of them. The following day, they explored another family of instruments. He figured he knew the instrument when he was able to play the classroom musical drills at the same level as his classmates, who had been working on only one instrument from the start of classes. Then he would repeat it with the next one.

Soon it was clear that there was no instrument in the room that Topaz could not pick up and play with facile ease. He figured out the mechanics of each instinctively, and when he was shown an example of the instrument being played, he learned even faster. He could feel the sound, feel how it was produced, how to manipulate it. He had little subtlety, of course, but it was still staggering for his teacher to watch.

After a couple more meetings with the School's administration and his uncle, it finally was decided that he had more than enough skill for him to be credited for the entire years- worth of this course, and that he would take private Music lessons outside of school to help him hone his talent. The Master-level performer Mistress Lumen was contacted for this, which was convenient for Saul and Topaz both since she was a family friend that they regularly visited anyway. Now he had get the chance to actually play on her wide collection of instruments, instead of being shooed away from them.

While he was in school, he would be assigned different classes now, so that he could maintain parity with others at his age-level. His uncle Saul helped him choose, signing him up for intensive training in Drama, Drawing, Sculpture, a new art-form every couple of months, to keep him from losing interest. His school day became a two-stage affair: the rudiments section, where he had to work a hundred times harder than everyone else to do what the teacher was asking, and the other half, where he was able to learn things at

HIS speed. This part of his days would always be where he shone, where he could almost feel like he wasn't disabled.

At least he was good at something. Maybe it would count for something when he got older. He certainly hoped so.

*

I knew that I would have to keep working at hiding him from all the prying eyes, but Fate seems to be hiding him better than I can. This world doesn't know what to do with him, and thus they overlook him. The Necromancers' spies and operatives are only seeking our brightest and best. They don't have time to waste with someone who can't quite master the Light. That's for the best. It won't hold up to scrutiny as he gets older, but by then he won't be as vulnerable. Till then, we are just going to have to . . . I don't know. He's become my joy and my hopes, but he learns so differently than we do!

> *From the personal journal of Saul Rallence, Councillor.*

Chapter 6 - Picnic
(Topaz Realm; 6 years ago)

"And then . . . then we made the electricity that we'd made with the generator dance in our hands!" the ten-year-old Toivo blurted out excitedly as he attacked the fruit on his plate. "I'm sorry we'll have to move to the Capital next week, 'cause this is the best place we've lived yet!" He stabbed another piece of succulent yellow melon with his fork and wolfed it down, barely chewing. Only a few dribbles came from the corners of his mouth, which he promptly wiped with his sleeve.

The trio of adults smiled affectionately at him as they picked at the remains of their picnic meal. The boy's uncle pushed his plate away from him, to the middle of the table, and covered his mouth as a most satisfied-sounding belch rumbled briefly. Smiling broadly, luxuriating in the cool breeze coming off the lake, he leaned back in his folding camp chair and took a sip from his dark, hot drink. The other adults grinned at him, the woman gathering the leftovers and covering them up, the man assembling the plates and utensils together, in preparation for the cleanup.

"That's what you said when we were camping out in that yurt on the Calorian Plains," his uncle answered, eyes half lidded as he sipped from his steaming mug again. "I'm glad you've enjoyed your time here. Finish your melon, then you can go play."

Toivo nodded, slurping down the last piece and tipping the bowl up to his mouth to drink the remaining juice. He placed his paper plate and plastic fork on the cleanup pile then flew out of his seat like a bolt of lightning. The adults watched him go, chuckling to each other and holding their drinks safely in their hands as the table rattled and shook with the departure. The boy sprinted over to the climber-playground in the field next to the beach where they had dined and promptly vanished within it. Several children there waved and clapped their hand, happy to have their playmate back.

"Oh, but that boy can move!" the woman said. "He's grown too, hasn't he? He's at least half-a-head taller than last time."

"Lumens, you're just annoyed at him finally being taller than you," Uncle Saul replied. "He's only slightly taller than last time. I'm just having a hard time trying to get his hair cut. He's determined to let that dark mop of his get as long as he can."

The conversation was allowed to fade, with only the sound of playing children and the gentle waves lapping up against the sandy beach filling the silence. Lumens finished wrapping up the bits of remaining meat and bread, then turned a businesslike face to the boy's uncle.

"Saul, did I hear him right? He did say that he's starting to learn the rudiments of manipulating electricity too, yes?" she asked, in a neutral tone of voice. "I thought you were a photic topaz color."

Saul nodded, eyes still half-closed.

"I am," he replied. "Light only. I can't even plug a machine into an e-m socket without worrying I'm going to get zapped."

"And did he mention the Calorian Plains region? Did he learn any of the brown topaz disciplines while you were there?" asked Edsol, Saul's best friend for many years.

"Oh, yes, he did indeed. Rudimentary at best, but he does have some Heat control too." Saul finished his now tepid mug of drink, and leaned his elbows on the table, head in hands. "You should see him when he tries to cook eggs *in* the shell, and melt candies into cups to make drinks out of them."

"Isn't he aware that he's not supposed to be able to do that?" Lumens asked, quietly. "If he's got to blend in, then shouldn't he . . . "

Saul held up his hand, cutting off Lumen's words. He inserted quickly: "He has no idea of that whatsoever. Nor will he. He'll learn soon enough that no one in the whole Realm can change the color of their Spectrum powers. For all our skill and power, we can't even begin to use other powers. For him, it's the most natural thing in the universe. And we all knew that he'd be like this." He looked at each of his friends and then finished his thought. "It's his nature to seek out diversity. It's in his blood. He is drawn to as many colors as we've got, and all the others that we don't."

These words hung in the air for a while, as all three pondered. They were able to hear the children in the playground, giggling and zapping each other with little sparks that made them squeal with delight; and there was the boy, Toivo, right in the midst of them, laughing -

"His heritage shines through in all these little ways," Saul replied. "However, I don't think that he'll ever learn about just one color of topaz power sufficiently to gain any kind of mastery in the conventional sense. "

"That's hard to say," Lumens inserted. "That could be the very form of mastery he's destined for, general mastery." She shrugged. "He has always been very passionate about what he's doing; that's what makes him such a gifted music student. He doesn't have the detachment most native topaz citizens possess. He is affected by what he plays, happy or sad. He might be prone to Emotional Lensing, once he gains a little more experience with whatever his Powers become."

"And if so, then he'll show his true strengths when his emotions are the highest, or lowest." Edsol leaned forward as he spoke.

"If I remember correctly, all of his people showed that tendency," said Saul, nodding and stroking his chin thoughtfully. "It was considered a weakness by many, right up until they discovered how versatile that particular trait could be." He shook his head. "It's been more than ten years since anyone has seen anything like him. Few now living on our world would even remember them. And certainly, the Invaders' spies would be hard pressed to know what they were looking at."

"For as long as he remains here, he'll be called clumsy and careless, then," Lumens said sadly. "He tells me that he's been teased by his peers since he started school. It'll only get worse as he gets older."

"At least, that will keep his emotional state lower than normal, till he's old enough to move beyond us." Saul said with the cold-bloodedness of necessity nipping at his words. He rubbed his forehead and sighed, weary of the task still ahead of him. "I just wish I could tell him even a little bit of his true heritage, instead of the half-true fabrication that his life is right now."

"Maybe you can," Edsol said, and he brought out an almost clear holo-rec crystal rod. It was easily as long as Edsol's hand. "Use this. Put it in your family safe box at the bank. Code it for when he returns, when he has his true powers."

Saul looked at the rare gift that his friend was offering, staring at it. This was a truly expensive recording crystal, one that only a senior Adept or a council member would have had the power to use, even with special devices. Given its size, it would have nearly infinite storage capacity, too, able to store holographic information within its very atoms. It represented a chance to tell his nephew the truth, the whole truth . . . now that was a gift indeed. He took the cold lump of crystal and pocketed it. He could only smile at his friends, in quiet gratitude.

"It's been long enough, now, that I think the Network cells here and those in the other Realms should be told that 'Hope survived the Fall', and that he will need to learn the *actual* skills of each, instead of what *THEY* try to teach him."

Their discussion was interrupted as the boy returned, eyes bright and clothes covered with dust and grass stains. He was dragging a girl his own age behind him, her long brown braids and blue jumper just as played-in and stained as his yellow one. In one, long, accelerated sentence, Toivo introduced the girl as his new friend; that her name was

Sollen; that she was a singer; that she knew some of the songs he did; that both she and he were thirsty and could they please sing a song for the three adults after they'd had a drink of juice. It took a moment for the grinning adults to actually hear what he was saying then all three laughed, and fetched clean cups for the children. Lumens sat down and listened to the two children sing a duet with beautiful clear treble voices, spot-on rhythm and pitch perfect. She asked them to sing it again, and she joined them. Her formidable vocal talents made the near-perfect harmonies turn almost visible to the others, like a crystal tapestry of sound that hung in the air above them.

What a lovely way to end the picnic, Saul thought, as he listened proudly to his nephew and this gifted little girl. Their voices rose to the wind, across the water. There was almost a resonance that he could hear, like an echo, but more so. It was like the ocean and the air was singing with them. No, that wasn't possible . . .

. . . not in this Realm, anyway.

*

When you learn more than you were meant to,
Your task becomes dealing with it.

All Knowledge leads to Wisdom,
Though the path is littered with Confusion.

> *Excerpts from Philosophy and Consequence, ancient*
> *Amethyst text.*

Chapter 7 - Meetings (Secret and Otherwise)
(Topaz Realm; 5 years ago)

Despite the distances that occasionally separated where they lived, Pho and Topaz did play together often, as they grew. They remained polar opposites, but their friendship bridged any difference. The strengths of one balanced the weaknesses of the other. Pho would help Topaz practice his basic light-power exercises again and again, and Topaz helped Pho see how to solve problems without them.

His uncle made sure that he always had a chance to visit when they were back in the Capital, regardless of his schedule. One time, though, when the boys were having one of their many sleep-over visits, they learned more than anyone could have predicted.

One day, when they were both about eleven years old, uncle Saul announced that he had arranged for a sleep-over. This suited Topaz just fine. It had been over two months since the last visit, and he was eager to catch up with his friend. He ran to gather his night clothes and toiletries together quickly.

"I won't be at the house tonight, Toivo," Saul mentioned as they walked down the road together toward Pho's house. "I have business to attend to."

"Oh? Okay." Topaz replied. "No problem." Just then another thought bubbled to the surface. "Uncle, you remember how I showed you that shadow-worm that was climbing on Pho's window?"

"Yes," Saul replied, turning his head slightly at the mention of it. "I remember. Do *you* remember what I told you about them?"

"*They represent our fears and doubts, and that . . .*" Topaz paused, trying to recall what his uncle had said.

"*...that any light can dispel them. Light will always banish Shadow, just as directly confronting what frightens us makes those fears disappear.*" Saul finished. "Every child your age had to learn that one for memory when I was younger."

"You're the only one that ever said that to me. Well, Pho finds them all over his window, almost every day now, and in the shadowy parts of his yard - dozens of them. Pho can blast the little ones, but they've been getting bigger. The big ones make me nervous. When we see them, Pho's the one that has to flash the light on them."

Saul did not even break stride, as he ruffled Topaz's hair affectionately.

"What a brave boy his is, then. Just remember that for a lot of people, it's perfectly natural to be wary of the Dark. The concept of living shadows terrifying most citizens of the Realm."

"That's for sure. Makes me jumpy when I see them."

"We are the children of Light, Toivo. Always remember that. Even a spark is enough to destroy a shadow. Learning to overcome a fear of the dark is essential for Apprentices, so that they can claim their full strength."

"Huh." Toivo mumbled, acknowledging the words. "My teacher says that we're supposed to go inside, into the light, and avoid them whenever we see them. She says that they're bad."

Saul snorted in disgust at this.

"Trust me, boyo, you know more about those shadows than your teacher ever knew. Just because people are being made to be more afraid of the shadows then they should be, doesn't mean you have to be."

Topaz smiled weakly then sighed. He really wished he could explain how the Shadow worms reminded him of his darkest nightmares. Maybe he would find a way someday; or maybe the fear would go away. He certainly hoped so.

When they arrived, he hopped up the steps to Pho's front door. His red-haired friend met him there and ushered his friend in. As Topaz dropped his travel bag around the corner, in the coat room by the door and fumbled with his boots, he could hear his uncle talking to Pho's father.

"Thanks for taking him tonight, Rhyol, I'll be gone for the entire evening." Saul said evenly. "Toivo tells me that you've been having problems with shadow worms?

"Now that you mention it, yes we have." Pho's father replied. "They show up almost every other day now. It's gettin' so I can't trim the lawn without a glowstone attached to the mower. You run over the pests, they gum up the blade and drain the power."

"Really?"

"Oh yeah."

"Are your neighbors finding them too?"

"Not so much. They seem to be focusing their attention here. And they really seem to like Pho."

"Like him?"

"Yup. They move mindlessly, right up till he shows up, then they all orient themselves on him. He moves around, they follow. He's a magnet. He can flash them to nothing, but it still takes a hand-strobe to clean his window off every morning."

"Hrmm . . ." Saul's voice took on a far-away tone, as if he were lost in deep thoughts, or memories.

"You ever hear tell of this?"

"Yes, but not in a very long time. I'll have to bring it up at the meeting tonight. You coming to this one?"

"Yeah, I'm almost ready. We can walk together."

Meeting? Topaz had never heard of these meetings before. His uncle had many during the day. It was the nature of his job, on the Council. But this was the first time that he had ever heard of his uncle having a meeting with Pho's father. He put his boots on the mat, quietly picked up his night-bag, and tip-toed into Pho's room, where his friend was finishing the last of his homework.

"Hey," Pho called out, closing his light tablet and facing his friend.

"Hey."

"So, what d'ya want to do tonight?"

"Actually, I was thinking we'd do something different." Topaz said quietly as he tossed his bag onto the camping cot he usually slept on when he visited, and sat down beside it.

"Oh?" Pho finished tidying up his desk and leaned in close. "Something secret?"

"Oh yeah."

"And not just sneaking around, trying to sneak peeks at the Cerulean girls in their nighties?"

Topaz had to blush as his friend reminded him of how inadvertently they had been – very - successful in their efforts to sneak a peek through the older girls' window, down the street. Both were about 3 years older than him, one a brunette with rich brown eyes, and the other a blond. The older girls had noticed them, but pretended otherwise. After a whisper, they proceeded have a fake argument, strutting around in their underwear. Both boys had been literally transfixed, filled with rich mixture of glorious accomplishment and a terrifying sense of the forbidden. The girls ended their argument by staring straight into the eyes of their observers, then soaking them both with a torrent of sapphire-power propelled water. Furious giggles could be heard as the window shades were drawn shut. It was a full minute later before Pho and Topaz had been able to move again; it had been weeks before the girls had stopped flirting outrageously with either Topaz or Pho, drawing a nearly fluorescent blush that went up to the ears every single time.

"Oh, yes. Very different. You still got that glow-band for your head?"

"Yeah, why?" Pho asked, eyes narrowing slightly. "Don't need it anymore, 'cept as backup now. Why?"

"Well," Topaz pulled out his personal chroma-chord, strapped it across his shoulders and slipped his hands into the gloves. "We've got a mystery, and we'll have to travel in the dark to solve it." He switched the sound box on and then switched it to its "mute" setting. Only light came from his hands, no sound. "I just overheard my uncle talking with your dad. He says that they've both got a meeting tonight."

"Huh. Dunno. My dad usually has meetings during the day, at the Power station. Without the sun, there's no solar to collect, so his job's done for the day."

"My uncle never has meetings at night, either, so I'm really curious. What are they doing? Maybe we follow them and find out."

"We'd have to find them then stay far enough back that they wouldn't notice." Pho mused, planning ahead as logistically as an eleven-year-old could. "I'm game, but how are you gonna cope if we meet any of those big worms out there?"

In answer to his friend's concern, Topaz tapped a contact on his left glove, and a narrow beam of yellow light stabbed out the bedroom window, impaling a tiny Shadow-Worm which faded to nothing.

"That's why we go armed."

"Oooo. Like that. Okay." Pho mumbled, mostly to himself. He made a fist, and shot a beam of light out the window himself. "I'll be real good at that myself someday too."

Topaz grimaced a little. "You already are that good, Pho. I'm the one who needs a musical instrument to cast light. You know that." He smacked Pho on the shoulder, just a wee bit harder than lightly.

"Right. Sorry." Pho apologized, rubbing the shoulder.

Toivo shrugged. "We'd better head out, if I'm gonna find the trail here."

"Eh? Oh, right."

The boys got to their feet, and moved toward the front door.

"Mom, can Toivo an' me go out the Treats store?" Pho called out. "I still have my allowance."

"Really? At this time of night? All right then. Have fun boys." His mother called out from the living room. "Be safe, call if you need something. Don't be too late."

"We won't," the boys chanted in unison. Slipping into their boots, they scampered into the cooler darkness of the evening.

*

As it turned out, it was easy enough to follow the adults. Topaz discovered that his ability to see those odd auras of light still worked at night . . . better even. His uncle always glowed in a brilliant yellow pattern that was distinctive to him. When they got out to the sidewalk, Topaz noticed a lingering haze that was the same pattern of yellow as the aura around his uncle. It led off, down the sidewalk. There was a different pattern of yellow haze, tinted blue that ran along beside it. Topaz started following it, Pho one step behind him, tapping his glow-band on with his finger. The gentle glow it emitted could be turned more quickly into an effective weapon for Pho than if he had to summon the Light himself.

The trail was not hard to follow, though it took quite a winding route. It led them out of the suburban neighborhood and toward the industrial district.

After following the trail for several blocks, the boys caught sight of their quarry entering an alleyway between two seemingly abandoned factory warehouses. With a quick run, they made it to the mouth of the alley. Peeking around the corner, they saw the men enter a dull grey metal door, into one of the buildings.

"Now!" Topaz whispered, and they scampered to the door. When they reached it, they saw no handle, knob or keypad. It was closed and did not seem to have any intention of opening for them.

"Okay, now what?" Pho muttered, combing the surrounding shadows with narrow shafts of light from his headband, to clear out any shadow-worms that might be there.

They both looked around and noticed the metal fire-escape ladder a little further on. It led to a window, around ten meters up the wall. Without a word, the boys moved to the ladder. Toivo started climbing immediately. He beckoned to his friend and popped into the window. Pho climbed about four rungs then froze, his eyes wide. He had peeked down and seen that he was he rest of the ascent was very slow, and white-knuckled. He reached the top with his face white and his back drenched in cold sweat.

Toivo helped him in the window, and noted his friend's expression.

"You're afraid of shadows, I'm afraid of heights," Pho whispered. "We're even."

Toivo looked more than a little puzzled by this, but shrugged. For some reason, fear of heights made no sense to him. He made sure to tap Pho's light-band, turning it off so they would not be noticed.

The boys were on a wide, metal catwalk above a large empty warehouse. There were some very faint glowstones glimmering near the exits, and at irregular intervals along the lower rafters. A small table sat in the middle of the floor. It was illuminated by a single, bright white hovering glowstone. There was a slight shimmer around it too, like a soap bubble. Seated at the table were five people. Their image was a little blurry, from the bubble, but a couple of them were easy to recognize.

<I see your uncle,> Pho sent to Toivo, via a tight-beam whisper. Toivo could understand them now, but only just recently. *<My dad, too. You know the others?>*

Topaz shrugged, moving closer along the catwalk until he was almost directly above the table. Pho followed. They peaked down over the edge, staying as quiet and inconspicuous as they could. The people were taking turns talking, that much was sure, but there was no sound escaping the bubble.

<Ok, what now? They took care of their privacy well enough.> Pho sent again. *<You don't have any distance-listening devices, do you?>*

Topaz shook his head, then his brow furrowed in thought for a moment. He looked at the table, looked at the controls to the chroma-chord that festooned the fingerless gloves he wore. He raised an eyebrow then his eyes widened. He flipped open a compartment on the chroma-chord's sound box, and a pair of tiny earpieces came out. He handed one to Pho, indicating for him to put it on. He popped the other one into his own ear. Pho mimicked him, not understanding, but recognizing an idea being tried.

Topaz adjusted the controls of the instrument to pick up ambient light from a very narrow area. He fiddled with the controls a little more, and the earpieces came to life. There were many ambient sounds now as the chroma-chord turned the light surrounding them into a dull ripple of low notes. Topaz pointed his right palm at the table, and the light receptors in the glove focused on the light reflecting off of the bubble. A sound representing this shimmer quietly rippled through the earpieces. Topaz fiddled with the controls on the sound box, and angled his right hand this way and that. Out of the ripples of sound, a faint but very clear version of the people's voices could be heard.

". . . has been diverting all of the best equipment to the Photic schools only," said a deep voiced woman, whose skin was a dark brown. "The galvanic, thermal and ultra regions are *still* getting castoffs and rejects. It's getting so that our children can't . . . ny new items from Sap. . . ethyst never makes it as far as us." The sound of her voice kept fading into a useless squelch at irregular intervals. Topaz frowned and kept his left hand hovering over the control panel on his chest, to make adjustments quickly.

"In other words, this is . . .wave. They're trying to . . . vide us . . . ." Rhyol said. Pho blinked, recognizing his father's voice, if not the words he was saying.

" . . . be starting soo. . ." Saul replied. "It's . . . ten years since th . . . They've been . . . their way into . . . We can . . . this . . . ." He turned to the dark-skinned woman and asked: "Dese, . . .region . . . ediate danger?" The longer patches of static were infuriating to Topaz, which drove him to more furious adjustments."

"No, we're all right," she answered. "The Blue Islands have their own culture, as well as the global one. . . . rovise." Here, her words became a long stream of noise. After a minute or so, the words returned: " . . . apphires aren'. . . ly ones who can . . .one sen . . .ck-start. We might come out . . . ."

A man with deeply tanned skin, in a long, dun colored robe with a hood and scarf started speaking then. His voice was lower than any of the others, so it took a moment to figure out how to hear him: " . . .nited our world, my people finally . . . e diplomats from Perid . . . Opa . . . helpe . . . find ways . . .ermal powers . . . veryone." For a brief moment, the static cleared: "If so much attention stays focused on the Photics, instead of the Realm as a whole, it will fracture us. Blue, Brown, even Clear regions would split off into separate countries again. We're vulnerable then."

<I've heard of those places, but I've never been to them,> Pho sent. <Did not even know Clear topazes still existed.>Topaz turned to his friend with an "Are-you-being-serious?!" look on his face. Pho shrugged helplessly. Topaz brought his left hand up and waved it in a small pattern in the air. A synthetic voice would be heard over the earpieces. The voice said, haltingly: <<Been to Blue and Brown. Best technicians and manufacturers in Realm. NEED both to . . . keep all machines working here. Don't know Clear. >> '

They turned back toward the table, as the conversation continued. Many garbled sentences were said, the boys catching one out of every ten words or so. A few kept repeating, though. "Charter", "influence", and the name of Councillor Pazos surfaced many times. Both boys drew in a worried breath when they heard the word "invasion" though. Neither could imagine what the adults meant by that, but it certainly helped them focus even more closely.

<You ever hear of this Charter thing?>

<<Sometimes . . . uncle . . . mention . . . never . . . notice-ed before. Important!>>

The meeting looked like it was coming to a close, as a couple of them were starting to put light tablets and documents back into satchels or carry-cases. Topaz, try as he might, couldn't clear up the static any more. He kept trying, though. He tapped Pho on the shoulder, giving him a signal to look around. His friend nodded, and cast about. He brought his arm over his friend's shoulder, and filaments of what looked like black spider-silk broke, blowing away in the wind. The interference vanished in an instant, and Saul's voice came through clearly.

"Your son is definitely the most promising photic I've ever met, stronger by half than some of the current Adepts in service right now." Saul said. "Makes sense. It's likely that we are all connected to the strongest children of our Realm, one way or another."

The others made noises of agreement, and finished packing. They pushed their chairs back and stood, some of them stretching.

"Us, yes, but you, Saul?" Dese asked bluntly. "You thinking your boy is . . ."

" . . . is something else entirely." Saul spat out quickly, cutting off anything more that the woman from the Islands was going to say. He looked significantly at her, bringing his hand up to his lips. Dese nodded, showing that she understood something. Topaz nearly cried out in frustration. What did Uncle Saul mean?

"We all know that they want to divide our Realm, making us all weaker by playing on the worst traits of each. The Necromancers have to kill all Hope in a Realm before they attack it. And make no mistake, we are watching that unfold."

Everyone nodded at this then they all touched their palms together, making a circle around the table. The shimmering bubble vanished. Suddenly, the voices became almost painfully clear to the boys. Topaz hastily turned down the volume. As he did this, he caught motion from the other side of the catwalk out of the corner of their eyes. He tapped Pho on the shoulder again, directing his gaze that way. With only the tiniest of ripples flowing across its immobile form, the boys saw the largest shadow-worm either had ever seen. It was as long as a grown man, and easily a meter in width. It was just beginning to undulate, ripples of motion in a liquid seeming shape. It seemed to be orienting itself. Pho saw it and caught his breath, his eyes wide. He gripped his friend on the shoulder.

Toivo saw the thing, and his mind went to a complete blank, his worst-ever fear brought to life. He unconsciously brought his hands up towards his face. His chroma-chord was still interpreting patterns of light as sound, and to his great shock, he could hear a gravelly whisper, speaking clearly.

{must report / find the window / must report / find the window / . . .} came the voice, over and over. Topaz could feel fear inside him like a living thing. It filled his chest with liquid ice, and made his legs tremble. His body was refusing to obey him, but a tiny portion of him was morbidly curious. Was he hearing thoughts from it, or did it have a voice? There were tiny filaments of its inky substance stretching across the

ceiling and walls. The boys could see truncated ends of these strands pulling back from directly over them. A shiver of revulsion went through both of them. Clearly, the creature had been the source of the interference that they had been experiencing. That implied that the shadow had to have some form of intelligence. A more chilling thought occurred to Topaz as he realized that the Shadow-worm had probably been able to intercept the sound signals that his chroma-chord had been using. It must have been spying on the meeting too. Why would a Shadow want to spy on a secret meeting like this? To whom did this great liquid spy answer to? The "Necromancers" that his uncle had mentioned? Topaz could feel the urge to call out to his uncle, down below, but when he looked down again, there was no one there. The meeting had concluded, everyone had left.

"That's a big one," Pho whispered, "Toivo, that thing is huge!"

"I know, I know, I know." Topaz replied. He could not move, he could not think. Pho took his cue and fired a small beam of white light from his right forefinger. It clipped the edge of the creature. Though the earpieces, both boys heard it make a sharp cry, and it recoiled from them.

{must report / way blocked / light kills / must report / way blocked / light kills . . .} it started chanting.

Pho heard the new messages, and tentatively tapped his headband. It started glowing gently. The worm's front end suddenly turned around and oriented on the boys. The message it was emitting changed too.

{must report / find the window / Spectrum child nearby / approach and contain / must report / find the . . .}

"Uh oh, that thing is trying to decide what to do about us, now," Topaz whispered frantically.

"Why is it babbling like that?" Pho asked, gathering the light from his headband into his hands.

"Sounds like a bunch of simple command that someone has given it, like a 'puter or an android."

The worm seemed to make up its mind, and all sounds from it ceased. It started moving, like a slowly rolling puddle toward the boys. Clearly its 'Spectrum' directive was higher priority than the 'reporting' one.

Topaz felt his entire mind begin to shrivel as Pho launched his ball of collected light at it. The creature opened its middle to allow the ball to fly through harmlessly. It kept approaching the boys, its surface rippling as it closed the intervening distance.

{. . . light hurting / consume / light hurting / consume . . .} the creature's shadowy whispers were actually audible now, with it being so close. Pho heard it, and started raking the length and width of the creature with as many light-beams as he had fingers: Core-Light and not the artificial light from his headband. The creature's substance parted as each beam hit it, then reformed immediately afterwards. Clearly the monster had learned how to deal with attacks of this nature.

"Er . . . Toivo, I think it's going to do something about me." Pho said tersely, as a slender black tendril shot out of the worm's side, and wrapped itself around his extended hand.

"Yee-ah!" Pho yelped in surprise and shock. The beams ceased instantly. "Ow, ow owowowowow, Toivo!" he cried out in pain as the tendril wrapped around his forearm.

Toivo heard his name called out, saw his best friend in the world being attacked by a Shadow, and suddenly his eyes started glowing with a bright yellow light.

"Hey!" he shouted, rising to his feet. "Let go of my friend!" With a flip of a switch, the chroma-chord became a flashing beacon of color and sound. With wild stabbing and slashing motions, Toivo aimed as many colors of light at his foe as fast as he could, in a completely random ways. There was not pattern to his attack. The tendril was sheared off in an instant. Each beam or burst of color shaved off a piece of the shadow, which did one of two things: the chunk fell to the catwalk and evaporated with a faint cry, or it wriggled around until it rejoined the main body. The worm rose up in front of the boys now. Pho backed up a step, cradling the arm that the creature had grabbed, but Toivo stood his ground.

"I don't think so," he said loudly, his voice crackling with anger. The light in his eyes got brighter again, and an aura of light started surrounding him. He punched both of his hands forward, and twin beams of light shot forth, many times brighter than what Pho had been using. The worm was stabbed through the heart by the sudden beams, and it was transfixed. His uncle had been right. You had to shine your light right into the heart of these creatures. The shadow substance that was touched by the beams evaporated into a foul vapor, so Toivo used the light like a paintbrush. Within seconds, the creature was gone.

Neither boy moved for several seconds afterwards. The dissipating smoke that the monster had become was acrid. Toivo's eyes slowly faded back to dark amber-grey, but they remained vaguely luminescent. He noticed that the gloves for the chroma-chord had been shorted out and somewhat melted by the beams he had fired. He pulled them off, and stowed them in his pocket. He turned to check on his friend. Pho gingerly rubbed his hand then cried out suddenly. He rolled his sleeve up and both boys gasped a little bit. Pho's hand, wrist and the top of his forearm had strange, raw-looking marks on them, like intense reverse-sunburns, as if the color in the skin had been drained away and replaced with greyish-white tissue and deep, intense, stinging pain. They corresponded with where the tendril of shadow had grabbed him. The boys stared blankly at damage to Pho's hand, shocked. Another stab of sharp pain caused Pho to draw his breath raggedly. Snapping out of their stupor, the boys looked at each other.

"Dunno if I can handle a ladder with this." Pho muttered.

"Let me worry 'bout that." Toivo declared, casting about and finding a staircase down to the floor just down the catwalk a little ways. "Go. Staircase is over there. Move." The tone in his voice brooked no protest.

The boys walked carefully to the stairs and went down to the floor. They wandered until they found what they thought was the door that they had first encountered. They opened it, and they were back in the alley again. When they were clear of the building, they both ran as fast as they could, back to Pho's house. They did not stop once.

They ran in the front door, kicked their boots off and ran to Pho's room. Pho did not stop there, running to the bathroom to run cool water over his discolored hand.

"Boys? Boys, what's wrong?" Pho's mother called out as she caught up to them. "Pho, Toivo, what happened?" She saw Toivo with a hint of residual glow in his eyes, and a very determined look on his young face. She looked over at Pho in the bathroom, and gasped when she saw his hand. She moved in, as only a mother can, and looked his hand over, back to front. She asked if he could move his fingers, which he could. She felt the starkly white skin, and he flinched as if he had been stung or burned by a hot flame.

"Boys, how did this happen?" she asked again, in that tone that said '*Ok-game-is-over-now-talk!*'

"There was a nest, ma'am," Toivo piped up instantly. "We were almost at the store when Pho fell into a nest of shadow-worms. His arm was stuck for a while. We got it out, but not before this."

Pho locked eyes with Toivo, and if he had been able to concentrate, he would have thanked his friend using a tight-beam. This cover story was believable, and entirely likely. His mother started rummaging through the medicine cabinet, pulling out several burn pads and soothing ointment. She had his hand bandaged up within minutes, and was feeding them both some reheated soup and crackers by the time Pho's father returned home.

"I'm home," he called out. "Anybody here?"

Pho's mother yanked him into the kitchen, to update him on the boys. Needless to say he was concerned, examining the burns right away. He quickly dialed up Saul's comm-number, and informed him of Pho's injury.

"Saul will be here in a few minutes, Toivo," he said. "I think it's safe to say that the sleep over is done for the night."

"That's okay, sir. We both kinda figured that." Toivo sipped his mug of soup as he spoke. He turned to Pho and continued: "My uncle will probably take you to the Council med-center. That's where I usually wind up when I get hurt." He realized he was still wearing the remains of his chroma-chord, destroyed gloves and all. He thought fast, then showed the damaged instrument and described how he had tried to pull Pho's hand out of the hole, only to have the shadow-worms in the nest short out his equipment. Pho's parents nodded, commending him for his bravery, knowing how much he disliked them. They had no idea how much more that was true tonight.

"I hope my auntie Lumens won't be too angry with me," Toivo pondered aloud, more to himself than anyone else. "I'm in the band for the arrival of some visiting diplomats next week. I'll need something to play on by then."

"Leave it with me," Pho's father beamed, picking it up in his calloused hands and looking it over. He popped the back of the center-box open and looked at the singed wiring and circuits within. "I know a few things about the workings of a chroma-chord like this. Maybe I can salvage it. Your aunt will never know."

"Really?" Toivo burst out, inordinately pleased. "Wow, that's *shiny*, sir. Thank you very much." Toivo did not have to feign being grateful. This would save him a Realm of trouble at home.

"Glad to help," he replied, then he turned to his son and said: "When it's light out, you are showing where this nest is. Must be pretty big, if it could do that to your hand. It's a hazard to the community."

"Yes sir," both boys answered.

Saul did arrive and whisk Pho off to the medical center. One of the few remaining Emerald Realm doctors examined his hand, shocked by what he saw, but more than capable of repairing the tissue damage. His powers over all things living knit his skin back together from the cells up. Saul kept images of the injury on his personal light-pad, a grim expression his only mask.

Toivo was able to play at the Welcoming, though he was at the back and had been told to accompany only. That suited him just fine. Auntie Lumens always told him the mark of a true Musician was that they made those that they accompanied sound better.

Toivo and Pho decided not to tell about their misadventure, but they both took a solemn oath that they would always stay alert for these shadows, and that they would destroy them with extreme prejudice every time they saw them. Toivo had come through this adventure changed to his core. His fear of the dark had been completely erased replaced by a steely determination. He was also extremely motivated to practice his light powers as hard as he could. His uncle was thrilled. He drew even more of the shadow-worms to him now, but they vanished in a flash of light from his eyes or fists every time now.

At the same time, though, another seed of self-doubt had been planted within him. He had found the power to destroy the worm-spy, but he had to loose emotional control to summon it.

*

"Yes, commander. The photic boy is getting more powerful every day. He's completely overcome any fear reaction to the Dark he might have had. Acrophobia took hold, though, for some reason."

"Then we will need to manage him with more subtlety, then. We'll try to bring him over with other elements when he's older, and more powerful than everyone. Arrogance perhaps, or maybe Pride. We'll revisit that when it comes time. Is there any chance that he is the missing TopazStar?"

"He's measures as photic only. He shows no sign of any other E.M. ability."

"Ah well, the search continues. Keep me appraised. And keep an eye on that bumbler that Saul is harboring. He does not fit any of the expected patterns for a child with powers in that Realm. He's doing a fine job of blocking himself, but we can't afford to take any chances. If we are to prevent him from achieving true Power, we will need to tailor his program more specifically than others."

"Agreed."

"What about the other children?"

"The blue girl has been found and is already proving to be useful as a singer. We'll be able to channel her into the Media program eventually. The boy from Calorian Plains is potent but contained by the social pressures on his people, effectively neutral there. There's one other girl who keeps showing up, now and again, but she's a clear topaz; not a person of any consequence, in my opinion."

"Very well. Continue as ordered. I will come to monitor the Ascension ceremonies for this generation of *students in due time. Make all the necessary arrangements. Command is pleased with your progress. Stay careful. Your realm is a potential flashpoint that we don't want to deal with until WE want to."*

"Yes sir."

*

"But, sirrah, you are but one. How will you survive battling so many?"
"Majesty, I am but one, but if I bear your favor, then I shall be many times more than myself."

> *From "The Peridot Queen and the Opal Knight", a children's tale.*

Chapter 8 - Connection
(Topaz Realm; 4 years ago)

His visits with Pho remained times of joy for Toivo as they grew, but in the intervals between them, he had to manage the best he could on his own. Some days were more successful for him than others. He had started being able to tell ahead of time how a day would be for him.

Today, it was quiet, for once. He peeked out from behind the bushes, and scanned the playground with his twelve-year-old eyes. He breathed a sigh of relief. There was no sign of the bullies; He had made it out of class before them. With luck, they'd overlook this particular bush in the Peace Garden by the junior grade entry door. The Garden was considered neutral ground for most, since it was closest to where the teachers emerged when they were supervising the outdoor playtime. Now and again, the ones who harassed him would be too engaged in their ball-kicking games to want to find him, but he could never predict when they would suddenly appear. Sometimes, they would chase him all-recess long. If they ever caught him, they would quietly drag him to an area of relative privacy, where they would throw him to the ground and punch him repeatedly as only twelve-year-olds can. Topaz worked very hard and ran very quickly to prevent this, whenever he could.

When they weren't beating on him, they would taunt him about anything they could think of. It used to be that he could not use light powers with any skill, now it might be that he was standing under a tree, or that he had answered a question in Mathematics class. It did not matter. Neither did it matter whether the duty teacher would wander by or not. They would simply pause, and then resume after the authority figure had left.

Worst of all was when they used their different gem powers on him. He knew that he could resist some of them now, but not reliably nor consistently. Everyone that had ever known him knew that he was barely able to make his hand glow - even now - and that meant that the basic Light Control skills that would deter them were beyond him. If he could use the Spectrum, they would desist because they had to. If an offense was made against a citizen of Light, then it would be reported to their parents, and that could lead to diplomatic embarrassment. After all, you don't insult your hosts when you are visiting somewhere. That was a moot point when it came to him though, since no one really considered him to have powers of note. No one had ever told them that it was all right to pick on the Powerless, but it was certainly the norm here in the play-yard. His disability made him fair game for everyone and anyone; whether or not that was fair was irrelevant.

"Hey, No-Glow," called a scrawny boy with wild blond hair, pronounced over-bite and raptor's eyes, using the nickname they'd given Topaz years ago. There were others they used, some silly, some mean. This one was a direct insult, and particularly foul language when aimed at any citizen in this Realm. The speaker knew this very well, as did his cronies. "Where'd ya go?" he shouted again, wiping the last of a messy lunch off of his hands and onto a maroon t-shirt.

"Not here," remarked a taller, deeper voiced boy, all in blue. "Maybe he's walkin' with the teach' again. Let's go look."

Topaz could not hear them for a few seconds. Two possibilities existed here for him: they were listening and looking for him or they had moved on to see if he was walking with the duty teacher. He did not dare peek out to check, the risk was just too great. His only chance was to be invisible. So he just sat, curled into the tightest, quietest little ball he could, under the shrubbery, hoping against hope.

Much to his sorrow, it was the former that turned out to be true, and the proof of that started with a rustling in the foliage he was under. At first he thought that someone was moving the branches aside to look in, but it was much more insidious than that. The bush that he was hiding under was shrinking. The leaves were pulling back into their buds, the twigs and branches pulling back together. Within moments, it was a sapling in the ground that was trying to burst back into adulthood. Of course, he was now utterly exposed. The boy wearing deep green pants and a black sweater who'd been holding his hands at shoulder level, put them down and opened his eyes. The four boys loomed over him, saying nothing. They did not have to. Topaz knew the drill here, it was so regular for him. He was not disappointed as they began by reaching down and hauling him to his feet roughly.

"Gotta love Emerald power," the boy in blue said to the one in green. "You were right, Lina. There *was* a little dark spot under that bush."

Topaz had stopped being startled by their vulgar words years ago but he could never avoid the flashes of helpless anger that washed through his mind whenever they used them. In his world, there was simply no need for that. He wondered if adults ever got used to this type of profanity.

"We're feeling generous today. Won't beat the sparkles out of you till I get to eight. One . . . two . . . "the sapphire boy grinned as he said this, eyes half-lidded in arrogant confidence.

Topaz looked at each of them: the scrawny Garnet lad whose powers over Force and Vectors could invisibly catch him anywhere in the yard and throw him to the ground; the tall black haired Sapphire boy who would do the same thing but with his arms, as well as soak him thoroughly in embarrassing places with his Water powers; the Emerald boy with the pale skin and greasy brown hair, who turned any plant or insect life around him into willing accomplices; and worst of all, the frog-shaped missile of a boy from the Diamond realm, who never participated, but always watched, his eyes only coming to life when Topaz was being beaten. He looked at his enemies arrayed before him, and decided to leave this scene as quickly as possible, since they were giving him the chance.

He turned away and ran toward the pavement at the other end of the school. If he could make it there, he would have relative safety. The boys played in the field. The girls ruled the pavement. At this particular Rudiments School, in the outskirts of Estan, the rules stated that he was not permitted to go onto the pavement - but that did not mean that he could not stand on the edge of it. The four would not assault him there, brazenly . . . he hoped. It was too public for their liking.

He reached the boundary: the coarse white gravel that was compacted and baked halfway to concrete by the one, two or all three of the suns. He checked the big clock over the door, and sighed. He still had twenty-five minutes to wait before he was safe in class. There, it was still a frustrating situation, but predictable at least. Out here, it was survival of the fittest.

He watched the girls playing, all in different colors of shirts and dresses, all skipping and playing quietly together. If there were conflicts and battles taking place, he did not recognize them. No one was getting punched, or shoved, or tripped. Compared to his usual experiences, life on the pavement seemed so . . . peaceful. He wondered what it would be like to be able to come outside and not have to fight, or to actually be able to have fun, like everyone else. It made him feel hopeless and useless to think like that, so he consciously tried to think of nothing at all.

He walked the length of the boundary then noticed a girl sitting off to one corner of the pavement. She was examining the sides of a little hole she had been digging through the gravel with a stick. She had light red hair, deep blue eyes and the beginnings of freckles across the crown of her nose. She wore a white top and a light green skirt. There was something almost familiar about her, but he could not place it. He watched her, curious, but not wanting to be rude.

"Hi," she called out to him, looking up. "Wanna come dig?"

Topaz blinked, his anonymity gone . . . but not in an aggressive way. He nodded mutely. She wasn't trying to tease him, nor be mean. And most of all, in his experience, a girl his age usually did not dig holes in the dirt. That was different enough for him to be curious about her. He sat down across the hole from her.

"I remember you," he said. "You just moved here, did not you?"

"That's right, how did you know?" she did not even pause in her digging to ask this.

"I was in the band that was playing the Welcoming song and the Anthem of Light when your family arrived here with the diplomats, last week."

"Oh? What were you playing?" she inquired, still focused on the hole.

"*Chroma-chord*. I was at the back."

"Ah, that's nice," she replied, clearly not knowing what a *chroma-chord* was. She continued to speak, brushing her hands off.

"My dad works for Peridot Financial Services. He was transferred here last week, and he's gonna be here for a while, so my mom, sister an' me came too," She said the words easily, but in a very weary voice. "We were here once before, when I was little, but that was years ago. My dad keeps getting transferred to different branches of the PFS, so we have to go too." She sighed a little bit. "This is the fourth school I've been to in the last four years."

"Huh," he said, moving the surface dirt around with the edge of his lucky pendant. "That's a lot of moving." He smiled sympathetically. She saw this, and smiled at him, relief clear in her face. Someone was listening, instead of talking. Her eyes lit right up, like blue topazes, and she sat a little taller. This was a different response for him again, but he understood. Despite living in the Realm of Light all his life, he had spent most of it traveling with his uncle. He doubted that the other students here could relate to that as well as he could.

"It sure is. I've tried to make friends on all sorts of worlds, but I just lose them again at the end of classes." She changed the subject abruptly here and started digging again.

"You know, you can tell a lot about a place by the rocks and fossils you find in 'em." She pulled out a medium-sized chunk of white quartz. "This stuff is on every world I've been to. Here, it's really, *really* white."

Topaz picked up a similar chunk, and noted its rough, milky surface. He had always noticed the different rocks himself, especially between the different geographic areas he had visited. This was typical quartz for here in the Photic regions. Some people polished them up and used them as pendants, or screens for smaller comm-systems. He shared what he knew about the stone, adding to the discussion. He did not feel that she was listening to him out of pity, or contempt, because she would contribute thoughts and facts of her own to what he was saying. It was an actual *full-bright-no-shadows* discussion. It was the first one he had ever had at this school, and it felt nice.

For the rest of the outside time, he sat there with her, just listening about how she had lived on Emerald, then on Garnet, how she had kept in touch with friends on Aquamarine. She eventually became curious about him.

"So, have you always lived on Topaz?" she finally asked.

"Uh huh," he replied, casting his eyes down and playing with the dirt again. "All my life."

"You're wearing yellow. That means that you have Light powers?"

"Yeah, but not so good. That's why my uncle got me a spot at the Rudiments school, and not the normal one." His cheeks became flushed suddenly as he spoke, but he kept going: "Thing is: I thing that I'm finally getting better. Watch . . ." He held his chunk of quartz in his palm, and squinted at it. With a tingle in his fingertips, he tried to send energy into the stone. As usual, his lucky pendant buzzed quietly, then he could feel the Light collecting where he wanted. The white

96

stone started to glow a dull orange, like a candle under a pink salt crystal. The girl drew in a surprised breath then clapped happily.

"Oooo . . . that was *amped*! Show me how!" she exclaimed in an excited jumble. She held out the chunk she had pried from the ground, and waited impatiently. Topaz showed her how to hold the rock, what the process was to call on the Light, just as he had been shown innumerable times, by innumerable teachers, and after a few minutes of her squinting and concentrating, the rock she held in her hand was glowing orange too. Topaz smiled then tapped her on the shoulder to see what she was doing. He was happy for her, and complimented her on learning one of the Rudiments skills so quickly. He remembered how nice it felt when his teachers said encouraging things to him when he made progress, even when it was a baby-step. He made sure to make her practice doing it a couple of times. Her eyes just kept getting wider and brighter as she mastered this skill.

"This is the best thing I've learned here," she babbled happily. Turning to Topaz, she beamed at him and thanked him for the lesson.

"You're better than the teachers! You used words that made sense to me. Thank you!"

Without any warning, she scooted over and gave him a quick hug before getting up to show a couple of the other girls the new trick she had learned. Impressed, they fell into discussion and started moving away.

Topaz stared after her, trying to grasp what had just happened. He had learned the stone trick only a few weeks ago. Any toddler of this Realm could make the white quartz chunks glow, of course, but to a girl from Peridot, it was still a neat trick.

And she had hugged him.

That had caught him off-guard. It had come out of the bright sky. She had been grateful and she hugged him. It was staggering to him. He could feel himself revising his opinion of the entire female gender in general because of this. He remained fixed there, pondering, catching the last of the scent of her flower-shampoo that lingered where she had been, only a short time ago. Her strawberry blonde hair and fair skin had etched their image into him. He could not put words to this mood he was in, but he knew that he felt amazing and that he liked it.

When the four bullies caught up to him, to their surprise, he did not even notice them.

*

The girl's name was Kayleigh. She and her younger sister had been born in the Peridot Realm and therefore that was that was the Gem that they were attuned to. Her father was indeed a Diamond citizen who was very influential in financial circles. Her mother had been born here on Topaz, though, and that is why they were here, staying with relatives while their father worked out the details of some great big financial deal between Realms. As Topaz got to know her over the next few weeks, he enjoyed a welcome reprieve from his tormentors. Whatever else the people born on Peridot could do, he learned that they were powerful. That was what they "did": Power, in any and all forms. It showed in many, little ways, like when different machines would pop to life when she walked by or when people got out of their way as they wandered the yard and pavement, talking.

They would talk about nothing and everything. He listened avidly to her, just as she encouraged him to talk. As it turned out, they shared many interests. They were both very creative, and able to spin silly stories till they giggled helplessly. She was a year older than he was, and a girl, so that meant that she was vastly more aware than him of how social nuances worked. Was that a function of her gem-powers, or that she was a girl? He couldn't tell - and he really did not care.

He was able to match wits with her, though. Since he had moved around so much, he had lots of experiences, in different areas, to draw on. Just talking with Kayleigh was enough to make Topaz feel like he was re-visiting all of his happier memories. He described the beauty he had seen around the Realm and explained about the other topaz powers. He even quietly showed her how he could make sparks appear between his fingers, and how he could warm up liquids in the palm of his hand. She was even more impressed, and promised to keep his other talents secret. She even listened to him as he detailed how he was bullied and teased all the time. This made her angry on his behalf, and she was not shy about letting him know that.

"That is not fair!" she would say, venting her frustration. "And it's not necessary! There are dozens of ways that you could avoid that." She would make several suggestions as to how he could prevent the issue that he had encountered. For example, he could change what he wore, so that they did not notice him (which worked some of the time); he could confront them directly in the presence of others (which worked less of the time). She was always willing to help him solve his difficulties, regardless of what they were. She was the most active problem-solver he had ever met. It gave her phenomenal drive and motivation, which she would lend to him whenever his strength was flagging.

When he walked home after school, his mind would review the time spent with her. Today, she had brought pictures and holos of her friends on different worlds, and of her sightseeing trips there. Images of dense jungles, huge futuristic cities and vast oceans filled his eyes, matching up with the tales she told that filled his imagination. He longed to go to these places, to smell the smells, to hear the sounds.

"If we go visiting, I promise to ask my parents if you can come too," she had said. When he had heard that, he had been suddenly so happy that before he knew what he was doing, he was hugging her. Even more miraculously, she hugged him back, leaning her head against his shoulder. They just stood there for a moment hugging each other, and Topaz could feel his heart become a thudding, racing beast. His head was utterly blank, but for the feel of her arms around him. Again, he did not have words for this. He felt strong enough to tackle a building, and fast enough to outrun a sunbeam. She let go of him, and waved. Did she have a bit of a blush in her cheek too?

*

For the rest the day, he was immune to any aggression, or snide comments the bullies could make. He simply ignored them, and they continued not knowing how to handle that. The Sapphire boy even tried to shove him into the wall, but only succeeded in smashing himself into it - Topaz had seen and dodged his attack with one step backwards at the right moment. When he got back to class, he even completed the Light Construct exercise his class was working on . . . it was weak and out of focus, but he had displayed enough skill to have received a minimum passing mark on the task as opposed to the outright fail that it would have otherwise been. The chime rang out, and he was out of his desk in a heartbeat. His feet moved of their own accord, and it felt like he was leaping all the way home.

He hopped over the low fence surrounding the garden of shrubs in front of his uncle's current house. He leaped up the steps to the porch and slid with unaccustomed ease into the front foyer. He spied his uncle at his light-desk, and waved cheerily, big ol' grin plastered across his face. His uncle Saul looked, then did a double take at his nephew's entrance.

"And hello to you," Saul said, rising from his seat, shutting down a holo-image displaying some thoroughly unpleasant fellows. "You're home early."

"Did not have to hide or take the long way, today," Topaz tossed his school bag into the corner and started toward the kitchen. His uncle had started putting up solid light barriers around the pantry, as his adolescent nephew's appetite was growing. Today, Topaz simply walked right through them, as if they weren't there, grabbing his snack amidst the shards and chunks of what once had been a photic lock and chain. His uncle blinked again then walked toward the kitchen himself.

"I see you've made progress in your 'construct' manipulation."

"Huh?" he mumbled over a piece of orange-fruit that he had nabbed, juices dribbling out a corner of his mouth. "What construct? Where?"

His uncle raised his hands and commanded the solid light bands that had been casually rent asunder, to dissipate. Topaz nodded, seeing them finally.

"Those," Saul said. "The ones I've been using to keep you from eating us out of house and home."

Topaz shrugged, with his "I-don't-quite-believe-you-they-weren't-there-a-moment- ago-you're -joking-with-me" face on.

"You must be in quite the state of mind if you could shrug off *my* constructs like that. How was your day?" His uncle always asked him this question, and listened to him as he unloaded his young joyful soul. He had not told his uncle about Kayleigh before this, because it simply hadn't occurred to him to do so, but now he shared every happy moment with his uncle, who listened, grinned and guffawed in all the right places.

"She sounds like a lovely girl," Saul noted. "I probably know her father from somewhere."

Topaz nodded, reliving today's events in his memory again in his mind. All the days he had spent with her were happy, so it did not really matter what they had done.

"Maybe we should invite her and her family over for dinner sometime, eh?"

Topaz blinked, then tackle-hugged his uncle. The older man was knocked back to the wall, then he laughed outright, hugging Topaz back. Clearly the suggestion had been met with approval.

By the time his assignments and practicing were finished, they had worked out an entire evening of dining and entertainment for Kayleigh and her family. Saul had to admit that he had never seen his nephew so motivated or so happy. It looked good on him.

*

This time together lasted the rest of that school year, with many other happy days, special dinners where his uncle would entertain Kayleigh's family. When he wasn't visiting Pho, he was visiting Kayleigh. He felt alive when he was near her.

Sadly, as before, her family had to move one last time: back to Peridot. Her father's company had an opening in their head office, and he was the man they wanted for it. When they met after school, in the park nearest to her house, both friends cried, then talked, then promised to stay in touch.

"Not sure how we'll do that, K," Topaz said, eyes red and puffy. "There's not a lot of inter-Realm comm service, anymore. I should know - my uncle was on the Council's Communications Committee for a bunch of years."

"You don't need comm service," she replied in a conspiratorial whisper. "On Peridot, we've learned a way to always stay in touch with someone, no matter where they are. It's called *mind-wave.*"

"Mind-wave?"

"Yeah. It's like Amethyst mind-talking, but not. It doesn't matter how far away you are."

"Not Amethyst, eh? You make it sound easy."

"Well, for the right people, it is." She pulled a personal holo-pad out of her pocket and handed it to him.

"If you are the right type of person, this will make sense to you. That's all I'm allowed to say."

"Allowed? What? There are rules about this?"

"Oh, yes. You can get into big trouble if you share realm Secrets with the wrong people. After all, knowing something is just a different type of Power."

"Gotcha."

"So, read it."

"Right now?"

"YES! Right now!" She slugged him in the shoulder in mock-anger.

"All right, all right. Slow the strobe down." Topaz flipped on the display and read the single paragraph there, thoroughly. It spoke like a textbook, but resembled . . . something else. He could not find the right words to describe it.

"So knowing how to send an impulse through dimensional space, from one mind to another, is a state secret for your people?"

"SHH! Just try it once. I have to go soon." She leaned her shoulder against his emphatically, then said in her serious voice. "I don't want to lose you, Toivo." She was using his real name to emphasize her point and the show him just how deeply she felt about this, about him. Only she, his uncle and a few others knew his secret, real name.

He nodded then touched his forehead to hers. Closing his eyes, he thought about her as strongly as he could, every detail, everything he had learned about her. According to the holo-pad, she was doing the same thing, engaging her Peridot gem-powers to forge a link. He could feel a tickle start to grow where their heads made contact, the sound of a dynamo and a waterfall filling his mind. He opened his eyes and saw that Kayleigh's eyes were glowing bright green. He could almost see filament forming between them. They pulled away from each other, and he could still see a tiny shimmering thread connecting them. To his surprise, he saw a green glow coming from his hands.

<Can you hear me?> he thought-spoke.

Kayleigh's eyes flew wide open, happy tears flowing from them.

<Yes! I can! >

<I'll be able to contact you, like this? >

<Yes! >

<Even when you go home? >

<Oh yes! That was the fastest that I've ever linked with anyone. It was as if you were another Peridot! I'll be here, now, till the Link fades.> She touched his forehead with the back of her fingers, gently.

<And so will I.> he sent, returning the gesture. They dissolved into a long hug, then parted ways: him walking back to his uncle's house; her walking to her family's hover-car.

*

They were able to speak via mind-wave as easily as any comm-system for almost a year. She had been right: distance made no difference. It had been as if she was speaking to him inside his mind. No one ever found out. He had more insight into the difficulties of his life than ever before, and no one could explain it. He liked that. It was as if she had given him some of her Peridot Power, and it filled him with all kinds of hope.

In the last minutes of their mind-link, they promised each other that they would find a way to get back together again, to re-forge the Link. He could feel the force of her titanic willpower agreeing to this. Neither one of them could predict when, but they both believed that this day would come. The memory of her gave Topaz an inner resolve he had not known. He *would* overcome his impediment and become an Apprentice. That way, he might be able to Ascend to the Academy then he would be able to travel to Peridot, and see her again. The force of the decision in him caused his eyes to glow brightly for a second.

*

Part 2

Changes

How to see what has not been seen
Is only possible when you use
Different eyes.
        Saying from the Opal Realm

Chapter 9 – Contrasts
(Topaz Realm; present day)

The light of Lesser Sun could be felt just below the horizon, like seeing bright lights through closed eyes. If he had been Thermal or Clear, he might have been able to see all of the radiant-invisibles dancing around in east-prime. Very few examples of Topaz Realm tech would actually be getting enough photic to do more than remain idle, given the dark oranges and deep reds of what passed for the night sky. Greater Sun, bright and blazing yellow-white, was not due to rise for another hour or so. Only those creatures that were adapted to *half-bright* were active.

He lay in the soft grass and let his eyes defocus and his mind wander. The deep condescension that followed him about daily was gone, as were the disappointments that plagued him every time he tried anything. Clearly, that was a big part of why he came. The people who were the source of his waking nightmares couldn't function in this predawn darkness, and thus his sanctuary stayed safe.

He lay under his favorite tree, a tall smooth-barked species that Uncle Saul received as a gift from the Ambassador from the lush Emerald Realm. Fast growing to its full height then staying tall and beautiful for many years afterwards, it thrived both in the bright sunlight and the half-bright. It even had a hint of luminescence in the leaves, which is why it was called a Moon-Leaf tree. You could only see the pale blue-green glow in almost complete darkness.

Not that it was ever *completely* dark here, but the muted colours of the night sky were as close as you got. Toivo knew that if he ever felt the need to move into true dark, the kind of blackness where you could only see outlines of things in a million shades of grey, he had to create it himself then dismantle it completely when he was done. The last time he had tried to make a "dark" place, he had been 5, and the shipping box that he had up-ended and used as an imaginary cave had been taken away the moment Saul had seen it, cut into pieces and tossed into the Re-Cycler. This was before he had known that there were Shadow Worms out there, roaming around. He knew now that he could have encountered one in there, which would have been dire for him. His friend Pho still had a scar on his arm from their encounter with a huge one. This meant that he would watch his classmates more closely now, imitating them when he could even if he sometimes had NO idea what they were doing or why.

Toivo kept his eyes focused on nothing, and thus he noticed it. One of the shadows cast by the branches of the tree moved. There was no breeze; the air was still. One long shadow was getting shorter on the trunk. When he turned his head to get a better look at it, he found himself blinking furiously for a few moments. When he stopped, his eyes suddenly adjusted and he saw clearly. It wasn't just a patch of obscurity; there was something about this shadow that had a substance to it. He sat up and looked more closely at it. It moved like a long bead of impossibly black ink slowly rising up the trunk towards the middle branches. It moved as if it were somehow alive, like a liquid/gel version of a worm or a centipede. The sight of it was enough to make Toivo shudder once, a chill flashing down his back. He knew this beastie: Shadow worm, albeit a tiny one. He and Pho had sworn to eliminate them whenever they found them, but he had never had a chance to examine one all that well. Up close, it really and truly did look like a liquid. It moved forward by orienting its front end in a direction and then ripples came forward, moving the thing in that direction. When it encountered obstacles, it would flow around or through them.

Toivo stared at it with a morbid fascination. He took a twig and poked it once. It was like poking a puddle, except that the substance of the worm crawled quickly up the twig. He let the twig go, and it fell to the ground. Toivo noticed right away that all of the colour had been leeched out of the section that had been touched. The worm continued on its way, unhindered. It turned and started moving out along the lowest of the big branches.

He picked up the stick and examined it more closely. The bark was normal coloured right up to the point where the worm had enveloped it, where it became as white as paper, just like Pho's arm had been. He touched it, felt it, nothing else had changed about it. Just to make sure, he tapped one of the tiny crystals imbedded in the bracer on his left arm, and a tiny glowstone lit up brightly. He held the stick up and confirmed that any colouration was gone, but not just gone. The pattern resembled that of a stick having been burned in a hot fire, only in reverse. This was the second time Toivo had ever seen this sort of damage. He now knew that these foul things could affect other things too, and that thought was not very comforting. He tapped another crystal on his bracer, and he could feel the tiny components imbedded within it hum to life. He held the stick up to the recording lens, and the bracer recorded the image. His uncle had to see this, so did Pho.

When he was done, he tried to find the worm. He thought he had lost it, but then he saw what looked like its tail end sticking out of a small, round object hanging from the branches. As he watched, it flattened into a ribbon then moved to add itself to the surface of the object: a compact little ball made up of many worms. The ball twitched a few times. Toivo knew of no reason why the foul things would do this, unless there was some living thing inside.

Switching his glowstone to as bright as it could go, he shined the beam at the object. The effect was immediate. First, there was a wild squiggling from the worms then with tiny wispy cries, the worms started dissolving into puffs of acrid smoke that faded to nothing almost immediately. When the last layer of shadow-worms faded from view, a small group of birds were revealed in a woven hanging nest. They were all bleached as the stick was. The smallest one of them twitched slightly once more then didn't move again.

Toivo stared at the family of dead birds in shock, their lives snuffed out. He felt a mixture of shock and anger now. He looked more closely at the pattern of feathers on the birds, and realized that they were flash-jays: little birds that could cause their feathers to strobe brightly in the event of danger. They were the most common species of bird for this part of the Photic regions. If a flash-jay landed near you, it was considered to be good luck or a blessing on your endeavours from the Heart of Light. They represented Hope. He had witnessed a true evil, live and up close.

"*Shade and Shine*, I don't think so!" he growled, shining the glowstone along as many branches on the tree as he could. Every few seconds, there was another little wispy cry and a puff of foul smoke. Within minutes, Toivo had cleared the tree of the shadow-worm infestation as best he could. He took a certain pleasure in watching the darkness fade. This tree was safe, at least.

But there were many more trees.

Looking about him, he saw that there were trees and bushes everywhere in the back yard. That was a daunting thought. If there were Shadow-worms on all the trees, then this was a much bigger problem. He would have to go back to the house to get a bigger glowstone. He would have to figure out a way to get over to Pho's house, then a way to wake his friend before *full-bright*. He could feel his mind beginning to buzz as it always did when he found a project to sink his teeth into. Admittedly, dealing with these worms would have been much easier if he could summon the Light from his hands, like Pho could, but if he could get a full enough glowstone, he could at least start cleaning them up.

He began to walk out of the garden when he saw a familiar sight just in-front of the stairs. Hovering there, floating in a rough circle shape, were several tiny glowing spheres of light. Toivo smiled and slowed down as he approached them.

"Well hi there," he said warmly. "It has been a while, little guys." The globes responded to his voice by flying over to him and rolling down his arms and zipping around his head a few times. Toivo grinned as the almost tickle that the globes always caused ran down his skin. He didn't see his little friends every night, but ever since he was a tiny child, they would come to him now and again. At first, they would play with him, but he began to notice that the games they played with him were helping him understand things: what was happening in school, truths about the Spectrum that you could only know if you weren't *skin-blind*. He never questioned it

111

when he saw them. For some unfathomable reason, these little balls of photic energy were always trying to help him.

Tonight, they greeted him, but then they shifted colour slightly. Toivo' brow furrowed slightly at this new display. He held his hand out to the lead globe land. It landed there, and pulsed between its usual happy white-blue light and a dimmer yellow-orange.

"Ok, there's something wrong," he said out loud. The globe blinked a couple of times, which Toivo had learned meant _yes_. It rose into the air again, and joining with its companions, pointed to a certain bush right next to the house. Toivo knew that it wanted him to go there, so he did. Pushing the outer leaves aside, he saw another shadow-worm cluster. This one was moving far more than the one that had killed the bird family. He watched as a bright globe would dash itself against the black substance, causing one worm to disappear, but another one took its place quickly.

"Aie, ok. I see what you mean," he said, switching his wrist glowstone on again. The resulting beam stabbed into the black writhing mass and once again, the shaft of light sheared away the worms quickly. This time, however, the worms fought back. They were actively trying to get out of the way. They were beginning to shield each other. He had to shine the beam across the same area a couple of times before any damage was done. This time, the Shadows actually tried to reach out and connect with his arm, aiming for the source of the light. His glowing friends were buzzing about like angry insects, adding their tiny light to the glowstone's.

Toivo kept at this until he found a pattern of slashing and cutting that forced the worms to retreat. It was in a rhythmical pattern that closely resembled one of the songs that his music teacher, Auntie Lumens, was having him practice this week. He unconsciously started humming it. The effect on the shadows of that little song was remarkable. It was as if someone had turned up the power on his glowstone, or turned down the strength of the worms, because the mass simply dissolved. Once they were all gone, he could see that they had been trying to consume another one of the glowing globes. It was very faint, its glow gradually dimming, flashing slower and slower.

Without even a moment of hesitation, Toivo caught the globe in his hand then shone the glowstone directly onto it. It stopped blinking altogether, and slowly started soaking up the light. Eventually, it lifted off his hand and its glow returned to the happy blue-white. Its companions zoomed around it happily.

Toivo stepped away from the bush, grinning. He had been able to save one of his secret friends, and that made him feel good. Each globe made a point of coming up and caressing his cheek before zooming off towards the rising Greater Sun. The one he had rescued made a point of staying back a moment longer. It came right up to his face, until it occupied his whole field of vision. It flashed once then vanished. Toivo blinked furiously in surprise, but then he realized that there was an after-image left in his eyes. Blinking continuously, he could actually read the words: *Thank you, Toivo.*

*

Yes, practicing how to hit your opponents is important
Of more value is practicing how to take the hit from them.

Saying from the Sapphire Realm

Chapter 10 –Practice

It took him a moment to grasp what had happened. These little balls of light knew his name. They knew how to write. They had sought him out to rescue one of their own. It was remarkable. And they had used a form of tight beam photic communication that was actually effective, given his disabilities. He had tried to tell his uncle about these little friends of his over the years. He dismissed the tales as fanciful stories born from his hyper-actively creative mind. He knew that this would simply be written off as another fabrication, so he decided to simply record the event in his personal journal.

He snuck across the living room floor, noting that he had once again forgotten to turn the furniture back on after his late night practice session. His reflective focus-mat was still on the floor, its carrying tube still over against the wall where he had tossed it. Sighing once, he knew that he really should practice a few more times before his Tests later that day. If it were less important, he would have crashed back into his bed right away, but these were his Rudiments Tests. If he finally passed those, he would finally be acknowledged as a citizen of the Topaz Realm. He would be able to graduate on-time, along with the rest of the children his age.

He would be able to graduate with Kayleigh.

Of all the people that attended the *Rudiments of the Spectrum* schools anywhere, at any time, that girl from Peridot was far and away his dearest friend. Sure, Pho and he were basically brothers-from-different-mothers, but Kayleigh was something special. Her return to the Realm of Light after a time on her home world had been the happiest day of Toivo's life. She would believe him when he told her about the Shadow-worms, the rescue of the globe. She would be busy today too. Since Graduation was so close, her family would be getting her as ready as possible. She didn't have Light powers, her abilities were Power itself. Thus, she graduated as a Peridot with specialized training in the aspects of Light that were connected with Power.

That reality sobered him a little bit. She would most assuredly graduate. She had more command of language and academics than anyone he had ever known. She made it a point of actively seeking answers from the instructors when she didn't understand. She studied furiously. She was truly gifted in more ways than just the Ways of Power. She was definitely moving on. Whether he was graduating or not depended on how he did today. There were only three options for someone like him: he could show the required Rudimentary skills, and earn his status as a Child of Light. This was his dream. Or he could show power, but not control of it. This had been the story of his life for the past several years. It would mean that he had to repeat his final elementary year, again, with the other students at the

Rudiments School, again, all of whom were from different Realms, and again he would be the only representative of the Topaz Realm to have ever studied there. Or, in his deepest nightmares, he fit into the category of students who never show the required Rudimentary skills, which would forever bar him from any positions of responsibility or influence for the rest of his life. He would be a *dim-glow*.

This was enough for him to settle himself down on the mat and close his eyes. He cleared his mind of distractions, as he had been taught dozens of times, and started the mantra his teachers had given him: "We are the Children of Light. It is our center. We are the conduits for it. We are the Light." He repeated this over and over. As usual, he felt the beginning of a crystalline buzz from gathering photic potential that he was building up. He brought his hands forward, palms upwards, then brought left hand over his right, and pulled the required image from his mind: a spiral galaxy made up of individual points of white light. Once that construct was in place, he would be able to manipulate this summoned light in specific ways – such as gathering them into a ball, stretching it into a rod, shaping the rod into some random geometric shape. The list of requirements was exhaustive, and only a full Adept was able to do all the forms, and that was only after having attended the Academy. How many you succeeded in showed which of the three categories you fit into. He knew this list very, very well. He had memorized the names of the different forms the first time he had seen them. Knowing their names but not being able to do them was . . . frustrating.

This year was the last chance for him. He was at the end of his primary education phase. If he didn't show progress this year, his group-three status would become official. He would have to get special permission to even travel from city to city. The fear of that officially sanctioned discrimination was enough to make him try even harder.

When he opened his eyes, he could see the barest beginnings of a galaxy-like shape outlined in points of light. They were all different colour and out of focus. He tried to concentrate harder, but all that did was smear the colours together into a swirling mass between his hands.

He had done this exercise so many times that this outcome was almost expected now. He sighed inwardly then rose to his feet. His lower hand was still in position, projecting the colour-haze above it. Quite a while ago, he had learned that looking around when he was concentrating this hard had its own benefits. His aura-sight was a lot easier when he was concentrating like this. Over the Cycles, he had learned that he could pretty much see where something had come from that glow. He glanced over at the physical shelf over where his uncle usually projected his work table. He saw the miniature sword in its scabbard, both glowing a bright scarlet colour. Toivo knew that his uncle had bought that souvenir on a Trade mission to the Ruby Realm. Beside it sat the tiny, intricately hand crafted spun-quartz hourglass from Turquoise which was always surrounded by blue-green waves.

He caught the sight of his own reflection in the mirror, and did a double take. He saw the tall, slender boy with a mop of dark unruly hair that he always saw, but there was a distinctly yellow glow around him that morning. To make things even more interesting, the reflection had a tiny, perfect image of a slowly spinning galaxy floating above his outstretched hand. He blinked and looked down. There it was, the first Form, perfectly projected. He could only stare. This was the absolutely first time that he had ever summoned the Spectrum in a focused way. He had to sit back down as his legs went a little weak. He wracked his brain trying to think of what he had done differently this time. He was not concentrating directly on the task, for one. He was moving about too.

Ah! He realized that he was not standing on the practice mat. That was different too. He squinted his eyes slightly in suspicion, then stepped back onto it. The closer to the center he got, the less focused the holo-construct became until it faded into nothingness altogether. Oh, that was a maddening thing. This mat was a Resistance mat, not a Focusing one. It didn't draw the energy of the Spectrum into him, it deflected it away from him partially. He stepped off again, and raised his hand again. He was still concentrating, still mentally summoning the power, so when he called the image of what he wanted into his mind's eye, it appeared instantly above his hand.

Letting go of his concentration, the construct faded again. He leaned against the doorframe of the once again dark living room, and tried really hard to decide how to feel about this new development. He was at the same time both jubilant and hopping mad, and he was stuck there. His eye fell on the mat again, and he came to a snap decision right then. He went over to it, rolled it up and put it back into its carrying case. Then he brought it quietly to the kitchen, where he opened the door of the Recycler and popped it in. He hit the _on_ switch, and the accursed tool vanished in a puff of molecule-rending Aquamarine energy. He was tempted to reset the unit's memory core, so that it could not be gotten back, but his uncle would land a transport's worth of trouble on him for the doing of it. It was School Property, after all. So he contented himself with grabbing a fruit from the basket on the kitchen table and munching away at it as he padded softly back to bed. Maybe he could catch an hour or two of sleep before the busy day got rolling.

Maybe his usual nightmares would leave him alone too. It wasn't likely, but there was always a chance.

*

A hidden truth revealed sometimes changes Famine to Feast ...though it might not taste as appealing.

From "Memoirs of an Imperial Spy", Garnet Realm Palace Library.

Chapter 11 - Breakfast

Saul finished pouring his dark black mug of morning beverage when he noticed the time. He leaned over the counter to bellow down the hallway once more.

"Toivo! Come on, boy. Greater is up and doing its job, so should you!"

This time, there was a mumbled reply from his nephew's room this time. In a few moments, Toivo emerged, shirt untucked and hair a bird's nest of tangles. Saul knew the boy had a hard time sleeping sometimes, but the dark circles under his eyes hinted at a deeper fatigue than usual.

"There you are," Saul chortled gently.

Toivo sat at the table, not really responding with more than a grunt of acknowledgement. He quaffed the juice set out for him. Next breath, he had already eaten half of the cereal in the bowl.

"Late night or early morning?" Saul asked matter-of-factly, sitting in the opposite chair. Toivo looked up and cleared his mouth.

"Both, sort of," he mumbled. He began to feel energy returning, so he turned a pointed look at his uncle. "I was practicing last night."

"Saw that," Saul quipped. "You forgot to turn the furniture back on, again,"

"Learned something," Toivo continued, undeterred. "That mat from school, the one I have been practicing on for the past five cycles? Remember it?" His uncle nodded, one eyebrow raised slightly. "It was a RESISTANCE MAT!" He hadn't meant to raise his voice, but his frustration was very near the surface. "It was actually making it harder for me to focus the Light for all this time!"

Saul nodded sagely, letting the boy vent. "Figured it out then, didja? Good." Toivo could only gape as his uncle downed the last of his drink. "Eggs or meat?" Saul asked, changing topics. Toivo was not about to let this go quite yet.

"Uncle," he began as calmly as he could. "Why have I been trying to summon the Light through a Resistance mat?" His voice had climbed a little in pitch by the end of the question.

"Oh, that?" Saul replied. "That, dear, was put in place to force you to learn how to focus your mind with absolute precision. Only that allows you to summon any kind of Spectrum powers. You needed the practice of that basic skill the most." He continued, despite his nephew's look of outrage. "We both know that control has always been your biggest problem, Toivo. This kind of mat is used when training Apprentices and Adepts. Consider yourself lucky. I had to call in several favours for me to get one in the first place, especially one small enough to carry around with you." With that, Saul considered this issue closed, and held up the plate of meat strips as well as a bowl of scrambled eggs. "Last call before I recycle these."

Toivo felt as if he had been run over by a herd of wild diffra. The two opposing feelings were slowly merging. He was still hurt and angry, but now there was an equally powerful confusion, as well as a little bit of surprised excitement. Adepts trained with mats like his? Really? The Champions of the Topaz Spectrum, the guardians of peace and order in their world, used Resistance mats to hone their skills? Of course, it would force them to come up with a million different low-powered ways to solve problems, instead of trying to overwhelm them with their incredible abilities . . . just like he had learned how to use the mantra and concentration to summon the energy of the Spectrum into himself before trying to use it. It was a staggering kind of thought. And no one at his school would have known about it.

His classes at the Rudiments schools were always populated by the children of visiting dignitaries and ambassadors from other Realms. It taught the educational basics, as well as giving these children with a myriad of other Powers a chance to learn about the Topaz Spectrum. Being the only citizen of the Topaz Realm there, only his instructors would have recognized the mat for what it was.

His pondering was interrupted by his uncle starting to clear the table. He realized he had to act fast, so he jumped up and interposed himself between his uncle and the Re-Cycler. With a grunt of surprise, Saul had to catch himself and rebalance the dishes in his hands. Toivo hit the reconstitute button on the machine. In a flash of Aquamarine energy, the Resistance mat and its carrying case re-appeared. Toivo snatched them up, and with a sheepish look at his uncle, moved quietly out of the room. He could hear his uncle's peals of surprised laughter all the way back to his room.

*

121

The sound of the front door closing behind him told the rest of his mind that it was indeed the day. Toivo waved to his uncle as he got in to his official hover-car, trying to keep his official Council robes from getting too rumpled. If he was wearing those, it meant that Uncle Saul was going to be in meetings all day, which meant that Toivo was on his own to get to the Testing Center. There was a time when that would have been a problem for him, but Toivo was more than capable of getting into to downtown Kalpa now. He could make most of the way by public transport then he would be able cut through his favorite part of town: the Performance District.

He shouldered his small backpack and walked down the block to the transport stop. He only had to wait a couple of minutes before the large, hovering vehicle came to a halt in front of him. He stepped off the sidewalk and climbed the few steps to where the driver was sitting. Toivo took out a small card from his arm-bracer, and waved it over the metal pad. The fare box registered his travel pass, and he was permitted to move back into the seating area. Most of the people riding this morning were clearly heading for the business or commercial sector. There was one very old gentleman in a hover-chair, wrapped in a faded yellow blanket. His face was deeply wrinkled and tanned to the point of being leather. His eyes were bright, though. He noticed Toivo staring at him, and laboriously turned his head to stare straight back, one eyebrow raised quizzically. Toivo felt his cheeks blossom into embarrassed blushing, and dropped his eyes quickly. He bobbed his head respectfully and quickly found and empty seat near the front.

Near the end of his ride, after many stops, he glanced once into one of the rear facing mirrors, He was only slightly relieved to see a wide, semi-toothed grin on the man's face. He was still embarrassed, but at least he knew that he had not caused any offence to the gentleman. His uncle would have tanned *his* hide if he had.

Stepping off the last stair, he oriented himself. The buildings in this part of town were a fascinating mix of old and new. The street lighting was both traditional glowstones with shudders, as well as photo-voltaic lights with black 'lector panels facing skyward. The buildings themselves were mostly concrete and glass here. Most were only about three or four stories high. He could smell the aromas wafting off of the food vendors on their pushcarts, the wet metal smell coming off of an atmospheric condenser placed just above one of the doorways. Clearly, that little restaurant wanted to gather its own water instead of paying to have heavily processed water pumped to their location from the other side of the city. There were tech-shops, newsstands, there was even a stand-by office ready for an Adept who might need the working space.

There were even stores from other Realms too, and those were always fascinating to him. He passed a shop boasting armour and weapons from the Ruby Realm, all heat-proof and nearly indestructible, so the signage said. Down further, there was a sports recruiting office maintained by the Peridot Realm. As he turned the corner, the Emerald Realm flower shop was receiving a tiny little rain shower from imbedded sprinklers.

This new street was a different place entirely. Here, there were theaters, and all the shops that provided supplies for them. Costumes, props, dance shoes, make-up, set-building materials, old books and resources…everything one could ever need to put on any kind of professional production was available here. The main theater had a large marquee sign that lay dormant in the morning light. A worker on a projected scaffold was removing the letters from the sign, and replacing tiny LED and glowstone-chip lights. He had already changed the poster at street level. Toivo paused to check out what show was coming up next.

Here, Toivo had the first of many surprises that day. He read down the list of names of the acts that were scheduled for the next few days. The first name on the list was a famous one: Sollen, teen singer pop-sensation and the idol of thousands. She had recorded more holos and vo-cordings than any performer in the past twenty Cycles. There was always a great hubbub and frenzy when she arrived and she always knew exactly what to sing to bring out the best in her audience. Her Powers were those of the Blue Topaz region – control of the electrical items around her through galvanic charges from her skin. Toivo knew that this meant that she could interface directly with the microphone and monitors around her so that she was always able to be heard perfectly clearly. She was really good at that. He should know, since she was a childhood friend of his.

He walked over to the main door and peered in. When he pulled on the handle, he learned that it was not locked. He glanced up at the worker who was now putting up new letters, then walked quietly into the theater. His uncle and he had been coming to performances here since he was just a little boy. For a couple of Cycles, he had volunteered as a student usher. More than once, he had performed here himself, as a member of the city-wide Musical ensemble. His chroma-chord skills were fairly advanced, and so in the past few months, his auntie Lumens – who was also his music teacher – had made arrangements for him to play with at least 6 different types of ensembles. It was a good thing that he was a quick study with music. Learning completely different styles of playing had proven an interesting challenge.

He strolled past the ticket kiosk, locked and darkened a tumbled stack of old-style printed show programs from the previous performances. Surely, Sollen's performance would have IR program feeds direct to the audience members . . . maybe even photic tight-beam. He would have to try and get tickets if he could. Admittedly, Sollen's popular music was a far cry from the classical training he had received, but he knew that she had an amazing vocal talent. This would be one show that he would really like to be part of, if possible at all.

He poked his head into the main auditorium, and to his surprise, Sollen was onstage, setting up her own sound equipment. Her only help was a tall, dark-skinned fellow wearing the colours of a Brown Topaz region technician. He was setting up the heavy sound-light panels and transduction cables so quickly it looked as if he were juggling. Sollen was busy setting up a stand-mic. She seemed a bit distracted as she worked, as well as more than a little bit tired. More than once, she paused to lean on the mike-stand, just letting the other arm fall to her side. Once, the tall dark boy saw her, and he hopped over to her side, helping her to a chair set up stage left. He clearly had Brown Topaz powers because with a wave of his hand, he drew the excess infra-red radiation from around Sollen, cooling her off. She smiled and nodded to him. He nodded back and returned to his tasks.

Toivo wanted to say hi, but she was clearly doing her initial set-up. He knew better than to disturb that process, so instead he went up to one of the dim lighting panels and set his hand flat against it. Granted he may not have had a lot of control over Light, but he certainly knew other tricks. Closing his eyes, he concentrated on summoning the Spectrum to him, but this time in the Blue ranges. This allowed him to cause a tiny spark to start jumping along his arm, into his hand then the panel. If Sollen was as aware of the electricals around her as she used to be, then she would soon perceive the equivalent of a wave and a smiley face transmitted in Galvan. Like his photic skills, this wasn't very advanced, but it was enough to make Sollen look up suddenly with a half grin on her face.

She cast about, and spotted Toivo, awarding him a wide grin and a wave. He waved back then indicated that he was only here briefly. She touched the microphone and sent a pulse through the wiring back to him. He felt the prickly shock of her message ride up along his arm.

    <<Hi there. You coming to the show tonight?>> her message said. Toivo had to shrug and send back: *<<Not sure. Will try. ClearSpark to ya!>>* She nodded, and blew him a kiss. He mimed catching it, and turned to leave.

    He thought about the first time he had met her, and this triggered his arm bracer's memory-filing function to scan for that moment. He could see her again, as she had been then, and grin. He only remembered playing, but these days, he was just a hint suspicious of his uncle and his secrets. Surely there was more to that picnic than he had known.

*

Practice your skills until you cry
So that in battle, you laugh!
>   *From "Philosophies of Battle from Across the*
>   *Dodecal", Academy Central Library.*

Chapter 12 –Testing

Back on the street, he passed between two larger buildings and appeared as if by magic on the same road as the Testing Center. He could see the school transports depositing students next to the large metal double doors that led onto the main floor. It was normally a sports arena, but it was off-season, and it was the only place large enough for the hundreds of parents and children that came. Even his school was here, he could tell. The contrast between the clothing worn by the visitors as opposed to the native citizens was easy to spot. This year would be different. He might have had to sit with them every year, but now he was doing his Rudiments Test. That meant he would only have to see them as they were entering the building.

"Hey!" yelled a grating high voice. "There's No-Glo now. Hi, Topaz." Toivo didn't flinch, he didn't grimace. He simply turned towards the voice, his face a controlled mask of neutrality.

"Hello, Garn," he replied. "Good to see you too. You Testing today?"

Garn, a short boy with greasy black hair and a sallow complexion in a deep maroon tunic, barked an ugly laugh and gestured towards Toivo with his right hand. Toivo felt the Garnet Force generated blow land against his shoulder, and allowed the pain it caused him to wash over and around him, then past him. He stood tall and didn't do more than flinch. Garn was a gifted Impactor, young as he was, and he always boasted that he would join up with the Garnet military, maybe even become a member of the Garnet Imperial Guard.

"No, I think I'll just watch you *shinies* do your best to make something out of nothing at all," he sneered. "Oh! And Topaz . . . I'll save you a seat too. I'm sure you'll be joining us again soon enough." A couple of cronies around Garn chuckled.

"Don't think so," Toivo replied, maybe quieter than he should have, but he was past being anxious about what the bullies thought. There were only two people here whose opinions mattered, and he couldn't find them. "I suspect that this will be the last time we cross paths. If we meet again, you will be speaking differently to me."

Garn's chuckles subsided as Toivo quietly responded differently than he had expected. Confused, the lad from Garnet could not do more than stare oddly at Toivo from that point on. The tall Sapphire boy beside him had not grinned during the exchange, and now that their usual prey was standing up for itself, he actually scowled a bit. He separated himself from Garn and disappeared into the crowded building.

Toivo entered the building himself, and the crush of people here was dizzying. Students of all different ages were milling about in every direction, their voices blending into a blue-white noise. The doors he had to enter were on a different floor, so he started moving slowly towards the stairs.

Essentially, he had to pass by all the different age divisions as he walked. Most children took their Rudiments Tests after their first formal year of schooling, so there were long lines of parents with five and six-year-olds all wearing their best clothes. The little ones were either standing there quietly, or more often scampering about from the excitement.

Toivo had watched his friend Pho perform here when they had both been that age. Pho's parents were good friends with his uncle, so he got to watch his friend play with the Light better than his Assessors could. They had placed him in the advanced track right away, which guaranteed Pho the right to attend the prestigious Photic Disciplines Collegiate. Almost every Adept of note for the past century had come from that school. Right from the start, Pho has known that it was his destiny to outshine everyone. Over the years, he had come to resent the expectations that everyone had of him. Granted, there was no Photic skill that he was not already master of, but it was tiring. His teachers never let him rest until he was eight to ten times better at the exercise than anyone else was. Gradually, his classmates started pulling away from him, since they knew that Pho was going to be better than them at anything they did, and they did not like that terribly much. He was the best, and he was always lonely.

His friendship with Toivo had become very important to him at those times. Toivo appreciated his friend, celebrated his victories, and always did his best to cheer him up when the world was too big for him. Pho in turn helped Toivo practice his Rudiments lessons repeatedly, showing himself to be infinitely patient. Once Toivo had started being able to call on the Spectrum even a little bit, he had become skilled at solving problems using the barest minimum of applied Power. This was always baffling yet fascinating for Pho, who suffered from using too much power for everything.

They had provided balance for each other.

Toivo passed by the Citizen's viewing gallery. All the most important people got to sit there and watch the children perform their exercises and forms. They would cheer for their own children, and clap politely for any who showed skill. On the ceiling in the center of the arena was a large view-screen that showed a different Testing area, with fewer people there. That was a shot of the Special Testing room, where he himself was going.

Pho was sitting with his parents in the front row, looking about. He spied Toivo walking by and waved. Toivo returned the wave. Pho raised his hand and summoned a six-pointed star-burst pattern of yellow light in his palm and raised it towards his friend as a sign of respect and wish for luck. Toivo grinned and raised his hand back. There was no star there, but then again, there was no expectation for him to do so.

All the citizens who saw who the 'burst was for, did a double take then looked more closely at Toivo. Pho, the Shining Star, acknowledging "Topaz", the bumbler from the Rudiments School? The more officious onlookers curled a lip in distaste, wondering if there was a scandal in the works.

Now he passed by a food vendor, then the line of off-worlders who were important enough to watch the Testing. Oddly enough, Toivo felt comfortable walking through this crowd. He had grown up surrounded by children from the other ten Realms. He could feel the different energies, see the various differently colored auras. A few visitors were speaking the regional languages of their worlds. Toivo never broke stride, but he listened closely to all the different sounds and reveled in them. Then his ear caught a particular lilt, a particular turn of phrase, and he turned his head. There was the delegation from the Peridot Realm: diplomats, Council representatives and the nearest they had to royalty – the president of the most powerful Financial firm in the Dodecal

Federation and his family.   The lot of them were making their
way to the plush seat at the front of the viewing area.
Standing a little ways away from the group, in the archway of
the door, stood the other person he had been looking for.
Kayleigh.

Kayleigh wore a light green skirt with a white blouse.
She now boasted a diplomat's badge, and she had various
attendants checking in with her. Her dark red hair was woven
into a complex braid, and her blue eyes were framed by info-
specs that gave her a continual feed on the various events that
she was monitoring. She was well and truly a Peridot
Apprentice, having shown incredible awareness and subtlety
during her Peridot Testing. She had the potential to be a truly
powerful Adept, so the Peridot Council made sure to give her
various leadership roles, even while she was off-world.

Kayleigh had been there when he had gotten the name
"Topaz" back in the Rudiments School, all those years ago.
She had stood up for him when the bullies came. She had
been a friend to him when he desperately needed one. She
taught him how to cope, how to see what the situation really
was, how to hear what was not being said. They shared a
bond, though he could barely articulate it.

If he passed his Rudiments, she would be so proud of
him, and he liked the thought of that: making Kayleigh proud
of him or happy with him for any reason.

She saw him her face lit up with her smile. She raised
a quizzical eyebrow at him and asked him a question over the
distance with her eyes. Toivo smiled roguishly back at her
and gave her a wink then a "no problems" hand-sign. She
nodded, sly expression on her face now. Toivo knew that he
owed her a great deal for all the moral support she had been
for him. She knew very well just how important it was that he
pass these tests, and so for the past few months, she had used
her Peridot abilities to help him find the last little bits of photic

energy in him to use for it. She mouthed the words "good luck" at him then had to find her seat.

He felt his soul lighten and he practically ran the rest of the way. He climbed the long staircase two at a time. He felt ready. For the first time in his young life, he felt ready for the challenges ahead of him.

Well, he thought so, anyways.

On the second floor, there were far fewer people. Only those who were receiving special Testing were on this level. The carpeted floors and art pieces decorating the bare concrete walls were a nice change from the grind downstairs. His uncle had meetings here, in the large convention rooms. This was an important place, for important people. His being here struck him as incongruous, which he found amusing. He followed posted signage to a tall pair of doors with a table set up to one side.

Sitting at the table, avidly reading a light-pad, sat a staggeringly pretty young blond woman in a crisp Council-representative uniform. Her almost violet blue eyes were flicking back and forth, across whatever she was reading. Toivo could feel his heart suddenly start thumping. He had not expected there to be anyone here, but it made sense. She was a receptionist. Surely, it was her job to make sure that only those with the right clearance entered. Toivo could feel his mouth go dry, and a cold trickle of sweat tracked its way down his back.

Then, to his great terror, she looked up and noticed him approaching. She set down her decorated light-pad and picked up a larger one. She also primed her shoulder crystal badge. Ack! On top of it all, she was an Apprentice or Adept? Ok, that almost freed up enough of his mind to be able to think. Now, as well as being heart-stopping-ly beautiful, she was an object of a different his admiration too. Oh, he was not coming out of this looking anything but silly, he knew that now. So many layers of "her" made his mind freeze up that he surrendered. He plunged through the ice that had surrounded his chest, and stopped in front of the table.

"Hello," she said in a high and fluting voice. He could smell some floral or fruit perfume come off of her, and his mind started recording details at a furious rate. She had a smooth jawline; a tiny dark spot on her left cheek, her hair was light blond, almost white. That could mean that she was a Clear from the Hidden Villages. He fought with every cell in his body to keep himself from staring at anything other than her face.

"Er, uh, hello," he stammered quasi-smoothly. He found that he had completely lost what he was supposed to say.

"Are you here for your Testing?" she asked, her delicate eyebrows raised in inquiry. Oh, but that was an adorable expression. He was certain that he was able to sculpt her face accurately now. In another second, he had be able to create a full holo' of her, trixel by trixel. Then he realized that he had been asked a question.

"Uh, yes," he answered, thrusting his brain in automatic. Conscious thought was so very much not an option for him right then. "My . . . my . . ." Ok, what was his uncle's name again? Oh yes.

". . . my uncle, Saul Rallence, made arrangements for me to be Tested here."

The young woman scanned the list of names on her official pad, and gave a tiny nod.

"Councillor Saul . . . yes, there we are." She tapped the screen once then beckoned to him. He stepped forward slightly then his universe shrank into an eternal single glorious 'now' as she took his hand in hers. His heart was punching the inside of his ribs, his face frozen in whatever expression happened to be there, and it was blazing like Greater Sun. The rest of his skin was ice and the pounding pulse in his ears rendered him deaf. She glanced up at his face then dropped her eyes to cover a slight grin. She turned his hand palm downwards then waved her other hand over it a few times. When finished, one very distant part of Toivo' conscious brain saw that she had attached an identification holo-glyph there. There was not one single connection in his mind between this and why he was here in the first place. She was touching him. For now, that was the only thing that mattered.

Her skin was extremely smooth and soft. Her arms moved gracefully and her fingernails were a pale pink that matched her pale pink lips. It was a floral perfume she wore, or maybe it was the conditioner she used. The scent of it was permanently etched into his brain now, and it was firmly attached to a feeling of intoxicating delirium. When she was done, she gently pulled his arm towards the door. He blinked a few times.

"Ah, yes, thanks," he blurted out, understanding very little of why she was moving him like this. He might have had other questions at one time, but they were buried under layers of hormonal overload. The girl was shaking her head now, a full grin plastered there. It was not a malicious smile, but one of genuine amusement. He was lightening her day, and all he had to do was stand there and try to act like a human. This pleased him no end.

"Go inside the doors," she finally said. "There are chairs along the wall to the left. Sit down there, and wait. The Assessors will be with you when they are ready for you."

"Ah, right. Good. Chairs. Right." Toivo had words again, thank the Light, but they were still very separate from each other. He finally looked into the room, and a spark of his rational mind surfaced. This was the waiting room. He was to wait here, in this room that the vision of beauty and light had told him to wait in. Great. Now he just had to enter the room.

Oh, that would require walking. After an infinitely long second, he started shuffling towards the doors, his gaze firmly fixed on her. He could almost think again, so in a moment of foolhardy bravado, he raised his hand to wave a cheerful goodbye to her.

That proved to be just one thing too many for him. He started to wave then crashed face-first into the edge of the open door. He could feel where his cheek and forehead had impacted with the polished wood, a dull throb blossoming there. He only blinked once then found he had to backpedal to pass the obstacle.

The girl let out a hoot of startled laughter here, then picked up her personal 'pad again. She made sure that he had cleared the door before starting to read again.

Toivo passed the door, and the pain he felt started to clear his head. The adrenaline that had rendered him a stumble-mumble was beginning to fade, and so his active memory was coming back to him. He thought about how helpless he had been in the girl's presence and had to laugh at himself. He knew that Kayleigh, who might as well have been a sister, would have giggle-tears streaming from her eyes seeing him so dumbfounded by a girl.

He was still mostly dazed when he started to notice the room around him. It was easily as large as the gymnasium at his school, only with carpeted floors, and skylights letting in the light of all three suns. It looked blank. He could see no sign of adjudicators, other students, or anything for that matter. The walls did not even have paint on them, just bare plasti-crete. He looked to the right and saw a row of chairs isolated from the rest of the room by a series of dividers. He saw four chairs lined up along the outside wall, with two adults seated there. They were clearly the parents of a child that was being tested, from mixture of patience and anxiety on their faces. He looked at the big, empty room, for any sign of the Testing in progress, but only the bare walls greeted him. He sat on the last chair, landing with a bit of a thump.

They looked up at him, and smiled at him. The woman looked a little puzzled by Topaz's flushed face and slightly widened eyes, and turned to the man. He, in turn, leaned in and whispered something to her. She looked puzzled for a moment, then she did her best to stifle a giggle of understanding. Her gaze became positively maternal.

"Here for your Tests, son?" the man asked, breaking the silence in a harmless way. Topaz didn't really have his voice working just yet, so he nodded in answer. The woman leaned into the man's shoulder, grinning widely.

"Our son just went in a few minutes ago," she said. "He's about your age too, I think. Did you ever meet him? His name is Stellan."

Topaz could feel the neurons begin to fire again in his brain, and he thought about what she had asked him. Did he remember ever meeting a boy named Stellan?

"I . . . I don't . . . don't think so, ma'am," he finally mumbled, through sluggish lips. He shook his head a moment to clear it, then answered more fully: "No, I'm certain of it. I've not known anyone named Stellan before. Which school did he attend?"

"Photic Disciplines Collegiate 12," the father stated automatically.

"Ah, that's it, then," Topaz replied. "My best friend goes there. His name is Pho." He paused a moment, to see if they recognized the name. Neither parent seemed to, so he finished with: "I attended Capital District R.S., so we would have only met during the Arts exchanges."

"Oh, the Rudiments school? Really? Ah, well, that's alright." the man flustered for a moment, changing what he was going to say mid-thought. "Well, maybe we can introduce you two when Stellan is done, then. He's always eager to make new friends." As an aside, the man flashed a projected message behind his wife's head, out of her line of sight. It read: *"Stellan was just as smitten by that dazzling receptionist as you were. Focused* Shiny *on you, boy."*

Topaz felt his cheeks go from hot to cold, as he realized that the man understood exactly how he had felt when he saw her, and approved. He felt a bit of kinship of a different sort with this Stellan and his father that he had not known before.

Before he could say anything in response, a cloud of light formed in front of them. Out of it stepped a boy about Topaz's age, with wild dark blond hair, blue eyes and strong features. His yellow and white formal shirt showed him to be a photic topaz. He walked over to the couple and gave them a nod.

"All done," he said, waving his hand at the cloud. It vanished instantly. "I told you there wouldn't be a problem."

"Good, good," his mother said, reaching out to smooth his hair absently. She turned to Topaz, then looked back at him. "Stellan, dear, another student came for Special Testing today, see." She pointed gently in Topaz's direction.

Stellan looked over at Topaz, and his eyes immediately scanned every part of him. That struck Topaz right away, as it was not unlike how he looked at people he was meeting for the first time. He came over and extended his hand.

"Hey there. I'm Stellan. Nice t'meet ya." he declared in a forthright tone. Topaz nodded, extending his hand. Stellan shook it firmly, and his eyes seemed to flash in an odd pattern for a moment or two. Topaz blinked, not sure what had just happened, then realized that he had probably just sent him a communication tight-beam. Sighing just a little bit, he formulated an answer.

"Hello. My name is Topaz." He took the extended hand and shook it firmly. He tried to send a flash through his eyes, but he was sure that it came out a garble. To his great surprise, he could feel a tiny spark of electricity pass between his and Stellan's hand. The only other time he had felt that was when he had been playing with children from the blue topaz Islands, with their electrical powers and their galvanic touch-language. He was just cogent enough to reflect the spark back to Stellan. He knew that in Galvan, he had just said the equivalent of a grunt, but it was something only a blue should have been able to do. It was Stellan's turn to look surprised this time. Now a new reality settled upon Topaz: this Stellan fellow had both yellow and blue topaz powers? Did he have brown and clear as well? This was interesting for him. In front of him stood a boy his own age who could use the Spectrum like he could, changing colors at will. Who was this guy? Topaz's curiosity almost got the better of him, till he remembered how easily this fellow had dissipated that light-field. His control was solid, then. Sighing, he recognized that Fate had just tapped him on the forehead again, reminding him to stay humble.

The handshake and introduction was cut short as an older man in a tan and yellow robes walked into the waiting area from somewhere near the doorway. He carried another light-tablet, similar to the one that the apprentice at the door possessed. His amber eyes were framed by neatly combed silver hair and a fine array of wrinkles. This was destined to be a day full of surprises for Topaz it seemed, because he recognized the man. Releasing Stellan's hand, he turned to face the new arrival.

"Student Topaz," the man declared. "By the Blue and the Bright, how you've grown! The last time I saw you, you were half as tall, and running everywhere."

"Representative Edsol, it's good to see you, sir," Topaz replied, feeling several layers of anxiety lift from him. "I didn't know you were on the Adjudicating panel. When did you change from the Ministry of Transport?"

Stellan and his parents said their thank-you's and headed out. Any mystery surrounding Stellan left with him. Topaz focused his attention back on his uncle's best friend, Edsol.

"Haven't been there for a cycle now. Got moved to Education and Assessment and never looked back." Edsol draped an arm over his shoulder and started leading him back towards the door. "So, Saully feel's you're ready for your Tests, eh? That's wonderful. We'll just have to get them underway then."

And with that, the pair of them walked back towards the doorway. This time, Topaz could see the edges of a Glamour field concealing the rest of the room. Edsol waved his hand, and a doorway of light open before them.

"I'll make sure that the five Traditional Tests happen at whatever speed you are comfortable with," Edsol whispered. "The other adjudicators are a little bit stuffy, but they mean well."

"Sounds good, sir," Topaz replied. Once they were past the doorway, it closed behind them, concealing them completely. The large multi-purpose room was empty again.

*

From under the chair Topaz had sat upon, a tiny shadow worm, no longer than a fingernail, crawled out and moved to the corner of the wall. It slithered quickly till it found the tiny crack in the wall, where it dove into the rest of the darkness there. It didn't make any sound as it urgently melted into obscurity.

*

Every now and again,
Keeping your thoughts to yourself
Is a difficult goal to accomplish.
      Amethyst saying.

Chapter 13 -Meetings and Lunch

Saul stomped out of the Meeting Hall with a scowl on his face, muttering curses in several languages under his breath, and his staff of office glowing faintly. He needed to get some air. The travesty of bureaucracy that the Council had become was simply too much for him to deal with right now. He passed into the bright noonday sunlight, and turned towards the Larger and Lesser Suns - almost *fullbright,* but for the absent Sister Sun hiding behind Larger at this time of year. He closed his eyes, and simply soaked up the raw light and radiation, his shoulder crystal badge glowing as the energy was stored. Though it was not as vital as energy from the Core, it felt good all the same. He could feel its warmth entering into him, and his mood softened a little. He would go back, listen to the provincial governors complain about this shortage of energy or that lack of resources. He was doing what he could to slow the tide of Chaos that was growing within his people, but there were days when he felt ready to send pulse-flashes right through the skulls of the more stubborn delegates. He sighed, and walked back in. Maybe he could quietly pump some of this solar energy into his allies. That led him to the decision that he would make a motion to get the shutters in the dome over the meeting room opened. He wondered who would object to sunlight streaming down on their discussions, though he suspected that he knew exactly who they would be.

Then, he realized that Toivo's Testing was almost finished for the day. All that remained now would be the Academic Assessments, which would be easy enough for him. This gained his attention far quicker than the petty squabbling and pointless rhetoric that this session had become. With a quick stride, he walked over to the Communications room, where he flashed his shoulder badge at the scanner beside the door.

"Welcome, council member Saul," the tinny voice from the scanner said to him. "Access granted."

The metal and glass doors whooshed aside, and Saul moved to the manager's desk. A young man in light blue overalls sat at the reception desk, his fingers flashing with electricity as he adjusted this system or that by interfacing his blue topaz electrical powers with them. He saw Saul then flashed him a welcoming grin.

"Hello sir. Welcome to Communications. Can I help you?" he asked politely, his young voice a little shrill.

"Yes, you can," he replied. "I want to observe the current round of Photic graduation testing, over at the arena."

"Yes sir. Not a problem. If you'd follow me, please," he piped up, rising from his chair and moving off to one of the larger cubicles. He taped a few buttons on the doorframe then opened the door.

"The display is tied into the Security cam and optical crystal systems there. The controls are touch sensitive, and voice-active. Please feel free to ask me if you have any problems."

"Understood. Thank you." Saul said, moving into the booth. The boy returned to his desk and the tasks waiting for him.

Saul sat down and adjusted the screen so that it was transmitting the visual data directly to his eyes, photically. This way, no one wandering by would be able to see what he was seeing. He touched the icon representing the arena and scrolled through the various views available to him. He finally found Toivo . . . no, Topaz . . . that is what he had to call him for the time being. The boy was exiting the Testing room, his face was neutral, but there was a hint of a spring in his stride. That bode well. He touched a few controls and a scanner picked up the image of his face, and transmitted it along the security line, till a call icon appeared in the air beside Topaz. The boy on the screen noticed the holographic request icon and tapped it with his hand. Saul's face materialized in place of the icon. Topaz grinned.

"Well, how'd it go?" Saul asked mildly, the image of his face duplicating the older man's features and voice.

"Not too bad, actually," Topaz said, continuing to walk. The image of Saul followed him. "I was able to do any of the forms that they asked me. I studied all the right things, it seems. Your doing?"

Saul shrugged, his grin deepening. "The perks of being on the Council. So, the adjudicators formally stated that you'd made no mistakes?"

"Well, they did not say much of anything, actually. They just pressed buttons on their personal displays and talked in tight-beams photic to each other while I was working. Councillor Edsol hinted at me that I'd done really well - you never told me he was going to be there, by the way. I'm glad for all of the standing that Auntie Lumens made me do during my music lessons. Once I started, I did not sit again for four hours!"

Saul nodded. "That's about right. You should have seen the Tests before they streamlined them. Back in the bad old days, the Tests were all day, and if you collapsed from fatigue, then you failed. It's why only the older students took them back then."

"The little kids taking them down on the arena floor would never have the endurance for that," Topaz muttered.

"The schedule I have here says that you've got an hour of free time now. Do you want to join me for some lunch?"

"I'd love to," Topaz replied.

"Good, then. There's a little diner, run by a woman from Amethyst - a friend of mine from back in the day. If you go out the main doors, turn right, then walk for about two blocks, you'll see it . . . impossible to miss. I'll meet you there." Saul said. "Do you want me to be conspicuous or not?"

Topaz raised an eyebrow at his uncle's image and grinned lopsidedly.

"Actually, my arrival here was enough to shake everyone up. I don't want to completely alienate myself by hobnobbing with council members in public."

Saul chuckled and nodded. He ended the communication with a palm star-burst of light. It was as habitual as saying hello/goodbye, but he cut it short, cursing at himself quietly.

"Sorry," he muttered. "Been dealing with some very stubborn delegates from all over the Realm . . . Narrow-minded tunnel-visioned fools mostly. Not thinking."

"No worries, uncle," Topaz replied, only a little tersely. He even tried to return the gesture, though for him, it was more like a sputtering spark.

Saul cursed himself again, having forgotten his nephew's limitations, but knew that there were no hard feelings. He switched off the comm-screens and exited the booth.

"Is there anything else you need, sir?" inquired the cheerful young man at the control-station desk.

"No, I'm finished here," he answered, adopting his friendly, quasi-fatherly expression and manner. Then he paused a moment and said: "Actually, there is something you can do."

He tapped her desktop a couple of times, and two holographic pages appeared on it. He quick-fired a note onto them with a wave of his hand, and then waved the other hand over them again, making the light-scribed notation to fade from view. The boy watched him avidly then blinked as he seemingly erased what he was writing.

"Have these notes delivered to the Estan Conservatory of Music, coded for Mistress Lumens," Saul said mildly. The attendant blinked, pulling the holo-pages closer to himself. Puzzlement was clear in his eyes, and he almost said something, but thought better of it. He nodded, and folded the pages with his hands, then moved them into the screen of his control terminal.

"Sir, do you send blank memos to people often?"

Saul grinned mischievously then replied "Only those I'm fond of."

With that, he strode out the doors and back into the hallways of the Council Building

*

Topaz found the diner easily enough. It was at odds with its environment: a tiny, ten-seat capacity eatery, decorated in shades of purple and boasting the most antiquated façade that Topaz had ever seen. Some of the most expensive and glamorous shops and restaurants that the Capital could boast surrounded it. It stood recessed from the sidewalk a little way, so unless you were looking for it, you would not see it. It also less brightly lit than the stores surrounding it, which meant that most citizens of the Realm would usually avoid it.

Topaz approached the door, set in an archway of huge, shaped cinder blocks, held together with grey mortar. He pushed the door open and a single bell attached to the doorframe rang. The smells of simple, savory foods wafted over to him from the door to the kitchen, behind the counter, making his mouth water. He walked up to one of the round stools that were set into the tiled floor and sat.

He looked around. On every flat wall-surface in the building were pictures, large and small. It was a wild array of images. Most of them were of people. Young, old, men, women . . . all the faces were clear as daylight behind dingy, aged frames, and every face was smiling. The more smiling faces Topaz looked at, the more he felt the corners of his own lips beginning to turn upwards.

"And a-hello t'you," called out a crackling, shrill voice from inside the kitchen. "Be right wit' ya."

Before long, a short, round little old woman hove out of the kitchen, wiping her hands on a dingy apron. Her grey hair was captive inside a light mauve hairnet, and her sparkling brown eyes danced as she caught sight of him.

"Hello, young man," she said again, cheerily. "Welcome to Amberyl's." She hustled over to the counter, and poured a glass of ice water. She placed it in front of Topaz on the counter.

"Er . . . hi," Topaz said, grinning, if puzzled by the greeting. "I'm supposed to meet my uncle here for lunch."

"Your uncle?" the woman paused a moment, then continued. "Well, if he recommended Amberyl's, then I know him."

"I would certainly hope so!" a strong voice from the entrance called out. Topaz turned to see his uncle, dressed as a street worker, safety vest and all, entering.

"Saul!" the woman exclaimed joyfully. She waved her hand at the windows at the front of the restaurant, and they all became opaque. The door locked itself too. Topaz winced, as he perceived that same subsonic rumbles that warned him of amethyst power at work around him. Inside his head, he automatically started shouting the lyrics to a child's nonsense song: "*One bright and shiny ball /sat there, upon the wall. . .*"

One the doors and windows had stopped moving, Saul let go of the Glamour field that he had woven around himself, then came forward to embrace the woman, his council robes billowing around him. She returned the hug heartily, kissing him on both cheeks.

"You rascal! You said that you would be right back!" she exclaimed, in mock anger. "Dealing with something took how long? Fourteen years?" She playfully cuffed him around the shoulders.

Saul laughed, deflecting the blows with practiced ease. Topaz watched his uncle's reflexive actions, blinking once. He had not seen his uncle actually fend off anything in a very long time, but it was impressive to see. The woman was laughing as she attacked him with fists, yet not one blow landed.

Seeing how quick his uncle's defenses were now, he could only imagine what he had been like in his heyday.

"Peace, 'Beryl, peace," Saul chortled. "You know why I had to leave." The woman nodded, and let him be. She twirled to face Topaz again.

"This young man here says that he's yer nephew," she drawled, her words leaning heavily into her distinctive amethyst Realm accent. "That true, Saully?"

Saul nodded, sitting down beside Topaz.

"And he's been keeping me on the bright and shiny path for a long time now." He ruffled the boy's hair affectionately.

"By his getup, I'm guessing that it's Testing Day again," she declared as she strode back behind the counter. She flipped up a few switches on the wall under a menu board then turned her head slightly towards her old friend. "So, Saul, you buying?"

Saul nodded then leaned in close to whisper to his nephew: "She's the best cook in the Realm, and I trust her completely."

Topaz nodded and sat there, watching. She was like nobody he had ever met before. He could not fathom her, and it was intriguing to him.

"All-righty then, let's get this meal started then." With those words, she turned and stared at Saul. The rumble of amethyst power surfaced again, and lasted only a few moments. She tapped a few things into a hand-held display screen. Then she turned to Topaz, and stared at him. The rumble came again, and he could feel the tickle in his head that meant that she was focusing her amethyst power on him. His mental singing became mental shouting of the same nonsense song. He could almost feel the power splashing around him, like waves passing around stone.

"Er . . . what's this?" she rocked her head to one side then tried again. Topaz was singing so loudly in his head this time that he did not even feel her efforts. Her jaw dropped, and her eyes went wide. She turned an incredulous stare onto Saul.

"He's Shielding himself!" she declared, more than a little shocked. "He's actually able to deflect a surface mind-probe. It's like he's not there. I picked up *nothing!*" She had to lean on a nearby table as she stared at Saul, her face a mask of confusion. "Saul, no offence, sweetie, but there's NO person, anywhere in this Realm, who can do that. Just not something you *shinies* can do unless you've visited my home-world."

Saul nodded, knowing grin flashing across his face.

"He figured that out all by himself, he did," he replied. "It was the most natural thing for him to do, when he was a young child."

Beryl paused then several expressions passed over her face. She looked at Topaz again with an unreadable expression then she came over and hugged him soundly.

"Oh, you clever boy," she practically sang. "I can't read your mind as to what you'd like to have for lunch. I'm going to have to ask you what you want verbally. Haven't had to do that since I was back home."

"Oh, sorry," Topaz answered sheepishly, his cheeks darkening slightly. "I meant no offence."

Beryl laugh crackled through a very wide range of happily discordant notes. She wiped a tear from her eye as she said "No offence taken, none whatsoever." She walked back behind the counter now, nodding to Saul. "Your uncle knows very well that I'm the strongest amethyst in the entire Shining Realm. I'm classified as a *Mind-Lady* Adept, back home. You, little man, are able to block me entirely. What I see of your mind is like a solid metal wall. When I tried the second time, I actually used some force. Your defense was so complete that I only just barely heard that silly children's song running round and round. Between that insanely distracting song and those mental Shields of yours, I would have to concentrate long and hard to read you."

All Topaz could do was shrug. This was the first time anyone had ever articulated what he was doing, or even noticed his little trick. .

"So, young man, what will ya have?" she asked, pulling out a stylus.

*

As Topaz ate, he could hear little rumbles of amethyst power flitting back and forth between his uncle and Beryl. She was an old friend, so they must have been catching up on things. He knew that he did not have to protect himself here, so he just ate.

<Saul, that's him, isn't it? >

<Oh yes, 'Beryl. He's the one.>

<Does anyone suspect who he truly is? >

<None of the known spies here have shown any sign of knowing, and I've been watching very closely for that. >

<He's really strong, you know. That second time, I did my best to read him . . . used actual mind-force in the attempt. He's as impervious as I am. >

<Really? I'd suspected. >

<Why? >

<Well, he's also able to walk straight through solid-light constructs as if they weren't there, when he's not paying attention, and he's got talent in all four colors of the Spectrum. Anything he sees, he can mimic . . . and he's gifted beyond measure at Music. >

<Of course he is. Makes perfect sense. Oh, Saul, if They *notice that, he might as well wear a target on his forehead! Is he going to be able to stay hidden from* Them *till he's old enough? >*

<I don't know. >

<I understand. Just you remember to bring some of those spy types around here for lunch sometime. I'll make sure they remember whatever YOU want them to. >

<I know, Beryl, and thanks. Let the Network know what you've learned about him. When he gets to Amethyst, he'll need all the help he can get.>

<I have a granddaughter about his age. To borrow one of your phrases, she's a sparkling talent too. I'll see what I can arrange, if he Ascends. >

<He has to become an Apprentice, first, and it's anybody's guess as to whether or not he'll make it. >

<We'll just have to hope. >

Both adults locked eyes for a moment on that last shared message. Old knowledge stirred in their eyes, and they nodded together.

*

Topaz just ate his lunch. What a fine restaurant his uncle had introduced to him. He would have to bring Pho here sometime.

*

At the end of the day, once all the topaz realm children had finally gone home, a familiar short, hunched little man in official robes of yellow and trimmed with black sat in a small control booth at the top of the arena. For sporting events, this is where the announcer sat, but it served well as a central nexus for the director of the Assessment Committee to mull over the results of the day. His dark, intense eyes darted over the lists of names and columns of data from their testing. The different panels of adjudicators were still meeting, so the numbers reflecting their findings kept changing, minute to minute. They were also discussing which of the students they would be record as worth watching. It was a time-saver for everyone, and it helped him make the necessary choices when they were of graduation age. Any child that was likely to be worthy of touching the Core would most certainly show the raw potential for power as a small child. Most of the time, it was this way.

He pulled up a listing of the current choices for candidates on a side display, and noted that the last slot remained empty, even now. That galled him. Four of the requisite five names were set and locked, and had been for months. That last wild-card slot always caused the Selection sub-committee the most grief. Choosing one student from each color of the Spectrum was straightforward enough. He scanned the names and the individual test scores that accompanied them. Years of assessment had sifted out the strongest from each region. Yes, those ones would do just fine. He would have to make sure that the diverters were really working well, as this group of graduates would be resonating with the actual Topaz Core really strongly by then. The very potential they possessed might actually guide them somewhere other than where they were *supposed* to go.

As he watched, the last slot started to blink on the screen. That got his attention. They were finally choosing the last name. Good. He tapped the screen a couple of times to see the choices. Ten children, all at the end of their elementary training like all the rest. Each had different faults, nothing new there, except that there was one boy had gotten a perfect technical score on his Rudiments. He grunted, noting that this bore a second look. He pulled up the boy's file, and read.

"Ah, ah! HA hahahaha..." he chortled loudly. He looked again, and burst out laughing, again. "Saul, you old boot," he guffawed darkly to himself. "Your little charity case has finally taken the Tests. Practically on his graduating day, he finally gets his baseline measure for his Rudiments. Now, after years of *lens-less* failure and abysmal levels of control, suddenly he's competent."

A hint of a smile came across his lips, as he input a couple of figures into his tablet, which adjusted the figures on the screen. With that little difference, Saul's nephew became the last candidate. It was the most perfect way he could think of to darken that bright day . . . to put forward the name of a boy who would never in a thousand years be chosen to become an Apprentice. The entire Realm would be watching as the Core rejected a duly chosen Candidate. The ripples of fear and doubt about the powers of the Heart of Light would definitely be helpful.

He took special satisfaction from the blow to an opponent. Take that Saul, he thought. Your nephew will touch the "Core" and it will destroy him. It would remove his old rival as any kind of threat, once as for all.

With that task complete, he started checking the arrangements for the grand Assembly next week and, of course, the Ceremony itself where the world would meet the Candidates. He knew that his superiors wanted him to do a good job, at this point. After all, the Plan needed all of the best from this world, just like all the others, and they would only be sifted out the masses if he was careful. He would have to check in with his superiors before too much longer, to report progress.

<No need, Pazos. We are here. >
"Ah good. All proceeds well."
<Good. Do you need any assistance? >

*

Talent is a marvelous gift,
Wasted on the young and naïve.
>   *From the newest training manual for the Stellar*
>   *Talent Management Agency.*

Chapter 14 - Suggestion

On his way home, Toivo made a point of going back to the theater. She was the one person he had met so far that was able to play instruments as he could - with facile ease. She was by far the better singer of the two of them. Her singing career had long ago propelled her into a state of Stellar recognition across the eleven Realms. Despite being able to harmonize correctly any song he heard, Toivo knew what kind of work he would have to do if he wanted to become as famous a performer as her. The thought of how much focus on a single aspect of his life it would take was simply too daunting. Other things in his life demanded his full attention.

He entered the front doors again, and immediately heard Sollen's voice pumping out of the speakers around the building. It was a ballad from Galvineth, her hometown in the Blue topaz regions. He had sung it once, a very long time ago, but as a folk song, the kind of ditty you would sing around a

153

campfire. Here, Sollen had taken its simple melody and transposed it into a higher energy, slightly faster popular style. Toivo had to admit that he was starting to like Sollen's songs. Sure, they were repetitive, the melodies were generic at best, but she was able to bring out the best in them. It may take her a while, but when the song feels right in a certain room, she quickly added it to the set she would sing that night.

He entered the auditorium and saw the dazzling show of lights and the pounding beat of her music. She was singing lightly, to conserver her voice, but the nuance was there. She wore a Glam-collar too, which struck Toivo as a little odd. She was a beautiful girl, with a beautiful voice. Why would she need to use the image-adjusting that the collar would afford her face and hair?

"No, Sollen, that wasn't quite right," said an oily voice over the speakers. Toivo looked around the room and found its source: a small man with narrow features and almost no hair, wearing a light purple suit jacket and slacks. He sat at the forward sound booth, just behind the floor seating area.

"Remember that you have to use the collar during rehearsal too."

Sollen heard the voice then made a sour face. Grumbling outside the range of the stage-mike, she flicked the collar on. Instantly, her hair went from slightly tangled light brown to beautifully coiffed shimmery blond. Her make-up was perfect, and her expression became one of neutral happiness. She turned to the man, and pointed to her face. The little man nodded and waved to her.

"That's better," he quipped. "Can't have the general public see you as you actually are." To his vast surprise, he could see Sollen's eyes go slightly blank under the Glam field then she nodded mutely. She started singing again a moment later, this time with her "show-face" on.

The snide comment was enough to make Toivo turn and stare at the man. Sure enough, he had a deep purple aura around him. Toivo could hear the deep subsonic rumble of Amethyst Mind-power in use. That manager-person was adjusting Sollen's thoughts for her. The flare of anger that rose in him was volcanic. He knew that he could not interrupt a rehearsal, but he had to speak to Sollen now.

He found a seat near the back of the theater, and thumbed his wristband comm-screen to life. He tapped a quick note to his uncle explaining where he was and that he might be late for dinner. His uncle sent a single pulse of light back to him, acknowledging the information and not forbidding the choice. Good. That gave him a measure of freedom to act.

Sollen sang three more songs in her set. Each one was more energetic than the last. That struck Toivo as odd too. You do not play a whole series of high-energy songs without a slower song or two amidst them. The audience gets over-stimmed and starts to lose the ability to appreciate what they are hearing. Sollen was a far smarter performer than that. Toivo rose and moved to the backstage door, waiting for the right moment to pop back to see his friend.

"You didn't maintain your energy level on that last song!" the voice of Sollen's manager boomed across the speakers again. "I am reading only a seventy-four percent of full potential in your effort. If you do that during the show, we will lose half of our audience before the night is out."

Toivo waited a moment longer then slipped backstage. He moved quietly around the cables and crates, towards the dressing rooms. He saw Sollen coming off-stage and sitting on a metal crate backstage, Glam-collar in her hands. She was leaning her head against the wall, her eyes closed. Toivo could see dark circles there. The male stagehand he had seen before was there, handing her a bottle of water and using his

Brown topaz powers to draw off any ambient Infra-red energy, clearly to help cool her off. Sitting beside her was a petite girl whom Toivo had first thought was a ghost. She was dressed in almost all white, and her hair was naturally white too. She had darkened lenses over her eyes, and she carried a transmission tablet in her arms. Few people dressed like that normally, and they were from the Hidden Villages. That meant that this girl was a Clear topaz. Intrigued, he knew that he had a dozen or so questions that he would ask her if he had the chance.

"He's pushing you too hard," the girl said, her voice high and fluting. "I monitor your ratings and popularity scales in real-time. Any show you do where he 'pushes' you to sing his version of a show, there is a marked drop in your post-show sales, and there is less buzz about you."

"Ebbella's right," the stagehand added. "The only thing that putting out that much power does is burn you out and drain the glowstones in the source-boxes. You have got to *stamp the ember* on this."

"Torch, 'Bella," Sollen finally said. "We have to follow his lead. Agency head office sent him. Yes, I am sick of him and his suggestions, but . . ." Her face went a little blank there. Toivo could see what almost looked like an actual Shadow flit over her eyes. That was all he needed to see. He strode forward, focused on his friend.

The other two saw him and rose to their feet as Toivo came nearer. Torch saw Toivo' features more clearly then relaxed a little bit. Ebbella just stared at him, her expression unreadable. She tapped Sollen on the shoulder and whispered something to her. Sollen opened her eyes, and looked at him. For a few moments, the Shadows ran rampant around her and she looked as if she did not know him. Then something clicked and her eyes brightened. Toivo could see a wisp of black smoke puff away from her when this happened.

A Shadow-Worm *inside* a person's head? The very idea of it made his skin crawl. It was different from the ones infesting the trees and dark places here, and for it to have been inside her head and not killed her outright meant it had to have a fundamentally different function. Maybe it was from another Realm, clinging to that Amethyst manager person somehow. It had been clouding her mind quietly. He was glad that it was able to be dispatched easily.

"Well, hello there," she said, rising to her feet and hopping over a crate to hug him. Toivo grinned and returned the hug. He could hear the echoes of that Amethyst power resonating in her still. Mentally gritting his teeth, he smiled and returned the embrace.

"Guys, this is . . ." Sollen paused a moment, looking at Toivo with a question in her eyes. Toivo returned the look with a slight nod. She nodded back then continued: ". . . Topaz, a friend of mine from way back."

He nodded and waved to the other two as Sollen introduced him. Though slightly puzzled by the name, Torch nonetheless shook his hand warmly. Ebbella declined to shake hands, raising a hand in greeting instead. They offered him a crate, and he sat with them while their discussion resumed.

"Heard you talking," Toivo said. "That manager is using Mind-powers on you, deliberately?"

Sollen nodded. "It's part of my contract. If he needs to tell me something mid-show, he 'sends' it to me. It's all right, I guess. Distracting, and I know he's *pushing* me now and again. It's all for the sake of the performance."

"Can I see your contract?" Toivo asked. "If you don't mind. I have never heard of a manager manipulating a performer that directly before. I'm pretty sure auntie Lumens would lightning-zap anyone who tried to tamper with one of her performances like that."

Both Torch and Ebbella chuckled at that image. Sollen just looked tired.

"Not like I have a choice in that," she muttered.

Toivo knew that feeling - bone-tired and drained from the "fight."

"Actually, you do have a choice," he said. "Amethysts can't influence you if they can't get into your mind in the first place. All you have to do is fill your head with some silly non-sense song or poem whenever you are around them. They try to tune into you, and all they hear is that, and not your actual thoughts. Once the door is closed to them, they can't force their way in. Only an Adept could forcibly read you then."

All three of them stared at him as if he had grown a 'lector panel on his forehead.

"I usually choose the most annoying little kids' song I can think of, and then I imagine myself shouting it at the top of my lungs."

"Yer serious 'bout that, aren't ya?" Sollen commented. "You've tried that and it works?"

"Last Amethyst who tried was cross-eyes for minutes after trying to pick my brains," Toivo crossed his own eyes in imitation. The others chuckled. "Can't hurt to try. Then that manager man will have to say what he wants instead of worming it into your mind the hard way."

"Try what?" asked the voice of the manager as he walked across the stage towards the group. Toivo started singing in his head again, an advertising jingle for an automated wall-painting invention. He saw that the others were concentrating too.

"My friend Topaz here," Sollen said first, choosing her words carefully. "He suggested a restaurant downtown that I've never been to. Wanna come 'long?"

The little man was very short and his eyes were so
blue they were violet. The hum of Amethyst power was
almost buzzing in the air around him, like angry purple wasps.
He looked at Toivo searchingly, his beady little eyes
narrowing slightly. He blinked once then his expression
became a mask of confusion. He turned to Sollen then did a
double take. He looked to each member of the group with a
growing look of concern.

"Something wrong, sir?" Torch asked, innocently
enough. He cocked his head slightly, a masterfully neutral
expression on his face.

By now, the little man was almost sweating; he
actually squinted at Sollen for a moment. Toivo could hear a
distinct rise in the volume of the deep hum, and the purple
aura around him brightened a touch. There was a moment
when he could almost see a shadow crossing across his
forehead. Then the aura and any visible trace of shadows
vanished.

"So you say this new fellow know a good restaurant,
hmmm?" he finally said, his voice starting out a little shaky.
"You only have two hours, Sollen. Don't be late. Your
contract states . . ."

"That I will be there to perform for any contracted
shows, or else there will be this consequence and that
consequence. I've heard it all before, N'stari. I haven't been
late once. Won't happen now."

Sollen rose to her feet and flashed the most brilliant
smile at her friends. Grabbing Ebbella by the arm, she danced
around the crates and headed for her change-room.

"You coming, boys?" she asked, towing a startled and
blushing Ebbella onward. "I'm grabbing my jacket. Meet us
outside in three."

Toivo and Torch looked at each other and shared a
grin.

*

After a magical meal at Amberyl's, Pho arrived for lunch himself. As the "star student" of the Photic Disciplines School, there were myriad and dizzying responsibilities he had to do. He was glad to meet Sollen, and his natural charm made the rest of the introductions easy for him. He was almost as famous as Sollen, in his own way.

"So, you guys play in our area much?" Pho asked. From anyone else, asking that kind of question would have come out at typical Photic-arrogant, but Pho was genuine in the asking, not one iota of condescension.

"Nope," Sollen replied. "This is the first of our big Photic Region tour. Sixty days, thirty concert."

"Ends in the Capital, in the big trans-system broadcast theatre. And, with Ebbella working her Clear miracles on the equipment there, Sollen will be heard in every Realm." Torch boasted.

"That's right." Toivo noted. "Clear topaz power is way up-frequency. All the long-ranges and invisibles."

"And let's not forget you, Torch." Sollen said. "The fastest Calorian mech-tech I have ever met. Able to fix anything that could even dream of breaking. Only a Sapphire Techno-path is faster 'n him."

The walk back to the Theater was one long fit of giggling as they compared differences between the four regions. Beyond the obvious differences of the different ranges of the Spectrum they used, the little differences were proving to be very entertaining.

"So why do they call it _dark-dump_ anyways?" Torch asked Pho and Toivo. "That's one expression that you _shinies_ use that always puzzles me."

Pho and Toivo looked at each other, a perplexed expression plastered on their faces. Then they both shrugged.

"Well," Toivo said, trying to find the right words. "I guess it's as simple this. When Photics go to the Hygienic room to ... to... excrete their . . . waste matter," The looks of morbid curiosity in the other three were becoming funny again. "Well, it's dark. You know, *dark-dump* and *bright-leak*?"

"*Bright-leak*? What?" Sollen asked.

Toivo could feel himself blushing a little bit, even as he started to giggle again. "Well, the solid matter that Photics excrete is dark, and . . ." He had to compose himself a bit here. ". . . and the liquid waste is luminescent."

"You mean your pee glows?" Ebbella said, as she started blushing and giggling furiously.

"Oh yeah," Pho agreed. "You walk through the parks and watch parents of young children checking to see how bright their babies' butts are glowing. Quite a time saver, that."

The group started laughing again. Toivo could not resist adding one last little image to the evening.

"Pho's such a strong Emitter that he really brightens up the whole bathroom."

The five of them were laughing all the way back through the stage door. Sollen bespoke the box office manager and got front row tickets for Toivo and Pho. The show was more than sensational.

Sollen's manager, N'stari, was conspicuously missing for the rest of the evening.

*

Sometimes, despite every effort to the contrary,
Things turn out right.
        Opal Realm saying

Chapter 15 –Grad

The time had flown by for Topaz. In no time at all, the last month of school was finished and the grand ceremony was upon him. He was attending after all. He was even looking forward to it. It had always been interesting to watch the holos of the ceremonies with his uncle and family friends, and he and Pho had pretended to be called to the stage many times in the past. Now that the real thing was happening, it was like a dream.

He moved to join the rest of the Topaz Realm's elementary graduates in the main hall. The members of his class from his *actual* school would be near the back of the room, of course, since they were all off-worlders. Tonight was not about other Gems. This was a purely Topaz Realm affair. He moved forward, until he found the last empty seat in the whole room. It was on the end of the very first row. Someone had reserved it for him - surely his uncle's handiwork. He was dressed as formally as everyone else was here, but all the Topaz Realm students that he passed murmured to each other,

162

wondering who he was, or if they had known him, why he was here.

The actual academic graduation and handing out of crystal medallions was a moderately lengthy affair, with proud parents recording the moment in myriad ways. Toivo received his medallion with good grace. He had received good evaluations in his basic subjects. The fact that his medallion was missing the self-sustaining spark of light that denoted mastery of the Spectrum skills was not lost on him. It would still be acknowledged across the Realms as proof of having passed his elementary schooling. Toivo took the crystal out of the medallion and placed it on his wrist bracer. Tapping a few tiny buttons on it, he watched as the device integrated the crystal into itself. Now he was a Citizen. No one could ever take that away from him now. For the rest of this portion of the evening, he simply closed his eyes and let waves of relief wash over and around him.

The next portion of the ceremonies began as five senior members of the Selection sub-committee processed onto the auditorium stage from the back of the room. The quiet murmur of the rest of the crowd diminished, but did not vanish. Five elders of the Council, their yellow and saffron robes sparkling in the spotlights, hoods drawn close over their faces, marched to the stage. They climbed the steps then strode toward the podium, center-stage. Four sat down on solid light stools, and composed themselves. The spokesperson, shorter and slightly hunched forward, came to the podium, pulling his hood off, revealing his dark grey hair hanging straight down on either side of his stern face. The podium adjusted itself to accommodate his short stature. He placed his light-tablet down upon it, and switched the display on.

"This year, has been one of many surprises," he said in a clear, cold voice. "We have selected those of you who have shown potential for growth and with that, the chance to ascend to the higher Academies, eventually."

There was a small rise in the volume from the students, citizens and guests. These were the traditional words, but with one significant difference. It was still somewhat shocking to the older people gathered when the Selection Committee mentioned the fact that there were more than just one higher Academy these days.

"We have selected the five candidates who will be given the chance to touch the Golden Core, and be granted permission to call on Spectrum Light." He touched a button on his tablet, and smiled. "The following students will come to the stage: Pho, of the Photic Disciplines Collegiate."

Topaz looked down the rows of faces and spotted his friend in his formal yellow and white tunic, pressed dark blue trousers and highly polished shoes. His usually unruly red hair had been tamed and he even wore his lucky light-band on his wrist as a bracelet. He waved, giving a thumbs-up sign of congratulations. Pho saw it, and returned the gesture, with a confident grin.

"Sollen, of the Azurine Schools." Toivo felt a pleasant surprise at hearing the name of another friend. Tall and dark-haired, she rose and followed Pho.

"Torch, from the Calorian Plains."

There was a bit of hubbub from the audience here. Toivo turned, spying Torch rising from the other side of the room. Once, that was something; twice, that was odd; this was the third person he knew getting called forward. He was now very alert. Something was *shaded* here.

"Ebbella, of the Hidden Villages."

That name drew an even louder response from the crowd. Petite, slender, Sollen's white-haired transmit-tech rose from her seat, and walked tentatively forward. She did not say a word, but her surprise was evident from her flushed face. Her diaphanous long-sleeved gown rippled gracefully in shades of pale yellow and off-white as she walked. The protective lenses over her eyes darkened as she approached the bright lights of the stage. Clear topaz powers made you sensitive to bright light, so this had to be painful to her.

The Hidden Villages were part of the only region of the Realm that Topaz had not visited as a child. His uncle had never traveled there, which made for an odd gap in his experiences. He had heard many stories about that mysterious race of people, most of which made the photics superior to them. Topaz had stopped believing those ones early on. He had no direct knowledge to the contrary, though, so he would ask if he could travel there himself, once he got the chance.

The selection committee spokesperson started to say the last name, then he stopped mid-syllable. He made a show of staring at his tablet incredulously, fiddling with the controls for several seconds before turning to his fellow committee members for a moment of heated and animated discussion away from the microphone. The delay gave the audience a chance to speculate about who would be next.

His unique *aura-sensing* vision began to invade Topaz's normal sight just then, kicking in more vividly than usual. It was faint and indistinct most of the time, but this time he did not have to concentrate or de-focus his eyes to see it. It snapped into place like a filter over a vid-screen.

In this case, he found himself examining the colors around the man speaking, since they seemed to be darker than usual. Right away, that struck Topaz as odd, since most of the members of the Council usually shone with an inner glow, in the different colors of the topaz Spectrum. A deep grey, shadowy haze hung around the man like a fog. As he continued to talk with the other members of the committee, the fog grew just a hint darker. Then, Topaz blinked as a shadow shot straight up from him, like an arrow. An answering shadow shot back down onto him. With a mirthless chuckle, he nodded and approached the podium again.

"And, due to his . . . uh . . . remarkable abilities in the fields of Music and the Performing Arts: Topaz, of the Rudiments of the Spectrum Schools," he said, a tight grin playing across his lips. It was as if he was savoring every syllable.

Stunned silence rippled into existence as the audience registered what the man had said. Topaz had heard the words too. They were so at odds with what he was expecting to hear that the boy sat transfixed.

"Topaz, come forward," the man said again, turning and beckoning directly to him, voice neutral but eyes betraying a puzzling excitement.

Topaz rose from his seat, totally removed from any sense of what was real or not. His head swam, and his cheeks blazed. How could this have happened? Someone had slipped his name onto the list of candidates as a huge prank. That was the only explanation that made sense to him. His uncle had wanted him to apply for a chance at the Core from the very start; his unfailingly belief in Topaz's abilities, despite his thirteen years of proof to the contrary, had been maddening to the boy. Had he called in all of his favors at once like he had when Topaz had been allowed to go to the Rudiments Schools in the first place?

He looked around, seeing the utter puzzlement that he felt reflected a thousand times on the faces of the people that had gathered. He was a puzzlement to everyone, Power-wise, and now the Apprentice Selection Committee had chosen him to touch the Core? A lone giggle came from the back of the room as he started walking toward the stage from his seat. Despite the joke being in poor taste, he had to continue. The further he went, the more the giggle started to spread. The hecklers from the back, who had started that had started it were pointing and laughing outright now. The room followed the cue, and raucous laughter filled the entire space. Thankfully, it faded to murmurs as he reached the stage.

He climbed the stairs at the side and took his place beside Pho. All of his acting skills were in play now, helping him to compose the expression on his thirteen-year-old face, though one frustrated tear did escape. The other candidates stared blankly at him, no malice in their eyes but puzzled beyond measure. He turned and nodded to Pho, who grinned and pumped his fist in victory.

"Way to go, Big Toe!" Pho extended his hand, palm facing forward toward Topaz, with a tiny sphere of light in the palm. Topaz grinned at this and tapped the offered hand with his own, unlit palm - he needed at least five or six seconds to focus enough light energy for this gesture of camaraderie.

Pho meant well, he truly did. Topaz knew that his friend was one of the strongest users of the topaz Spectrum of his generation. He certainly would become a powerful Apprentice. He might even Ascend to the Academy for his skill.

Well, that is what they were all here for, these five, after all . . . a chance to Ascend. To that end, the Selection Committee summoned them to the center of the stage. The chosen ones walked in a line to where the Council members waited for them. Each member of the Committee greeted and shook hands and hugged the students, ushering them to seats beside the podium. When they got to Topaz, he recognized two of the Committee members: Godfather Edsol and his auntie Lumens! He had always known that they were important people to the Realm, but the Council? That put them both at the same sort of rank as his uncle. He grinned, and hugged each of them warmly. Clearly, they must have had a hand in getting him here too.

The spokesman of the committee was the last in line. When he grasped Topaz's hand, a stab of cold seemed to shoot through the boy's arm. It has settled somewhere between his shoulder blades. Topaz saw the vision of an aura of shadow return, surrounding the man. He recognized the man's face from his past.

"Clearly, you are here as payment of an enormous debt that was owed to your uncle Saul, boy," Pazos growled. "No other reason." He squeezed Topaz's hand harder than was comfortable for a moment. "You are a joke, a *dimglow* and an insult to your Realm. You will provide some entertainment for us as you pose like a clown, trying to touch the Core . . . and fail. After that, I promise that you will vanish." Topaz listened to the words with only half of an ear. Pazos had been an aid to his uncle for a long time - an agent for the forces of Shadows even longer. Given what Topaz had learned about him, the threatening words made sense.

The cold grin returned, as he released Topaz's hand. Topaz moved over to his seat, touching it first, as always, to make sure that it was solid, and not a hologram. The bullies had never tired of playing that trick on him, ending him up on the floor because he could not distinguish holograms from real at a glance, like everyone else.

Pazos moved into a position behind the podium, and several things happened. Firstly, the stage itself descended slightly. A large, multicolored disk hove into view from the side. It moved as if on an invisible track. Seven or eight meters across, it rippled and shimmered in shades of blue and green across its surface. It did not look metallic, nor wooden. It did not even seem solid. It was vital in a way Toivo had never seen. It resembled nothing in his experience, and this more than commanded his fullest attention now.

"This gift from the lost realm of Opal will now bring you to the Core," Pazos said into the microphone on the podium. The crowds grew silent again at these words. "Walk through the disk, then proceed until the Light allows you to enter. Touch the Core, and return the way you came in. You go as graduates of your elementary training. You will return as Apprentices of the topaz Light."

To the growing applause and cheers of the audience, the five students rose from their seats, and approached the disk, which had started to become a maelstrom of silently swirling colors. The first four strode up to it, and walked right into it, vanishing from sight, their passage marked by a silent smear in the colors that moved across the disk's surface, which resolved after a moment. Topaz stopped just before entering it, struck by the beauty of the device. He could feel the power coming off it, very keenly, like the shimmer above a fire, or the almost visible movement of a deep, swift river. He knew it, and somehow, he could tell that it . . . it was recognizing him too. He could not say how, but he just knew that this device was just waiting for him to make contact. He touched it with his fingers, and a brilliant star-burst of colors flashed out from where he had touched it. The gentle hum from it changed too, rising in pitch melodically. He started forward, and his arm vanished as he entered the . . . the . . .

<Portal,> it answered him, as he passed the boundary. It was a type of surface tension between one place and the next. He turned to see the auditorium fading from view, the sounds of the crowds dwindling as that scene moved back, dwindling into a bright yellow speck. He turned to face forward again, and took stock of where he was.

A streaming kaleidoscope of shapes and colors streamed out in front of him and behind him. He could feel the pull of his destination drawing him forward through the tunnel of light . . . no. It was . . . a . . . a fixed wormhole connecting two points in space. It caught him off-guard that he could name this, but a moment of reflection told him that he knew this because the device had given him the knowledge directly. He knew that he wanted to study this, and wondered how he could slow his progress down. The portal "acknowledged" his mental request and let him come to a stop.

This had been some impressive gift, Topaz thought as he reached out and felt different destinations call out to him. No matter which direction he looked a tunnel of light that ended in a destination came into focus. Whatever point of light he was looking at directly became his new destination. He saw bright red specks, flashing green ones, all the colors one could imagine. There were some that looked and sounded vibrant and alive. Some were dark and decaying. He wondered if his companions had been as distracted by this display as he was.

Uh oh, he thought again. Just like me to wander off at a time like this. Better to stay with the group. He searched for a moment then found what he deduced was his original destination: a brighter yellow speck than the one he had come from. He stared intently at it and concentrated. He willed the device to speed him there as quickly as it could, just like the rest of his friends.

As quickly as he thought it, his destination zipped forward. The sudden speed did not make him dizzy, but it was a little bit disorienting. One jarring transition later, he arrived.

*

The same moment that Topaz arrived, a silent blinking red light started flashing on Pazos' tablet. It signaled something to Pazos that had not occurred in many years. He glanced down, and his eyes widened ever so slightly. He tapped a query into the tablet, and the resulting answer made him raise both eyebrows.

*

He was standing in the glittering central chamber of the Core of the topaz Realm. The archways and walls were

170

one enormous topaz crystal that had formed around the Core, and it glowed on all surfaces with reflected light. There were different colors of crystals inset into the walls, and a distinct pattern in the crystal on the floor, marking the exact center of the room. Other than that, the room was empty. His footsteps echoed in the wide-open space deep under the surface of his world. He was in the Arrival hall. He had studied its layout for weeks now, as part of his schoolwork. It was breathtaking. He just stood there, dazzled. He looked behind him, and short hallway that led to a staircase lit with glow stones, going up. That must have been the old way of getting here, before the Opal Realm had given the portal to his people. He could imagine the great quest that the graduates must have had to undertake to walk down to the Core chamber. The journey must have been arduous back then, a sort of endurance test for the candidates.

*

From the podium at the center of the stage, Pazos watched the arrival of Topaz at the glittering central Core chamber on the screen of his tablet. His face was neutral, but his mind was flying furiously.

<*He's at the Core!*> he thought darkly.

<*That should not have happened.* > answered a dark mind-voice: his superiors were indeed watching. <*The Diverters were in place?* >

<*Yes. I tested them myself just this morning. Standard procedure. He should have gone to the secondary site.* >

<*How did this happen, then? No one on that planet should be able to alter any kind of setting on the portal.* >

<*Don't know. I am recording everything. I will report when I have an explanation. By now the candidates will have joined him there, and I see that the rec-broadcast crystals are already registering their arrival.* >

<Nothing further to be done, then. We must let this proceed, as it will. One crew of actual apprentices will make little difference in the overall Plan. Note their names. We will have to maintain closer surveillance on them now. >

<Understood. >

A tiny bead of sweat dribbled down his forehead as he switched on the relay systems.

The assembled people in the auditorium all exclaimed happily, as the huge monitors came to life. The figure of Topaz, looking about, filled the screens. Lumens and Edsol were holding hands, watching very closely.

*

Far away, on the other side of the city, watching the vid-screen in his personal hover-car, Saul saw it too. He sighed deeply, and mopped profuse sweat from his brow. There had been no way for him to help his nephew here. Pazos had most assuredly taken care of that when he slipped Topaz's name onto the list. He had had to trust that Fate would help the boy find the right place to be, which it had.

*

We are the Children of Light
We are the Chosen conduits of the Light of our world
We are the Beacon that guides the lost out of Darkness.
We are the Children of Light.

Core Philosophy of the Topaz Realm

Chapter 16 – Apprentice

As he pondered the candidates of the past, he remembered that he was one, himself. Then he realized that he was alone here. Cursing himself quietly, he started walking toward the center of the room, where he supposed the others had already gone, and been transported somewhere else, through some hidden doorway. If he were too far behind the rest of the group, would the Guardian of the Core even let him near it? He was just about to push open the doorway on the far wall, when suddenly his peers arrived through the disk. They looked around then jumped when they saw him standing there on the other side of the room."

"An' just how did you get here first?" Sollen inquired, eyebrows raised in surprise. "We entered that thing 'fore you did." A shrug was all Topaz could answer with before a blinding golden light from the center of the room dazzled them all.

173

When they could all see again, they saw a tall, bald man in white robes, trimmed with every color in the Spectrum, standing next to an immense golden imperial topaz crystal. Five people could have spanned the distance across it, and ten could encircle it. It sparkled and shone like a star, yet it dimmed at the touch of its attendant. Topaz hastened to join the rest of the group, just as impressed as they were.

"This is a manifestation of the very Heart of our world, the source of all our powers," the ageless seeming man declared solemnly. "If the Core deems you worthy, it will unlock within you the fullest potential of your powers, and share with you what it intends for you to do with them." He stepped away from the core and moved off a little way. The five graduates stood stock still, not sure of how to proceed. The guardian now stood to one side of the crystal. He touched the crystal again, exaggerating his hand motions, the barest hint of a smile on his lips. The crystal now pulsed lighter and darker, like the gentle beating of a heart.

"My name is Pho, and I'm not waiting anymore!" Pho shouted. Before anyone could say anything to him, he strode right up to it and placed his hand on the Core. Everyone held their breath, anticipation quivering in them. The crystal itself went dark around Pho's hand a moment. He kept his arm immobile, waiting for the judgment that was surely happening.

After another interminable second, he got an odd look on his face, as if he was hearing something the others were not. After this, his face took on a look of startled joy then his entire body started to shine like a beacon. His flesh of his whole frame was shining brightly, his clothing filtering the glare a bit. Beams of yellow and orange light shout out of his eyes and mouth, and his back arched as the power of Light filled him, changed him. The rest of the group watched, immobile, both terrified and excited. Pho's hair was standing completely on end. After several long seconds, he was flung

from the Core like a glowing comet. He flew a couple of feet
away, and landed on his side. His body dimmed until it was
almost his normal coloration, except for his hair, which was an
almost luminescent red now. Topaz rushed over to him as he
started to pull himself into a seated position. There were still
the odd freckle or two on his face that was shining brightly,
but they faded quickly too. He shook his head a few times,
trying to mutter a few stunned phrases to himself. Topaz
checked him over visually, checking for injury. With an
excitement that bordered on callous, the other three ran up and
took turns touching the Core themselves.

"Th . . . thththt . . ." was all he could say at first.
Topaz kept watching him closely, making sure that he was
safe, and that he would not injure himself by falling again.
With a visible effort of concentration, he cleared his throat,
and said in a small, reverent voice "Th . . . that was . . .
intense!" He looked up at his childhood friend, and his face
split in a wild grin. "It spoke to me. It spoke to me." A
mixture of awe and excitement mingled around him.

"Very *shiny*, Shade-boy," Topaz replied. "What did it
say?"

"It told me that it was happy to lend me its power, and
that it was proud to call me Apprentice of the Golden Light!"

Topaz grinned and helped his recovering friend to his
feet. Once standing, Pho started walking around in little
circles, muttering things to himself, clearly beyond himself
with what he had learned and become. The others were
coming back from the Core, looking just as dazzled. Sollen's
hair had arcs of electricity dancing around it and bits of metal
were circling around her. Her electrical powers now extended
into the magnetic ranges. Torch was radiating light from his
eyes that ranged from deep red to almost orange and a haze of
smoke seemed to surround him. Topaz had seen holos of
Ruby warriors who looked like him, and was duly impressed.

Ebbella did not look as if anything had changed for her, until Topaz saw her vanish completely! She reappeared a few feet along the path she had been walking. Then her image shifted, and became that of Sollen's, then Pho's. Her own image returned just as quickly. Her clear topaz powers now granted her control over how any light hit her now, which meant that she had utter control of what others saw when they looked at her. There had to be more to her than that, but he just did not know enough about clear topazes to hazard a guess.

"Young man," the guardian said gently. "The others have been granted their gifts. It is your turn now."

Toivo gulped deeply and took a steadying breath as he started toward the Core. Everything in his life had led to this quintessential moment. His doubts were screaming at him to stop, run away, not to sully the Core with his unworthiness. He stopped more than once on his short walk. His uncle had said that he had the potential to become something magnificent, like no one he had ever known - he believed in Toivo so completely that it humbled him. Well, if his uncle, the strongest Adept the Realm had known for a century, thought that he could touch the Core, then he would. He pushed his fears aside and, though his chest and limbs were full of ice and his face full of fire, he took another deep steadying breath, and stepped forward, placing his left hand on the warm surface of the Core.

The golden light of the Heart of the Realm enveloped him. He could feel the glow as warmth that ran in tickling rivulets through him. He watched as several wisps of acrid black mist rose up from him as the cleansing power of the Core flowed. He had had shadow-worms inside of him? The relief he felt as the last cry and puff of smoke faded to nothing merely added to the glory of the moment for him. Then he heard a voice as old as time, as deep as space and as kind as sunshine start to speak.

<Little one, you are not one of mine,> it said. Topaz could actually feel his heart skip a beat in terror as those words flowed into him. *<Though you are not of this world, I recognize you, boy-who-is-called-by-my-name. For your own safety, you may use my name as your own, for as long as you need to. A loyal friend told me that you would be here, one day.>* Relief flooded through him at this, though it was *not* accompanied by even a mote of comprehension. At least, now he was certain that the Heart of Light did not object to his adopted name. That counted as a good thing. Topaz could hear, or more feel, the voice speaking to him again:

<I will gladly honor the promise made to him, as well as the one I made to my Brothers and Sisters. Since the beginning, we Twelve were One; our voices different but unified. Our strength was unity through diversity. Nothing had ever been able to prevent this communion, until recently.> There was emotion coming across in its voice now . . . sorrow, loss, fear, and anger. Topaz had never conceived of the Cores as being able to feel emotions.

<For almost 15 years now, I have not been able to communicate with my family. I have been lonely for them, and them for me, I am sure.> Topaz felt a pang of sympathy at these words. If a bright light could smile, then the Core certainly did, sensing Topaz's response.

<You, little one, are the key. When you Journey to the other Worlds, speak to my brethren. They will be able to hear the echo of my voice in you. You will be my Messenger to them. Bring my Power with you, to Shine for them in their darkness.>

Journey? What did that mean? Only the very rich or the leaders of the Council ever traveled to other Realms. He was neither. The Core expected him to travel? Though the idea of it was one of his dearest wishes, he just could not conceive of how to accomplish it.

He could feel something change about him. On his left shoulder, a clear crystal the size of his fist formed. This was the sign that he could summon the Spectrum independently now, a badge of office showing his status as Apprentice. If he checked the others, he was sure that they would have similar crystals on their left shoulders. He could feel it. It was a part of him. It would appear when he used his powers, regardless of what he wore. It felt like a vast storage room, devoid of content . . . until the Core poured Light into it. Vast torrents of Light energy flooded into him like a tsunami. All the colors of the Spectrum danced and swirled through his entire being. It overwhelmed him.

From the outside, the visible light coming from the crystal suddenly changed to all the colors of the rainbow, in a swirling spiral pattern. No one had ever seen this, in any display of Spectrum power. The four new apprentices could feel the energy of the Core entering Topaz wildly. The yellow portion of that rainbow shot forth and struck him in the shoulder right about where his new shoulder crystal badge had formed, with the sound a thousand crystal chimes ringing,. It only lasted a few seconds,

The Core pulled his consciousness back, and said *<You have far to go, little one, before you can return to your true home. You will visit it at least, before you know what you will need to do to save her. I am the first to aid you on your way toward that goal.>* The words it spoke seemed to grow louder, filling his whole being. *<I grant you permission to call on my Power without let or hindrance, to the fullest extent of your understanding of it.>*

He could feel that his hand had left the surface of the Core now. In the last few moments of contact, the voice said one last thing:

<You are now an Apprentice, but not one of mine. Your Powers are very different from what I can grant. I

have only awakened that part of you that sings with me. Go now, you have much to learn, and even more to do.> The ancient voice faded from his mind, and a parting image of a very old, regally dressed man, sitting on a multicolored throne, smiled and waved to him then faded.

His puzzlement grew cosmically large now, with the questions that blazed in his head. How was he going to Journey to the other Realms? What did the Core mean by only waking a part of his Powers? What did it mean when it said he was the key? Key to what? If he was not 'of the Topaz Realm', then where was he from? And who was that old man? Nothing in his experience could even begin to answer them. Now, if he could only find his eyes, or his arms, he might be able to start finding the answers. Wait a minute, where were his limbs? Or his entire body, for that matter. Several dark, confusing moments followed for him.

When his senses gradually returned, he found himself lying on his back, staring up at the other four graduates. They all wore expressions of confusion and concern.

"Toivo, you ok?" Pho asked, using his real name out of concern. He helped his friend into a seated position.

"The Core went crazy: all swirls and rainbows." Sollen said, her voice nervous still. "You stood there, longer than any of us, then just walked away from the Core."

"A nimbus of Power connected you to the Core for at least another five seconds before it suddenly disappeared, and you fell flat on your back, glowing like a spotlight." Ebbella added, her high voice ringing like a gentle bell. "You went dark real fast. No pulse or breathing. We were all sure that it had killed you, or rejected you, or something." Torch nodded agreement to this.

In response, Topaz shook his head groggily, and tried to stand. With help from the others, he rose to his feet, now dizzy from the feeling of new energy coursing through his veins. He thought about what the Core had said to him, and with a raised eyebrow, raised his hand . . . and a small sphere of yellow light rested there, in the center of his palm, as cohesive and strong as one from anyone else. Pho blinked, returned the gesture, and for the first time in Topaz's life, a bright star-burst flashed when their hands met. Pho let out a loud whoop of victory as he grabbed his friend up in a fierce bear hug. The incredulous look in Topaz's eyes was echoed in by the others, who each came up, in turn, and *star-bursted* with him, sharing with him a fuller measure of respect than he had ever known. He could even feel each person's power briefly connect with his, conveying congratulations and pride.

"Apprentices of the Realm, welcome," the Guardian intoned just as he and the Core started to fade from view. "Shine brightly."

The five young people all bowed deeply to him and the Core. No one spoke for several long seconds. The light glinting off the crystalline walls and pillars just danced about. Then, at some unspoken signal, all five of them leapt into the air, cheering and screaming for joy. They hugged each other, and became the fastest of friends in that moment . . . all five of them.

After their private celebrating, they decided that they really should return to the Auditorium, to complete the Ceremonies. Taking their time, they strolled back the way had come, toward the shimmering portal. In little ways, they were each exploring the range of their new and considerably amplified topaz Powers.

"Watch this!" Torch said, as he vanished from sight completely with only a quiet ping. There was no telltale shimmer of distorted light - he had well and truly vanished. A brown topaz skill this was not, and he reappeared with a knowing grin on his face.

Sollen grinned, then a globe of visible light surrounded her for a moment. When it faded, she had altered her appearance to that of Ebbella's. Both versions of the girl from the Hidden Villages drew in surprised breaths then laughed out loud. Sollen returned to her normal appearance then looked at each of them, excitedly. She was a galvanic blue topaz, electricity being her usual area of E.M. spectrum strength. Performing a Light-based trick was as much a novelty for her as he was for Topaz himself.

Pho grinned, then extended an arm, and a very powerful ray of yellow-orange light shot forth from his fist, impacting the far wall and pushing the center of it back, quickly and effortlessly. Then, he fired a bright red beam from his fist, which melted a hole in the wall beside the first one. He actually repeated that one several times, melting several fist-sized holes into the wall with newfound heat powers. Grinning wildly, Pho closed his eyes in concentration. Within a heartbeat, his entire form flashed brightly for just a second. When they were able to see again, Pho stood before them, clad head to toe in glinting silver and gold armor. It bent and flexed like cloth, clinging to him. He touched the brim of the helmet, and a faceplate flashed down, sealing him in a seamless protective skin of solidified light. He touched the faceplate again, and it flashed up and out of the way, revealing his face, flushed and wide-eyed, even more speechless than before.

"Whoa," Ebbella said, watching with her fingers covering her mouth "That's battle armor, new-style photic battle armor." The others looked at her then nodded.

"It's stronger than any metal forged, and regenerates when hit." Torch added. He came over to touch the cool metallic-seeming surface of Pho's shoulder. "There are Council members who don't know how to summon this."

They all admired Pho for a moment longer, before he dispelled the shining armor with a quiet crystal ping. Topaz had to admit that this was the singularly most impressive photic display that he had ever seen. The fact that it was his best friend performing it made the moment more than a little surreal. It was an amplification of his natural skill. All of them were stronger, and the sharing of the colors between them was the most unexpected outcome that he could imagine.

"Oh, but this is *full-brilliant-star-clear*!" Pho cried. "S*hard and Shine*! Everything feels so different! We've been given the power to save the Realm!" He reached his long arms around the shoulders of those nearest him. Soon, the entire group was walking, arms on each other's shoulders, matching step.

His words were true, Topaz thought. Nothing was the same now. These displays of incredible power signaled the end of their old lives and the beginning of a shining new chapter. Topaz had not known that Apprentices were this strong in the Spectrum, and he liked it. This cross-color sharing of abilities was also a new discovery. He was inordinately pleased by that, even more so than Pho's new armor. He had to tell his uncle about this. Looking up, he saw the rec-broadcast crystal imbedded in the ceiling, and understood that it was more than likely that his uncle already knew. He could not stop grinning, seeing how his friends' powers had been changed and amplified.

Then his face went neutral as an idea occurred to him.

He stopped walking and disentangled himself from the group. They all paused, looking at him curiously. The Core had said to him that he could call on the Spectrum "without let or hindrance". That meant that he should now be able to do Light tricks now that had eluded him for his entire life. He tried to remember the most impossible topaz power lesson he had tried. Hrmm . . . must have been when they were trying to teach him how to create a functional shield out of solid light. The best he had ever done before was taking full sunlight and spinning it into a sewing thimble-sized pad that crumbled when touched. That seemed like a good place to start. He visualized what he needed to then called on his Powers. With breathtaking speed, a round buckler constructed of solid yellow light instantly appeared, attached to his forearm. There had been no straining, no resistance, just the willpower and then the reality. With a cry of shock, he backed up against the wall for support. He could actually feel the weight of it on his arm, the texture of the holographic metal and rivets. He was rendered mute by it. In fact, he could barely breathe. With a slight tremor, he looked from one person to the next. They all bore looks of joy and encouragement for him. He ended with Pho, who stood especially proudly. Just to be sure it was not a fluke, he dispelled and reformed the half-meter sized buckler a couple of times more. He tried to summon the same kind of armor that Pho had summoned, but the malformed plates of solid light didn't join together, roaming over his body randomly instead for a few seconds before sputtering out. Disappointment filled his chest again, as it always did.

"Topaz, I've never seen you able to call a light-construct together as quickly as you did with that buckler thing." Pho said as he strode forward to where his friend leaned against the wall. "You've gone from Shade to Shine!" He pulled Topaz forward, back into the group.

Topaz let a smile return to his features as the truth of the words sank in. That shield-construct had been solid, no doubt about it. He was no longer a *dim-glow*. He could call on the Light. This was his photic skill. And if this part of him had been improved, the other colors he could call on might also have been increased as well. It wasn't the same victory that his peers had experienced, but it was one for him. His uncle would be so proud of him.

"I think I'm going to like this," Topaz said, quietly. Pho and the others agreed with him, pounding his shoulders and back. They entered the portal back to the Auditorium together, their arms linked as they traveled. Topaz noticed that the others became immobile as they went through the tunnel. That must have been what happened to them on the way to the Core. He sent a mental _thank you_ to the portal itself, for bringing them safely back and forth. Again, it actually answered him with a happy sounding rumble. The noisy yellow circle of light that was their destination approached now, the cheers and applause of the crowd reaching his ears even before they had arrived. Their trip to the Core had been seen by everyone throughout the Realm. So now, the whole Realm itself was happily welcoming its newest Apprentices of the topaz Light. For the first time, Topaz was not the stranger, the outsider. He was an Apprentice. He felt that he was part of something. He felt like he belonged . . . that he had a place . . . and he liked it.

*

Part 3

Apprentice

The powerful magnetic force between student and teacher
Only comes into play when both are ready.

Peridot truism

Chapter 17 – Orientation

"Of course, you'll have access to any transport you will need, during your term as working Apprentices," droned the guide, his official uniform looking somewhat less than pristine. "When you are on call, you will have full planetary resources available to you. When you are not, you will connect to the edu-net, for direct instruction on your duties, your responsibilities."

Topaz nodded, big silly grin still stuck to his face. It had been two weeks now, and his new reality was still keeping him mute with jubilation. The turnabout that his fate had experienced in the past week was a never-ending source of wonder for him. The other members of his squad were looking around the somewhat worn-looking rooms of their new apprentices' quarters with more than a touch of apprehension. The news media always showed that the Adepts lived in the best rooms, in the best towns, ate the best foods. Clearly that didn't apply nearly so much to

186

Apprentices. Instead of the newest, cleanest, brightest
domiciles in the Realm, Topaz, Pho, Sollen, Torch and Ebbella
had been assigned to what had to have been a slum that had
been cleared out only just recently.

"The Council has decided that since you are the
newest Apprentices, it would be more advantageous for you to
be as near to the central transport hub for the entire Realm,"
the guide continued. His voice never really got louder or
softer, higher or lower. It was as if he had said this a thousand
times. "You will learn in how to recognize the call of the
Council when you go for your orientation." He finished
entering the final codes into the keypad by the door, then
started walking out. Over his shoulder, he said. "A piece of
advice, youngsters . . ." All five graduates turned from their
exploring to pay heed. The man scratched his cheek, and in a
half-whisper, said: "That's the official line. I've housed every
apprentice for the past 40 years, and I can say that these
quarters will serve you better than any other. Watch, learn,
and walk with the Light. The Realm needs you." Then he
passed out the door, which closed with a slightly grinding hiss.

The five of them stood there, surrounded by their
luggage. They looked at each other, with the same expression.
This was going to be an adventure, to be sure . . . whether it
was a good or a bad one remained to be seen.

*

Their first call from the Council had come in the very
earliest part of the next morning. The message flashing on the
screens and holos of their residence stated that they had to
report to the Central Council complex for the first of their
orientation training.

They finished a hurried meal together, and left the
dishes sitting on the table as they ran out the door. It took
them all of two minutes to arrive at their destination. They
could see a group of people their own age gathered at a small

door to the side of the main entrance. A moment later, they were sitting amongst the newest apprentices from around the Realm, listening intently.

"You will be assigned schedules of duty, for each of your rotations, until you've completed your initial period. You will be granted clearance to go anywhere you need to, in your roles as Apprentices." The lecture was a recording of a bland-looking man, playing from a large holo-player inset above the door. Topaz could count about thirty brand-new apprentices seated around it. "All citizens and law officials must assist you when you performing your duties. They will not, however, help you to break any of the Laws as laid out by the Council. If you abuse your power as an Apprentice, then the Adepts corps and the Council will deal with you."

Topaz wrote furiously on his light-board, in his irregular scrawl, all the details he could. He already knew all of this, and had for years. He was surrounded by young men and women, all of whom had touched the Core. That made for a true sense of camaraderie that was a welcome change for him. Only his first day, and he had already struck up conversation with several people sitting nearest to him. It seemed that in his own mind, his new abilities had given him permission to speak with anyone now.

Once the preliminary vid was out of the way, the door opened, and the apprentices were ushered in. It was a good thing that Topaz had brought his light-pad with him, because the next six hours were spent learning all that there was to know about the Council and how it interacted with them. He caught the important bits as they flew by, but he made a point of finding out how to replay this orientation when he needed to, so that he could catch the rest of the information at his own speed.

When it felt as if every fact in the universe had been stuffed into their heads, from Council sub-committees to the frequency of comm-lines around the different cities, they were given time to refresh themselves - a short time, though, with instructions to assemble outside of the door they'd entered in one hour. Most of the apprentices crashed onto couches that they either found or constructed themselves from solid-light.

When they exited the door, there were actual people waiting for them now, though it was still the hologram that led the proceedings. Within minutes, the entire group was divided up into smaller squads. Topaz and his friends were officially grouped together. Once the groupings were recorded and filed, the orientation leader began assigning an experienced Adept who had volunteered to help out to each squad. There were seven truly famous Adepts, from around the Realm there, and they each took a group of five. Pho and Sollen were asked if they wanted to go with some of the more glamorous teams, but they refused, knowing that their original team would probably be the best place for them. The other Adepts shrugged and took their teams with them. Oddly, none of them looked all that excited to have a team of Apprentices with them. The last advisor was very old, grey-white hair cut short and wrinkles dominating what once had been a dashing face. He hadn't spoken during the whole selection process, giving all the impression of dozing. He had remained seated there, in his hover-chair, wrapped in a thick blanket, watching. He looked around him with eyes that still shone brightly.

"And the last of the apprentices will go with Adept emeritus Dellas," the guide said curtly. "Fare well. Walk with the Light." With a brief shimmer, the instructional hologram faded. The old man remained motionless, looking at his new charges. They sat in their seats, equally motionless. Only Topaz seemed to be processing the situation.

"Sir," Topaz started, in a quiet, respectful tone. "Adept Dellas?" The ancient, shining eyes turned on Topaz, like twin beams of light from a focused glowstone. "Sir, are you the same Dellas who taught Council member Saul how to tame a wild diffra with his bare hands?" The twin beams of light remained focused on him. "Or the Dellas who found and charged the prime lens of the Council chambers in Estan, all by himself?" Now the others were looking at him, confused.

"If you are the same Dellas who led the Radiant Knights to victory against the Dark beasts, the man who was reputed to be the TopazStar, then I am more than honored to meet you sir." Topaz rose from his seat and moved toward the old man's hover-chair. He dropped to one knee in front of him, and bowed his head. "My name is Topaz, as I was named by the Core itself. I am the nephew of Councillor Saul, and I am humbled to be a student of yours." He kept his head down, and waited.

<What are you doing? > Pho asked Topaz, in a tight beam inquiry. *<How do you know all this, and why are you on one knee in front of this fossil? >* The girls had risen, and stood behind Topaz, the boys staying in their seats.

The old man's hover-chair slid forward, and a skeletal hand emerged from the blankets. It reached forward and rested on Topaz's head for a moment. In a glowing cloud around him, the old man answered Topaz's words with a projected holographic reply: *<Young Topaz, I haven't been greeted in this way since before you were born. Your uncle was one of my most brilliant Apprentices, and remains a close friend. You are well-come, boy, well-come indeed.>* The shining eyes rose to encompass the others and a question formed in the projection: *<And are you others as ready to learn as this one is?>*

Pho, Sollen, Torch and Ebbella all dropped to one knee, as Topaz had. The old man smiled and his hover-chair started to glide toward the door. *<Then, come, all of you. I will try to show you what it really means to be an Apprentice of the Light. >*

*

When they entered the pedestrian traffic near the Travel hub, the young people formed a protective phalanx around Dellas. His mastery of the Spectrum was shown in dozens of little ways as they traveled. He spoke to them in tight-beam speech continuously, describing how the Adepts were first formed, how they were organized at the beginning, how they'd changed as a group over the years. Gradually, the young ones started asking questions back, and they were genuine ones. Dellas answered each one, thoroughly and in just enough detail to satisfy the curiosity of each. They had not been issued their apprentices' uniforms yet, so Dellas lead them through the Hub, to a small clothing shop, in the outskirts of the city. It may have been similar to the other metal-and-glass towers shops that the city contained, but it had been designed and built many decades ago. Its proprietors, a man and wife with deeply wrinkled skin and grey to white hair, were only marginally less old than Dellas himself. They saw the old man coming up the walkway of their little shop, and started a loud argument with Dellas over something that had happened twenty-years prior.

<Look around, young ones. This place is unique. The founders of this shop have made the best Apprentice garments the Realm ever known. Not everyone knows about this place, and those who do usually underestimate it how well the Sardony's know their craft.> Dellas sent to each of them, as he continued a vigorous discussion with the shopkeeper.

Topaz nodded, taking his cue. He moved away from the group, and started looking at the walls of the little store. There were robes, tunics, outfits of all sorts. Almost everything had to be more than thirty years out of date.

"Well, if they are apprentices, then they need to get rated and measured then," the old woman said brusquely. She came from behind the wooden counter bearing a long wooden staff. It was unadorned, but rounded at both ends. The wood itself looked ancient, polished to a high gleam from many hands holding it, its dark grain contrasting the slightly green coloration of the wood. Dellas used holographic arrows and pointing hands to guide the five youngsters over to a spot in front of the counter. Dutifully, they moved into place, lining up beside one another, starting with Ebbella, then Sollen, Torch, Pho, then Topaz. The woman brought the staff up to Ebbella.

"Wager you thought I'd be using some new-fangled sapphire-built power gauge, didn't ya?" she crowed, a wry grin on her face. She let out a bark of laughter at the blank expression on the girl's face. "HA! Course you did. No such luck here, girlie. Only the tried and true methods used by the Peridot Adepts for the past millennium. No mechanical glitches here.

The staff started to glow a pale green as it got closer to Ebbella.

"Well, now, that's different," the old woman muttered to herself. "Every so-called apprentice that has come through here didn't even have enough power inside them to light a candle. Hrmm . . ." she pondered, as she passed the staff in front of all of them. The wood glowed gently for each of them.

"By the glow of my staff, from the Peridot Fields, / I now know to say that your Powers are real," she intoned, ritually. She turned back to Ebbella, and with a raised eyebrow, and almost a smile on her lips, she offered the staff to the girl, to hold.

"Take this with one hand, and place one end of it on the ground." The puzzlement on the white-haired girl's face was so clear that the old man behind the counter, on his high stool, answered her silent questions

"The last test was to confirm that you had the requisite Power level needed to purchase clothing here." he said. "This test will tell us just how much power, and of what type it is. With that, we'll be able to make the right type of outfit to compliment your particular abilities." His eyes were as glittery as Dellas', and he was clearly as interested in the results of the testing as the woman was.

Ebbella blinked, looked at Sollen, who shrugged, then nodded. She gulped once then took the staff. It began to glow with a bright green light now. When she touched it to the ground, a line of white-yellow with a rainbow of thinner colors swirling around it rose from the rounded end on the ground, and rose smoothly to the rounded end at the top. Ebbella watched it go up then nodded as it filled the rounded end with the colors of the topaz Realm.

"By the ... I can't ... Dellas, is this a joke?" the woman said, sputtering. "This child has more pure topaz power in her than I've seen in any person on the planet for the past fifty years!" She examined the colors on the staff more closely. "She actually touched the Core, this one. She has access to the entire clear range of the Spectrum, with virtually no hindrance. Only her understanding of it limits her. You are from the Hidden Villages aren't you?" This last question she blurted directly into Ebbella's face, who blinked again, then nodded. "She's the first from that region to have ever been given this kind of Power Gift in my memory." She took the staff from Ebbella then shook it several times. All of the luminescence faded, and it returned to its light green state. She handed it to Torch, who accepted it and placed it on the ground as well. The same effect happened for him, only this time, the two yellow lines were on either side of a smoky brown line.

"TWO! Two children have touched the real Core! This one is a brown topaz. He must have unparalleled control of the infrared range. That would make him able to manipulate Heat, almost as well as the Ruby people!" the old man crowed from his spot behind the counter. "Dellas, you were right to bring them here."

The staff was passed to Sollen, who made it light up, but with the center line a brilliant blue. Pho, on the other hand, had a solid yellow line, with only filaments of the other colors present in his display.

"The strongest Blue I've ever seen, and the most powerful Photic in a dozen generations!" the old man was nearly weeping. He never moved from his seat, but was now busily entering figures and data into the terminal on the counter. His fingers were a blur, clearly excited beyond measure

"And finally you, young man," the woman said, handing Topaz the staff. He examined it, felt it, and sniffed it first before he put it on the ground. It felt like it was vibrating in his hands, and the color of it was reminiscent of the clothes that his dearest friend Kayleigh would wear. He smiled at that, and jabbed the staff down onto the floor.

A loud clap of what could have been thunder boomed throughout the store, rattling windows and upsetting displays. The staff itself didn't send of a yellow shaft, but what seemed to be an open braid, with every different color that you could imagine climbing up the entire staff with pinprick threads of brilliant color. The yellow strand was the thickest of these at the moment, but clearly, the empty space in the braiding showed that there was room for more.

"Oh, my . . ." the woman said, stunned by this. "This can't be. They were all killed."

"Not all, it seems, and this one an Apprentice already," said the old man.

"Agreed. This is what we've been waiting for." The woman first turned to Dellas, who gave no physical reaction, then looked at Topaz avidly. "He's got as much potential as you did, Dellas, but it's unrealized as of yet."

Then both man and woman stopped, and looked at each other. Topaz heard the light buzz of Peridot energy passing back and forth between them for a few moments. This must have been what it looked like when he and Kayleigh had used that secret Peridot Mind-wave communication trick. He could almost see the haze of light green passing between them, then toward Dellas.

"You know what they are talking about?" Pho whispered in Topaz's ear. "Lots of words, yet none of them are sayin' much."

Topaz shrugged, still pondering the colors that the Peridot-wood staff had displayed.

<There's a lounge at the back of the store, with periodicals and entertainment vids from eras gone by.> Dellas projected. *<Go, read. You might learn something. Your official uniforms will ready in a little while. From what I saw, I think that making uniforms for you lot will be an interesting challenge for them.>*

With nods of acknowledgment, the five young apprentices moved through a curtained doorway behind the counter. When they were gone, the adults were joined by a robed figure who had been standing in the corner, invisibly.

"He's the one, your charge, the one you saved," the old man muttered. "The one-who-must-be-kept-safe."

Pulling back his hood, Saul nodded.

"That's him. It's because of him that this squad of apprentices had the chance to touch the Core at all." Saul whispered, coming to stand close the counter. "He doesn't know anything of his past, nor of his true potential. He can't learn any of it until he's safely out of range. Remarkably, he's found a way to emulate our powers so effectively that the spies

195

and agents who know him think that he's simply a very lucky bungler."

"That stands to reason," the old woman mused. "I've never known one at such an early stage in their lives." She had to grin to herself. "The last one I outfitted was that youngster who raced on Sapphire, but she was fully realized by the time she got to me."

"We'll have to make his uniform very differently from the others. We haven't made a suit for an apprentice like him in decades!"

"It has to resemble this Realm's current designs, even if it's . . ." Saul interjected strongly, but he stopped short as both shop owners looked at him, raising their eyebrows in slightly amused disapproval. Saul bowed his head, taking the silent rebuke in good grace.

<They're already trying to manage him, you know. They assigned me to them, after all . . . and we all know how 'old' I am, don't we?> Dellas' ancient, wrinkled face split into a wide grin as he projected this. *<We must be doing something right, because I would have grouped them like this myself. Finishing their training will be a joy. >*

Saul nodded, and pulled the hood back over his head.

"There's no one I'd rather have working with them, Del. This Realm's current GemStar is the right one for the job. Speaking of GemStars, how's Stellan doing? He must be ready to graduate by now."

<Thank you for asking. My grand-son has been advancing in all areas, and he's been very busy. I took your suggestion, too. He and his parents have been traveling continuously since he was four. He's learned just like your Toivo has, only with no limitations. For both our boys, using all the disciplines is as natural as breathing.>

"His identity is safe still? You've kept him hidden?" Saul asked

196

<Oh yes. He's the youngest active member of the Network too. He's aware of what he is, and what he will become when I finally pass on. By the time the new apprentices are ready to Ascend, he'll be ready to assume his proper mantle.>

"I tell you one thing," the old man behind the counter mentioned. "We'll have to all watch ourselves as these children start to change things. They are exactly what the Enemy is seeking. The Realm of Light won't survive if they are found any time soon."

<That's why I've kept Stellan from Apprenticing. If my instincts are right, then this little squad here will be exactly the team to form the next . . .>

Saul raised a hand to silence his old mentor.

"Dellas, don't say it, not yet," he said, seriously. "I think the same thing, and I'll do what I can to keep them together, or at very least connected. My nephew unique powers and luck will help each of them in many subtle ways, so that they will be ready when the time comes."

They all nodded in agreement.

"Things are starting to glow now. We are the first ones to help, and our job will set up how the rest of the Network will help, when their time comes." Saul growled quietly. "For all our sakes, we HAVE to do a good job."

*

Sometimes,
There is nothing more confusing
Than how other people organize things.
Therefore
Look and see what is not there,
This will tell you a clearer story.

From *"Organizational Strategies for Non-Linears"*,
Academy Central Library

Chapter 18 – Plans

With one final heave, Topaz lifted the last dusty storage container onto the shelf. He looked over at Pho, who was using a tiny welding-laser beam projected from his finger to fuse a supporting strut onto a new shelving unit, then over to Sollen and Torch, who were busily entering file codes and locations into the terminal on the wall. Ebbella was out of sight, again, bringing the next box of random files for them to sort. The Council had assigned his squad to this painstaking task to them, despite the fact that normally it would have taken a small army of bureaucrats to sort and store all the files that they could find in this wing of the Council Building's basement. From the layer of dust that had coated everything, it was clear that no one had thought about these physical files for a very long time. It was also clear that the last person that had been responsible for keeping this archive in order had been seriously overwhelmed by the task. The great piles of randomly sorted physical pages, recording crystals of all shapes and sizes, light pads sat in their thick coating of dust and almost seemed to chuckle at them.

The chaos had clearly underestimated this squad of Apprentices.

Though they had all agreed that this task did not require the skills of Apprentices of the Spectrum, their ability to talk silently and instantly and to improvise around the lack of tools to do the job made it at least possible. Sollen would walk into a room and get the Council Interface Terminal up and running, which took some time due to neglect, outdated software or plain-old damage. Torch would create thermal air currents, to start removing the dust from all the surfaces. Ebbella turned out to be truly able to find the little code clues that told them where the pages went. Pho would use his light constructs and muscles to move the piles of paper about, as they got sorted. He was also recruited to rebuild the shelves that were falling apart. Topaz floated from job to job, helping where he was needed. That gave him the freedom to notice patterns that the others were missing as they worked.

"You know," he mentioned to Sollen. "I don't get why the terminals need you to restart them each time. Are there signs of vandalism?"

"Dunno," she mumbled. ". . . 'm having to improvise around missing parts, though, as if they've been scavenged. Why would anyone take parts from an interface terminal, of all things? This is the Council Building!"

Topaz nodded, lending his hands to hold a couple of finer components together while she ran electricity from her fingertips into the right spots to make them work together again.

It made for interesting thoughts as they waded through the mess.

By the time they had sorted four of the ten rooms, Topaz could tell that they were ready for a break.

"We're done here," Torch called out as he finished removing the last of the accumulated dust with a wave of his hand. "Every record, file, holo-file and news-film clipping has been entered and confirmed in the Council database."

"How many more rooms are left in this wing?" Sollen asked with a tired voice.

"Six," Ebbella said over the pile of light-pads in her arms. "And this one was tidier than they are."

The group moaned together. Pho signaled that it was time for a break. Topaz checked the time, noting that they were well overdue for their midday meal. They all put their various tools and tablets away and headed for the door. If they wanted to catch any sunlight at all before nightfall, then they had to get topside fairly soon. "I'm officially sick of this job," Pho muttered. "We've become Core-gifted janitors and filing clerks! Does anyone know if the other Squads had to start like this?"

"Dellas said that we've more power between us than any Apprentices in a very long time," Topaz mused. "Maybe this kind of task was the safest for them. I'm sure Dellas and my uncle will be getting us assigned somewhere else soon enough."

"I've got to meet this uncle of yours, Topaz," Torch said. "It sounds like he lives a busy life."

"That's for sure," Topaz replied. "It's why I moved around so much as a kid: he was transferred all over the Realm as I grew up." Then, he grinned, remembering something.

"He took me to a little diner called Amberyl's right near here on my Testing day. Anyone hungry enough to grab a meal?"

There was a general agreement amongst them, so when they finally got to the ground level of the Council Building, they walked out to the road together. Yes, they were dusty, but the uniforms that Dellas had helped them acquire became resplendent in the light of the sun. To their surprise, each outfit turned out to also have fairly efficient solar collecting cells woven throughout the material. The energy that they gathered was channeled toward their shoulder crystals. Each of them could feel their lethargy and frustration fading as a warm, contented feeling began filling them. Even Topaz could feel the energy entering his crystal, and the positive feelings that came with it.

"These are NICE outfits." Sollen remarked, her crystal crackling gently with blue topaz energy. "We don't have to concentrate to transduce sunlight any more. These clothes do it for us. Hee!" She had to giggle a little bit as her powers caused a model hover car in the window of a very posh toy store to slowly rise into the air, much to the surprise of the staff inside. Sollen blinked and then dimmed her electrical output back down to normal.

Each of them in turn had to dial down their innate powers as the suits fed them energy. This made Torch less of a heat-lamp, Pho less of a blinding beacon, and Ebbella less of a source of interference for the invisible EM waves in the air all around them.

"We've got to talk to Dellas about this," Pho said in a quiet voice. "Apprentices don't just walk around with this kind of uniform. It's some Peridot trickery at work here."

"Hrmm . . . I dunno," Topaz thought aloud. "If we ever get off-world, then we'll be too far from the Core for us to access its power. My uncle says that after the Gates between the Realms were closed the rest of the way that the

Cores could no longer shunt Gem power back and forth. A suit like this would make it possible for us to use our Light powers from stored energy, as opposed to simply being a conduit for it."

"Huh. That makes sense," Torch said. "In my village, back home, there are these bright red vests that we keep charged with any stray heat that we generate. They are intended for any Rubies that need to use their powers while visiting. They can't call on the Ruby Core here, so I guess we can expect the same if we travel off-world."

"Yet another set of questions to ask Dellas, or your uncle," Pho said. "I wish there was a way for us all to talk, and get all of our questions out at once." He eyed Topaz significantly here. Topaz caught the look, and understood what his friend was actually saying. Only he and Pho knew anything about the dark secrets that were hiding in the Shadows. Maybe it was time for them to bring their friends up to speed with their suspicions. In that case, Amberyl's was just the place for them to chat.

"I could call my uncle, see if he could join us," Topaz offered. "If anyone knows about Adept powers, he does. I'm sure he could pick up Dellas and meet us for lunch."

They all nodded at the idea, and turned to corner onto possibly the busiest street in the Capital. The throng of people walking back and forth was a great river of humanity, swirling and flowing along the walkways. The Apprentices walked in a loose group, but it tightened into a phalanx as the crowds pressed in. They locked step and marched forwards, Topaz at the point, guiding the group.

*

"This is Sahn Lelleliam, channel 31, broadcasting to you live from in front of the financial buildings here in the heart of downtown. We were sent here to cover the release of this year's Energy Rationing rates, but something more is

*happening. Just a few minutes ago, the newest squad of
Apprentices came walking down the sidewalk. Their shoulder
crystals were all glowing and responding to any and all of the
energies around them. This is the first time that such a
powerful group of Light-users have walked among the people.
There is no sign of any emergency, so they must be acting on
orders from the Council. Yes, I can see their faces now.
There's Pho, and his golden light is almost blinding. Beside
him is the blue Apprentice Sollen. Her powers are causing all
the electrical systems to flicker. It's unheard of for Photics to
walk around in the company of Galvans, or even Thermals,
like that brown Apprentice Torch. This has to be the most
mixed-up squad of Apprentices in history. And who is that in
the middle of the group? It's hard to say. His powers are
clearly photic, but wait . . . oh my, it's that Apprenticeling boy
that calls himself Topaz. What's he doing here? I've heard
tell that he still can't even control the powers that the Core
has given him. What a joke. It's a sad day in the Realm of
Light when a buffoon like him is to be granted equal rank to
someone like the brilliant Pho. We'll have to see."*

*

By the time they were nearing the old stone facade,
the broadcast crystals and hover-cameras were buzzing around
their heads like annoying insects, though they never got close
enough to be affected by Sollen or Ebbella's abilities. Soon,
the reporters and tri-photographers started snapping holos of
them, calling them each out by name with requests for a pose,
or to answer questions.

*<By the Light, how did they zoom in on us so
quickly?>* Pho beamed to the others.

<We walked out with our crystals exposed,> Torch
replied. *<This is why Pazos said we should only walk around
in public when we've shut them down, I guess.>*

<The Apprentices are always among us,> Ebbella added. *<The only time we notice them is when there's an emergency.>* '

Topaz knew she was speaking the truth. That is why you got out of the way when an Adept's crystal is glowing. Could he remember the last time he had seen an Apprentice on duty, flashing their crystal? Try as he might, he could not.

They gave the reporters one last wave then entered the tiny dinner through the deep purple front door. Topaz looked about, searching for Amberyl herself. The five of them waited at the doorway by the cashier.

"Dellas told us to keep our shoulder crystals powered down when walking in the streets too," Sollen said as she willed hers to fade back into her shoulder. "When I put on the Glam field and sing on stage, the crowds react like that. That's why I change to a Stage-look, so that I can have a private life too."

"Never thought I'd need to have an alter-ego," Torch muttered.

"I'm sure if we had our Powers active, the feedback making our crystals glow, then folks would move," Torch replied. "After all, if there was an emergency, we'd need to move."

"We haven't been called to an emergency yet, folks." Ebbella muttered. "And at the rate we're going, Pazos will keep us in the dark for as long as he's able"

Topaz heard her, and knew that they had to bring the others up to full-glow about what they knew.

"Toivo, come here and let me hug you!" Amberyl cried out, dumping several glasses of drinks onto the floor behind the counter. The resulting crash of breaking glass made everyone jump, but when the dust had settled, the round little amethyst woman had Topaz by the hand and was pulling him into a firm hug. The others in his squad were covering their mouths to keep the startled giggles from escaping.

"Good to see you too, Amberyl," he replied, hugging her soundly. "I brought some friends for lunch."

"Ah!" she said, taking in the four others with a sweep of her deep brown eyes. "Any friend of young Apprentice Topaz here is more than welcome here. Come in, sit anywhere." She ushered the group in, complimenting them all on their spiffy Apprentice uniforms, how pretty the girls were, filling the air with a friendly, harmless babble. She was talking to them as if she had known them forever, like an old auntie. Clearly, she was picking up surface thoughts passively from them, which guided her conversation. They all blushed, grinned, nodded politely and all sat at a table for six. Amberyl left the empty chair in place.

"You never know," she said. "We're a small diner. Might need to plant someone here."

"Like me?" came a voice from the door. They all turned to see Council Member Saul entering the room, his traveling cloak closed and his hood drawn up. The group saw him, and all stood, coming to attention, facing him. Topaz rose too, but his posture was more relaxed.

"Figures they'd show up on your usual lunch day," Amberyl noted. "Come on over. I've got your usual table ready."

"Many thanks, 'beryl." Saul said. "And stand down, you bunch. This is lunch, not an inspection." He extended his hand to Topaz, who star-bursted in response. Saul then shook hands formally with each of them, smiling. He moved to sit at a table for two, right next to the group. He looked over at Amberyl intently, who looked him in the eyes, then nodded. She walked back behind the counter.

The Apprentices, except for Topaz, looked at each other in puzzlement at her departure.

"She's an amethyst Adept. She specializes in bringing you the food that you are actually hungry for, whether you order it or not." Saul said. "You'll see."

The meal that followed was delicious, of course. Amberyl's mind powers, as well as her culinary skills were right on the money.

"So, how is the life of an Apprentice treating you?" Saul asked. "I've not spoken with Dellas for weeks. Is Pazos treating you well?"

The responses he got ranged from an indifferent shrug from Ebbella to a tirade of frustration from Sollen and Torch. Only Pho and Topaz said nothing, and that was noticed by Saul right away. He gave his nephew a look of inquiry, raising an eyebrow. Topaz's responding look of vague frustration didn't help Saul feel any better.

"Er, Uncle," Topaz asked. "I know that there has to be a more private place for us to discuss things." He jerked his head to the front of the store significantly. Saul's expression changed to one of guarded curiosity now.

"Just how private do you need our conversation to be, Apprentice Topaz?" he asked formally.

"Very. There are some things that I think that you need to know, uncle. And the rest of my squad needs to know what Pho and I know." Topaz said quietly.

"Boyo, there's no more private place for us to talk than here," Saul replied, beckoning to Amberyl. He tapped his temple a couple of times as she walked up, and immediately the rumble of amethyst energy blossomed from her like a fountain. After a second or so, Amberyl turned to face the Apprentices, and her brow creased a little bit in concentration. The tickle in his mind meant that she was trying to contact him, despite how he instinctively deflected any mind-probe.

The others started turning to each other, with baffled expressions on their faces, but no words came from their lips.

"I've created a temporary telepathic link between the Apprentices, your uncle and your teacher, Dellas." Amberyl said, maintaining her creased brow. "I think that your uncle would like it if you could join them in it. You could ask all of your questions, and get answers for them." She patted his shoulder gently. "Not all amethysts are out to harm you, Toivo. This could save you a lot of time."

Topaz could feel the cold sweat forming in the small of his back as he recognized the logic in her words. He would have to let that mind-tickle enter him, let it connect with his consciousness, and that made his shudder inside and out. Then again, with his uncle here, and Dellas connected too, he knew in his mind that they would look out for him. He resigned himself to the inevitable and did his best to relax enough to allow Amberyl access to him. Part of him enjoyed the contradiction of working very hard to relax, but eventually, he could sense that she was succeeding. The nearest sensation to this experience for him would have to have been a med-tech slowly sticking a needle into a vein in your arm, only instead of your arm, it was the sides of your head. There was a moment of dizziness as his perceptions were guided toward the fabricated link. Amberyl held him steady, to keep him from falling to the floor in a dead faint.

<What's happening with Topaz? > he heard Pho's voice ask.

<My nephew has always had a natural resistance to mind powers of any type,> his uncle's voice answered. *<For him to actually have allowed himself to become part of the link was very stressful for him.>*

<You ok?> Sollen asked him, putting a hand on his other shoulder. Topaz couldn't tell if it was virtual or real at this point.

<I'm . . . fine . . . Thanks, > he answered back, each word feeling like another twist of the needle in his head. At no point would this meeting-of-the-minds be easy for him.

<Pho has shown us how the two of you followed me that one night,> Saul drawled casually, swatting his nephew on the shoulder gently in reproof. *<The injuries that Pho sustained make much more sense to me now. Everyone on your team knows how the two of you have sworn to wipe out the Shadows whenever you see them. >*

<And we'll dispatch them when we see them, too. > Torch said. *<These Shadows are counting on us not to pay them much heed, so that they can grow unchecked. >*

<Good . . . But, uncle . . . you know more . . . than . . . we've figured out, > Topaz interjected. *<Please, we are . . . Apprentices of the Realm, now. There's a threat to the world of Light, so . . . we have to . . . try and deal with it. >*

Saul eyed each of them in turn then nodded.

<ClearTruth, we didn't think that you were ready yet. I didn't think you were ready.> Saul assumed a neutral expression, but his eyes were tired. Topaz noticed that, and the sense of fatigue that rose off of him.

<Ready for what?> Sollen asked.

<The reality behind the Glamour that has been woven around you from the day you were born.>

The young Apprentices reacted with surprise, and many questions burst forth from them simultaneously, in a wave in inquiry. Saul gestured for them to wait a moment, then he continued speaking.

<From what Pho has said, you five already know more than enough to be considered a threat to Them. So, for your own safety, and that of the Realm . . .>

<You're going to tell us about the Necromancers,> Topaz muttered. *<I remember that word from what I heard that night. That word has been surfacing in the old records*

*that we've been sorting, the really old ones. Every time it
surfaced, something bad was recorded officially: a flood, a
power-outage, missing persons.>*

Saul looked at his nephew and the deep lines around
his eyes seemed to grow.

*<Yes, Necromancers . . . the name of a group of
Invaders from outside of the Twelve Realms. They came to
our little corner of space over a thousand years ago. They've
been a threat to us all from the moment they arrived. Their
ultimate goal is to destroy all of us and what we represent.
Records show that when they first came, they were repelled by
the Adepts of the Twelve Realms, working together. They were
so soundly defeated that they reconsidered their plans and
began a much quieter campaign of conquest, based on subtlety
and manipulation. Only in recent years have they surfaced
again, and they are much more ready now than before. They
hide on every world. They watch, listen, learn and wait. They
are trying to cause the Twelve Realms to destroy themselves
before their Second Invasion.>*

Saul pulled up memory-images of soldiers dressed all
in black, holding powerful-looking weapons. They were
flying in pitch black landing craft, and they moved with
wicked efficiency. Any living thing that they encountered was
killed in a heartbeat.

Topaz could feel his breathing become very shallow.
He knew that form. He recognized the distinctive glint from
their drawn weapons. This was a very clear picture of the
nightmare that had plagued him since he was a little child. He
only started to feel his chest unclench when his uncle banished
the image.

*<I would remember if I'd ever seen somebody like
that,>* Sollen whispered, shuddering.

*<That was the only image we have of the shock troops
that they use. However, you've seen spies and agents all*

around you,> Amberyl added. *<They are almost as good at hiding in plain sight as I am. >* She scowled a bit as she said: *<Many of my brother and sister adepts back home were forcibly recruited to help them stay hidden, too. >*

<Pazos.> Topaz blurted out. *<Pazos is a spy.>*

Saul nodded. The others tried to contain their reactions of betrayal and anger.

<When you were just a little one, Topaz, he was my aide, > Saul recounted. *<He made it his business to learn everything about me that he could, then he moved on, transferring somewhere else in the bureaucracy. Back then, the Network wasn't nearly as organized as it is now. Plus, we didn't anticipate just how ambitious he turned out to be. He's in a position now to create all manner of trouble in the Council with delays and distractions that take forever to resolve. Lately, there's very little that I've been able to do to stop him. I don't even have a sense of when they will be moving against us more directly, and that has me very nervous. >*

<Hold on.> Ebbella said. *<Are you saying that we're about to be attacked?>*

Saul shrugged, then shook his head. *<No, I'm pretty sure that it won't be anytime soon,>* he replied. *<They don't attack unless they know that the world has been broken from the inside, so that they meet with minimal resistance. Our world is more of a challenge to them that.>* Saul's mind-voice dropped to a whisper. *<They have already destroyed one Realm, and have rendered a couple of others virtually helpless. Thus far, we have been able to stop their advance, but they are insidious and amoral and have all the patience in the universe.>*

<Well, this invasion is not going to happen,> Pho voiced strongly. *<We're aware of them now. Once we figure*

out where their leadership is, we can take it out of action, and be done with it. >

<Pho, if we knew where the actual enemy stronghold was, don't you think that an attack would have been mounted already?> Sollen asked.

<You're right, Sollen.> Saul interjected. *<We can't challenge them directly yet. Our Network here is not positioned well enough to strike at the heart of their operations elsewhere. And you five have not had a chance to learn the depth and breadth of your new powers yet. We're not ready, but we will be.>*

<You said Phase One earlier. Do you know anything more about what they intend to do?> Ebbella inquired, her luminous white eyebrows raised in curiosity. *<No, not with any kind of certainty,>* Dellas chimed in. *<Don't have any idea yet. The first world they destroyed using orbital bombardment. We're proof against that, thanks to the Security forces and firing range of our Adepts. We know the shadow-worms are part of their plans here, and the social oppression of blue, brown and clear topazes. If my hunch is correct, they will try to tailor their attacks to our weaknesses, which means it'll be dark when they do it.>*

*

Though he could still hear everything that everyone was saying around him, Topaz could hear the distant sound of voices. Thinking a moment, he decided to try something. He willed most of him to keep looking at the images of his friends that were in his mind. He nodded at the right times, made all the little sounds of someone participating in a full conversation Then, with a shift in his thinking, he lifted his physical head, opened his actual eyes and looked around the restaurant. It was like seeing two channels overlapped on the holo-vid, manageable if you concentrated. He could see that they were alone, and that the crowds of holographers and reporters were still outside the door, trying to peek in through drawn blinds. He could see Amberyl sitting down now, her eyes half lidded. He turned his chair to face her.

"You ok, Amberyl?" he asked out loud. "Can I get you anything?"

The amethyst woman looked up, at saw that he was looking at her.

"Oh, but you are a surprise, Toivo." she said in a distracted tone. "You've just shown that you can divide your mind into two different modalities. You're still part of the 'link too, aren't ya?"

"Yes ma'am." he answered politely. "I just thought you might be getting tired, maintaining a mind-link this long."

"Just how long do you think you've been in the link, huh?" she asked with a hint of a smile

"I dunno, maybe half an hour."

"You've been in conversation for all of seven or eight seconds so far."

"Oh! Well, then, if you're ok, I'd better get back there."

Amberyl smiled at him, and gestured for him to turn around in his chair again. He let his attention drift back to the group.

*

<*Up till now, we've not had any Apprentices in the Network.>* Saul paused, then amended himself: <*Well, that's not true. We do have several people who have the rank of Adept, but not a one has the power that you five possess. You actually received Gifts from the Core. Not one soul has been empowered like you have, not in at least a generation. You are the first ones to come back from the Core fully powered in a long time.>*

This fact shocked Topaz just enough to put a few details together differently in his mind.

<When we were traveling to the Core, there was a second when I felt like we were about to be sent somewhere else. We made it to the Core just fine, in the end, though.>

<You felt like you were being sent . . . somewhere other than the Core?> Saul asked, somewhat rhetorically. *<Did anyone else feel that?>*

The others shook their heads.

<We didn't feel anything, > Pho said. *<One second we were walking into the disk, the next, we were in the crystal chamber.>*

Saul looked in turn at Amberyl, then towards Dellas' voice before speaking again.

<That would imply some sort of diverter technology had been installed on the portal. We have suspected something like this - that the Candidates were being sent but there was no way to ever prove it. It's not an area of expertise we possess in this Realm.>

<Who all is 'we', anyways?> Pho interjected.

Saul shook his head and grinned lopsidedly.

<Pho, m'boy, I can't reveal too much about the Network. It would compromise us, and endanger you. Nope. Can't risk that.>

<Saul, is it time to introduce them to each other, yet?> Dellas' voice could be heard by all in the link, even though the Apprentices' advisor was nowhere to be seen.

<Yes, old friend, I think it's time,> Saul concluded. All of them could see an image form on the surface of the table. It was that of a tall, gangly, older youth, about their age. His light brown hair was long and pulled back into a ponytail. His blue eyes were alive, and darting everywhere. He wore simple clothes, and was busy repairing a wall-mounted vid-camera. He zapped part of the supporting arm with a spark of electricity which spot-welded it in place. Then, he took his other hand and an intense red glow came from his index

finger, and finished welding the plate to the pole. Then he
fired off a couple of bright yellow beams of light from his eyes
at console on the far wall, which powered up. The vidcam he
was mounting came to life, and began moving back and forth.

    <Who is this, and what are we seeing?> Topaz asked.
*<He's used three of the four topaz colors so far. You said to
me that I was the only one who had ever been able to do that.>*

    <Topaz, you can do this too?> Ebbella asked.

    <Not as well as he can, it seems,> Topaz replied,
more than a little impressed, and a wee bit intimidated. Then a
flash of memory flitted through him, connected with the
feeling of insecurity. He had met this fellow before.

    <This is my grandson, Stellan.> Dellas said through
the link. *<He's about two years younger than all of you. He's
been a member of the Network since the day he was born.>*

    <There's a reason for that, I assume.> Torch said.

Saul took over from Dellas now.

    *<Stellan has been Gifted by the Core already. It has
chosen him to be the next TopazStar. When he graduates, he
will have a chance to become the most powerful user of the
Spectrum in the entire world. His grandfather is the present
TopazStar.>* Saul tipped his head in the direction of Dellas'
voice. *<When the Gates closed up tight, and we in the Radiant
Knights squad had to come home, Dellas settled down, got
married, and had a family. If the Necromancers ever found
out that the next TopazStar had been born, they would stop at
nothing to track him down to either recruit him into their army
of darkness or to kill him. He will become our world's
greatest defense against the darkness, and you lot will be the
squad best suited to support him.>*

They mulled that over for a few moments before
speaking again. Topaz could see why Stellan had been hidden
for his entire life. Then a thought occurred to him.

<Uncle, I know how to use all four colors of the Spectrum, like him. Did he travel to the different parts of the world too?>

<Yes, he did. He actually traveled to all of the ancient sites around the world, to learn everything that he could.>

<And when he finally is old enough, we will be able to help him reach the Core secretly, to finish his training.> Dellas declared. *<We'll even be able to use the same Portal disk you all used, since we know that it's reliable now. None of the others around the Realm seem to work properly. >*

<And so there are no Adepts who are fully powered now,> Sollen shook her head as she spoke. *<That's shady, for certain. What zaps me is that there's no one in this Realm that knows the least little bit about Portal technology. The most any of us could do is damage a device like that, assuming that it's even possible to do that. How could these darkdump spies manipulate them to keep people from the Core?>*

<Our only clue about that is that the world that they outright destroyed first . . . was Opal. I think it's safe to assume that they stole what they wanted before the end.> Saul's mind-voice was a gravelly whisper.

<That still doesn't explain how we got to the right place, > Torch murmured. *<I guess we were just lucky that whatever diverters they have in place malfunctioned just as we were traveling.>*

Saul, the image of Dellas, and Amberyl all glanced at each other knowingly, but kept their peace. Topaz could not help but notice that.

<Would it help if we tried to help the other Apprentices to touch the Core too? You know, after-the-fact, sort of . . .> Topaz asked.

Saul turned to the virtual image of Dellas, and thought a moment.

<I'd never thought of that,> he said. *<It's never been done.>* then he got a frustrated look in his eyes. *<We would only be able to help the Adepts that are in the Network. All the others out there are being managed and manipulated by the Enemy now. If we started empowering them, the Necromancers would get unwitting accomplices with vast power. I don't want to give them that sort of advantage.>*

<What should we do, sirs?> Sollen asked. *<We've got the power. How can we do our duty without compromising Realm security?>*

<Well, clearly you five have the power to stay in contact, even if you are sent to different areas.> Saul mused aloud. *<And being Apprentices, you can contact me through official channels anytime there's a problem. It's in the Charter of the Realm. They can't go against our laws directly. It would alert the masses to their presence.>*

<I'll make sure that the official reports that I have to submit to the Council are filled with good things about each of you. I'll try to suggest that you get sent to places that really could use someone with your skills.> Dellas' voice finished. *<I'll need your backing on that one, Saul.>*

<You've got it. And you five will have to keep your eyes open. Let us know if you suspect that someone is a spy or not. We can keep track of them, once we know about them.>

<And we will try to do our jobs just as we are told to, so as not to alert the Enemy that we know that they are here. The people of our world still need us, that's for sure.> Topaz nodded

*

They finished their meals, and made sure to conceal their crystals on their way back. From years of hiding from the bullies, Topaz was an old pro at trying to be inconspicuous. Ebbella had him beat though, going completely invisible for the return trip. They didn't talk much as they walked, full to the brim with new thoughts and dangerous ideas. The Realm needed them now, more than ever. They all agreed to learn everything about their powers that they could, so that when it came time, they would be ready for the fight.

*

Never assume that a machine will fix itself.
Sapphire Techno-path saying

Chapter 19 – Mission

"No! *Turn, turn, flash,* THEN *fade!"* the managing Councillor cried. "Apprentice Topaz, please! It has to be done right if this is to work."

"Yes, Council member Aobh. I understand," Topaz replied, repeating the movements necessary to recharge the huge generator above him that provided power for this isolated town. It was a fine piece of sapphire ingenuity that converted light from the sun into usable energy. Granted it was not as efficient as a glowstone array, but this area was very poor, and the only solution had been for them to purchase this from a traveling sapphire-realm Merchant.

One last time, Topaz ran through the long sequence of useless-seeming motions, building up the photic potential within him, paying close attention to the last stage then he placed his hands on palm-shaped panels in the center of the control console. This time, it worked and all of the energy that the exercises had gathered in him was channeled it into the machine. All the displays came to life, as his energy coursed through them.

Topaz had performed the actions, as he had been shown, and the council member nodded as each was completed. He thought about the motions, thought about this machine, and its function, and pondered another solution. Since he was essentially part of the machine at this point, he figured he stood a chance of figuring out why it needed to be recharged like this every year. He was glad for his small amount of practice with electrical problems.

With a small zap of galvanic blue topaz power, he could hear the insides of the machine answer him. After a few sounds he could only hear with his mind, the machine engaged a diagnostic function then flashed an analysis towards him. Topaz could not make sense of the data that filled his mind's-eye, so he willed a copy of this information to be printed here, and a copy to be sent to the Council chambers.

"Eh? What's this?" muttered the council member as the console came to life. He examined the information on the screen and then his eyes began to bulge. "Apprentice, you can stop now," he said to Topaz, still gazing at the screen. "It seems we've been going about this all wrong for years now." He adjusted a few controls here and there then flipped a switch. The generator hummed back to life.

"Sir?" Topaz said, raising one eyebrow in inquiry as he removed his hands from the panel and quelled his powers.

"Young man, I was here when they installed this sapphire-built thing, and the technicians who worked didn't ever mention the fact that these units have remarkably deep storage batteries in them, for when it gets dark. When they were installed, someone disabled that function. All the energy we've been pouring into it was simply being stored. I've re-engaged that system, and this unit is autonomous now." Fiddling with the controls one last time, Aobh asked. "Did you do anything differently once you were connected? Once you started transferring your power?"

"I don't think so," Topaz pondered. "My best friend's father works for the Capital Power Grid. He uses his blue topaz to talk to machines all the time. If they have processors, then anyone with galvanic powers can talk with 'em."

"I didn't know that," Aobh remarked. "This is so far away from the Islands that we don't usually get anyone with blue topaz powers. Topaz, my boy, I think that you've done very well. You didn't quite do the job I asked of you, but what you did do will save us all from ever having to do this again." He patted Topaz on the shoulder, affectionately. "Please, don't tell anyone about this development . . . quite yet. Tampering with Council property is a serious offence. I need a little bit of time before I can do anything about it."

"Yes sir, not a word. I understand."

*

It took Pazos and his subordinates quite a while to quell that particular fact. Long enough for some of the underground media sources to get hold of and broadcast the truth of the situation to a wide audience. Damage? Yes. Fixable? Yes, but that would take time. At least the councillor responsible for the leak, Aobh, had been removed easily enough. Such were the wrinkles of the Plan.

*

How many tragedies
Have been prefaced
By the word: Oops.
> *Councillor Saul Rallence, in response to a report*
> *presented in-session, Topaz Realm*

Chapter 20 – Accident

The day started out as normally as most for Topaz. His squad's four month placement at the Luminus City's Transport Hub was almost finished - only three weeks to go. He thought he had been doing fairly well, despite some surprisingly familiar stumbling blocks.

From his the first moments of his time here, the senior manager, an intelligent and abrasive man named Citran, had not made any attempt to recognize him as an Apprentice. He could understand why. He didn't use powers for every little thing, as most Apprentices did, getting up to fetch the tool from across the room whereas Pho might use a light-construct to grab it. Sollen would galvanically control the load-lifters; Topaz would use the physical controls. His friends weren't trying to make him feel bad, it was just their natures. That had given Ebbella the idea that he should stay hidden like that, not using powers for anything.

"You learn more about people when they don't know you're there," she told the group in the workers' bunk-house, next to the Control Tower. "If I wanted to weaken a Realm in subtle ways, I'd mess with its Transport Hub."

The others conceded her reasoning was sound, though none of them would have thought of that. The plan was approved of, so they all started talking about their own interests again. It was more talking than listening, but that was normal enough for topazes.

"Clear topaz saying - *Hide from plain sight /Learn what ye might.*" Ebbella said to herself. The others missed her quiet words, but Topaz caught them, and nodded at her, acknowledging the Cultural wisdom of her people. Ebbella's face went bright red when she saw that he had heard her, but then she giggled nervously. Topaz had to grin. Someday, he would have to convince Ebbella to take him to the Hidden Villages. If everyone there was as quick-witted and subtle as Ebbella was, then he could learn a lot from them.

When they had been assigned their duty rotations, Citran had placed the visiting Apprentices where they had wanted to be. He was falling over himself to be helpful for them. If "mighty" Pho had wanted to use Citran's office as a private grav-pool, then the man would have made the change within the hour. The rest of the new arrivals were less "powerful", and thus deserved less respect. He delegated the task of placing the rest of them to his lieutenant, while he went back to catering to every little whim, real or imagined, that he thought the Apprentices might like

"Think I'm going to be sick!" Pho said to Topaz as the groups moved off to their assignments. "Please, may I photo-sail this guy into orbit when we're done here!"

"We stay in touch and compare notes each night," Topaz replied. "If ever there was a need to expose someone, it's here and now. Let's see how things go."

They parted ways with a quiet star-burst, then Topaz broke of and followed the rest of the technical crew. The older man who was their foreman was a straight-forward kind of fellow who was very experienced in his trade. He judged Topaz as capable enough, and set him to work sweeping up every mess that was produced by the workshop. He was forbidden from touching, or even looking too long at, any of the heavy equipment or the various high-powered off-world hand tools. Truthfully, Topaz had been grateful for this. Sweeping up metal shavings and soaking up spilled lubricants would not require him to use his powers too much, and it would afford him the time to talk with the other members of the ground crew, the foremen. He would likely learn more from watching them do their job, and asking questions, than he ever would otherwise. And, in a way, it was safer for him, being able to melt into the background when he needed to.

He made sure not to let his shoulder crystal show whenever he had to use his powers. His anonymity would be gone if he were identified by that badge. It would change what he was able to learn. He would be shuffled off to the imaginary world that Citran was keeping his friends in. The longer he could stave that off, the better. That meant that he had to take the harassment from the Tower with no complaining. With a sigh, he knew that this was something he had had many years of practice doing.

Citran himself was the most insufferable micro-manager that Topaz had ever had the misfortune of dealing with. The kinds of things that he had the ground crews do showed that he knew less about the care and maintenance of the machinery at the Transport Hub than Topaz did. The experienced crew-members received their orders, nodded, then went about doing the job that needed doing. Most of the time the Tower would see that the trifling or imagined problem had vanished, and that would be the end of it. The only time feedback was ever given to the workers was when they did something wrong.

Topaz saw this pattern right away, and tried to do the same thing . . . once. He had been sent out to pour some patch material onto a crack that was forming in one of the airship runways. It was a hot, smelly job that took a very long time. When he got there, though, there was more to the problem. The crack ran deep into the concrete of the runway. Throwing some patch on top of this would only hide it, not solve the problem.

So, on his own, he ran back to the tool room, and grabbed a garnet-made field-effect hammer, and went back. By fiddling with the device a little bit, he was able to guide the Garnet Force that it used to widen the crack just enough to see where the foundation of the concrete had been compressed from an impact somewhere - the crack was simply a side-effect of this. He poured the patch material down into the widened crack then reversed the energy from the tool and forced the crack closed. The resulting pressure forced the patch material into all the tiny nooks and crannies of the concrete, which made the repair more solid than the original. Whatever had impacted here before would bounce harmlessly off of that patch now.

When Topaz reported back to the yard foreman, the man had nodded, and patted him on the shoulder. When he reported to Citran, he was criticized harshly for having used official equipment for which he had never received training. No mention of his solving the original problem better-than-effectively ever came his way - only the inflated offence and resulting disciplinary days of scrubbing exhaust vents and waste chutes by hand. The knowledge that this rotation at the

Hub was of only a few months longer gave him the resilience to cope with this unfairness.

This situation became Topaz's new normal. No matter what he did, he was criticized. He would follow the orders without question and repair whatever it was exactly as he had been told to, which usually meant that there would be a cascade of breakdowns later. He would get blamed for that too. When he actually solved the problem - as he had with the crack in the concrete - he would be reprimanded for overstepping his authority. There was no happy medium. Topaz really had to work at not flashing his shoulder crystal during these uncomfortable times. Was there any way to end it?

It was a familiar feeling for him, being called incompetent, or belligerent, or disobedient. He had lived through that all through his elementary days. In this new guise however, the bullying hurt again. The difference this time was that he was *choosing* to endure it. That fact empowered him enough to maintain his dignity this time.

The experienced workers tried to help him, explaining what his mistakes were, and how to prevent them. Topaz was reminded of steps that he had skipped when he was in a hurry, and why they mattered. The foreman made a point of making sure that he understood what was being said. Topaz appreciated that and earnestly tried to apply the recommendations. On the other side of things, there was Citran, who disapproved of him if his tool belt was crooked, or if he smiled at the wrong time.

That day, he was just finishing his daily sweepings when he heard the control tower hailing an approaching craft. His headset was tuned into the main comm-channel for the whole Hub. There were many times when knowing what ships were coming in made his job somewhat easier. What he heard today puzzled him.

"Luminus City Control to approaching transport, hold and identify. You are entering restricted airspace. Please respond."

Topaz knew the controller on duty was Citran. He always took himself far too seriously when he acted as the voice of the Hub. Since it involved how he was being seen by outsiders, Citran was in his "stickler-for-the-rules" mode. Topaz relaxed a little bit, knowing that nothing would be aimed at him for the next little bit.

"Approaching Transport, your flight path is approaching the automated cargo transit system for the Hub. Change your vector immediately!"

That was different. Usually any approaching ship would answer by now. This was unexpected. Topaz noted the touch of worry in Citran's voice that time. He adjusted his earpiece to hear the conversation more clearly. Citran's repetition of the warning came through clearly, but there was only static where the other ship would have responded. Even a robot barge would at least put out an ID blip when queried like this. Something was not right here.

He walked over to the open bay doors and looked down the runway towards the matter transfer cargo system, controlled directly from the Tower. A steady stream of energy from different transfer stations around the Realm flowed into the huge shining receiving platform, where it was either materialized, sent into virtual storage or, if it was rubbish, converted into light energy and sent to the planetary batteries. He had worked there a couple of times, under careful tutelage from the experienced technicians. They told him that these devices were a combination of different technologies and that they maintained themselves fairly well. As he washed off the debris from a load of fruit that had materialized too soon, He had been able to feel the immense energies that coursed through it, even when it was in stand-by. His aura-sight abilities showed him much higher levels of power in play here than anywhere else in the Hub. There was a swirl of deep blue that flowed around the inner workings, sure sign that it had been built at the Foundries in the Sapphire Realm. The receiving plate itself radiated a lighter shade of blue, which he deemed to mean that it had come from the molecule-bending world of Aquamarine. It was powered by the largest photic power cables he had ever seen, coming straight off of high-energy transformers. In other words, this was not a place that a stray ship should be flying towards, for any reason.

By squinting, he could see the approaching transport now. It was a smaller ship, a personal craft of some sort. It was most definitely crossing the pathway that the energy stream from the other cargo stations used for E.M. transfer, since it was now being dragged through the air at a strange angle. Yep . . . He could almost see the violent streams of electromagnetic energy coursing around the foreign object in its way. He watched closely for a minute then his vision snapped over to his aura-seeing mode unexpectedly. The ship was surrounded by a deep green glow that pulsed rapidly. Deep green? Emerald? This was an emerald transport?

"What are you doing here?" he mused, walking out the doors and down the runway a bit. The sound of a straining engine could be heard now, and it matched no engine that Topaz had ever heard.

"Ok, you are from Emerald," he thought aloud as simultaneous possibilities flashed through head. "One, if you're a drone, then there's only a slim chance that your systems would try to correct your flight path. Two, if you have a live crew, then they would know that they were in serious trouble right now, and be trying to make corrections and sending out distress calls." He tapped his earpiece / microphone a couple of times, and still heard nothing but static. "So, why can't we hear you?"

Then, in a flash of insight, he realized that their comm-system had been set to a different frequency than was standard here. This presented another puzzle, as surely the control tower would have all the standard communication frequencies on file. Of course, this was assuming that the controller was paying attention. It was Citran up there, and Topaz had learned not to expect too much from him, as a leader. So, this was a real problem, then. He knew very little about the tech behind comm systems, but he suspected that he knew a couple of people who did.

He ran over to the Apprentice station of this facility. It was cluttered, dusty, and generally used for storage by the Hub, since it was rare for the Apprentices to ever appear here. Still, he shoved aside boxes and broken machinery, and placed his hand against the dark panel in the center of the screen. It came to life, becoming a comm-screen that blinked in readiness. Using his terminal caused his insignia crystal to appear on his left shoulder, and a yellow glow started inside of it.

Tapping the center of the screen, the image of a uniformed operator appeared. She looked up, and nodded once.

"Council-comm acknowledges Apprentice Topaz," she said crisply.

"CC, connect me to Ebbella and Sollen," Topaz stated. "Priority one." It was the first time that he had ever had to use the emergency code. He hoped that it made things easier for him, as he had been taught.

The operator nodded again, and the faces of his two friends appeared in separate windows on his screen within moments of each other. Topaz actually blinked. He had never been able to connect that fast before. The girls greeted him warmly, if suspiciously, as they had clearly been contacted out of the blue. Their duties kept them deep inside the

Administration offices for the Hub. Apprentice Priority One
superseded pretty much everything else, though. Topaz
informed them of his situation as succinctly as he could.

"Frequencies of field gear can be changed pretty
easily," Ebbella said. "Most of them can be adapted to the
needs of the user. You just have to know what frequency they
are using, then the headset should adapt."

"Didn't know that," Topaz replied. "Thanks. One
problem, though. I have no idea what frequency that they are
using. It's definitely not in the standard comm frequency
band."

"Can you hear the ship?" Sollen asked

"Oh, yeah. It's screaming out a very shrill E - you
should be able to hear it yourself soon."

"Good." she continued. "Most ships have all of their
main systems tuned to the same E.M. frequencies . . .
corresponding to their gem type. If the engines are
overloading so badly that they're making audible noise, then
you can probably use the pitch to guestimate the frequencies in
question. Just start at that pitch then go up by about a
thousand Hertz or so."

Topaz's eyes widened a little, as he realized the
possible connection that Sollen was describing. He
understood exactly what she was saying.

"Thanks, girls," he said, still thinking. "I'll flash you
a vid of how this goes."

Both girls wished him luck, and broke the connection.
He ran out to the runway again, and listened more closely to
the sound of the approaching ship. Yep, it was crying out at E,
all right. He reached up to his earpiece, and scrolled the
frequency down. Every now and again, there was a more
intense burst of static then suddenly a man's voice became
clear. He locked that frequency in place immediately.

"...MAYDAY! Luminus City control, Mayday! We are unable to escape. Please help!" came the frantic, heavily accented man's voice.

Acting on purest impulse, Topaz made the fastest decision of his life. He started running back to the Apprentice panel as he answered the call: "Emerald transport, this is Luminus City ground-crew. I read you, loud and clear. Repeat, I read you."

He tapped the screen again, and typed in a Priority One summons for Pho and Torch, the other two members of his team. As he got confirmation of them being en route, he spoke into his microphone again: "What is your status?"

"L.C. ground crew!? Thank the LifeSpark! This is the consular transport *Veridian*. We are five people aboard: myself, my wife and our three daughters," the man's voice cracked with near panic. "Our propulsion and navigation systems are non-responsive, and we are approaching your cargo transit platform. Please advise!"

"Transport *Veridian*, if you've already tried your main engines and failed, then I suggest you shut them down and prepare for landing," Topaz got a signal back from his friends then started running towards the cargo center. "Apprentices of the Topaz Light are en route right now," he said quickly, not breaking stride. "They will assist us in getting you out safely. Suggest you extend your landing struts and start firing your retro-thrusters. This might get a little . . ." he fumbled for the right word here. ". . . bumpy."

The transport beeped once in acknowledgment then the comm signal squelched, then silenced. The cry of the engines shifted in quality, becoming more of a rumble, as it started preparing to land. With the resistance gone, the magnetic flow into the cargo Hub simply carried the ship inwards now, into its perimeter of influence. Topaz knew the sequence of events now, having seen a few times. If the automated systems registered the ship as a threat, they would protect the Trans-mat disk by de-materializing the offending matter in a puff of Aquamarine energy, and hold it in stasis for a short time. If a controller did not specify what to do with it, it would then be converted into energy and dispersed safely. There was no recovering the matter after that point.

He ran towards the Hub's control booth as quickly as he could, hoping that Fate would allow him the chance to reset the resolution of the disk so that living things could be stored safely. If he, Pho and Torch stood a chance of making this rescue, then they would have to hurry.

*

"Ah, Councillor Pazos. I was just about to call you."

"Good, fine. Tell me, how is your assignment proceeding?"

"All is going as planned, sir. The jamming field crippled the transport's systems just as they entered our airspace. I made sure that the Mag field caught them as they started to make corrections. Within minutes, they will crash onto the receiving disk, and get stored at the lowest energy resolution. Even if rescue crews retrieve the ship, the people won't have survived."

"Excellent. The Ambassador and his family are well worth sacrificing for the sake of the Plan. Be sure to entangle any official rescue with procedures and regulations long enough to seal their fate."

"Yes sir. The ship is landing now. The Aquamarine systems are revving up, and there's only one technician logged in."

"Citran, monitor this to its conclusion."

"Yes, sir."

Switching off the tiny black comm-box, Citran turned back towards his display panels. He looked out the viewing windows at the Hub, and the spectacle that was starting to happen. The transport was beginning to fade from view, the closer it got to landing. Something didn't seem right, though. It was dematerializing far more slowly than he had expected. He checked, and noticed that the cargo system had been manually set to full power. Another view was pulled up, and he saw the emergency matter buffers coming to life. Someone had anticipated this accident?

Inconceivable.

His brow furrowed slightly as two more signals entered the airspace around the tower from the farthest part of the most remote landing strip of the Hub. Both were broadcasting Apprentice Priority clearance codes.

"How did they find out so quickly?" Citran muttered as he automatically cleared all traffic out of their way. He would not be able to hamper them directly any more, and maintain his cover at the same time. All he could do was play the role of the clueless manager again. Maybe he could misdirect . . .

*

Topaz met his friends as they exited their travel pods. Pho and Torch nodded to him then the three of them ran towards the machinery section of the Trans-Mat. Topaz briefed them en route. They had all summoned their shoulder crystal symbols, and everyone got out of their way fast! Topaz wore his proudly, his charade well and truly over now. The technicians that he had been working with were more than a little surprised, most of them grinning.

"Any idea how we're gonna do this?" Torch huffed as they ran.

"Nope," Topaz replied. "This is new territory for me. These kinds of accidents shouldn't happen - too many built-in redundancies."

Pho just shrugged a shoulder and said: "This is the first real situation we've ever faced and it's a *lens-buster*. Must be our lucky day."

Topaz thought the same thing, but there was too much at stake for him to ponder it too long.

The three of them came to the fencing surrounding the inner workings of the Cargo Hub. Pho tore the gate off of its hinges with a flash from his eyes. The whine of the machinery was a scream now. All three donned protective ear-guards, and looked at the tangle of technology.

<Oh, Shade it!> Pho tight-beamed to his friends. *<Topaz, your show. What now?>*

Topaz looked at the conduits, displays, valves and regulators then closed his eyes. He tried to remember where a control panel might be. He had been shown the layout of this facility once, but that had been several weeks prior.

<Over here!> Torch sent. *<This panel is a master control for the teleport disk.>*

They gathered at the panel and examined the readings.

<Not much help here . . . this is a display only,> Topaz sent back. *<Any of the functional controls have been locked out. It's telling me that we still have a chance to save the ship, though. The matter is safely in storage. We'll just have to do this . . . >* he paused, then grinned slightly. *< . . . the hard way. Back outside.>*

<Plan?> Pho inquired.

Topaz nodded, his face a mask of concentration as started to chew on his new idea.

*

"Apprentices Torch and Pho, please respond!" Citran shrieked into the intercom panel, to no avail. He turned to his security monitor and saw the technician boy and the two Apprentices gathering at the power lines that fed the cargo systems. It would take hours for them to figure out how to rescue that ship, and by then he would have been able to shut down the buffers, thus dooming the Emerald Ambassador. He started entering commands into his console.

*

Topaz had a working plan, but that didn't mean that he felt confident about it. He was duty bound to try. He nodded to his friends who were holding parts of the machinery: Pho at the lens which channeled the photic energy that ran the entire array, and Torch at the heat sink assembly which recycled the thermal energy of matter conversion back into usable photic energy. Both of them closed their eyes and their shoulder crystals started glowing brightly.

Topaz stood near the main disk and waited. He was touching the disk, trying to guide it as he had once before, at the solar battery installation months before. He was asking it to reverse its process briefly so that he could rescue that family. The machine indicated no objection to helping them. It even allowed Topaz to 'see' the orders from the tower.

Topaz watched as Pho's energies started surging through the Hub's conduits. Every now and then, a tiny puff of black smoke would rise up, accompanied by a tiny cry. So, the Shadow Worms were here too? Well, flushing the whole system with light from the Core would deal with that soon enough.

Finally the flow of power reached the disk, which started to glow pale blue again. The ghostly figure of the ship started to appear. Pho's efforts were paying off, and so Torch kept everything balanced by making sure that the excess heat from Pho's task didn't burn him up. By redirecting all of the infra-red energy, Torch was adding a fair amount of power back into the disk himself. The two of them had slightly crooked grins of accomplishment as they pushed the limits of their Apprentice specialties.

Topaz waited and waited until the disk systems signaled that the living matter re-integrated. The rescue would be a failure if he tried to yank the family out too soon. However, the disk systems also showed that there were override commands coming in, that were cancelling his requests of it. Topaz's brow furrowed in frustration when he learned this. That could only mean that Citran was trying to reset the disk from the Tower. That was unbelievable! Did the man not realize the urgency of the situation? On another level, that infuriating manager was interfering with Apprentices who were doing their duty. A very paranoid part of Topaz's mind thought this was intentional too.

<Keep it up, you two,> Topaz sent to his friends. <The system is trying reset itself. I'm going to have to improvise.>

*

Pho could actually feel the vast energies flowing through him as if it were a stormy wind. The heart of Light was happy to lend him its power, which it sent to him in torrents. He was the Light, he was the Power. He could feel Torch's control over heat drawing that invisible radiation out of him and the air around him, too. Different, but both were part of the Spectrum, and since they were using this much power, it afforded them a form of communication.

<<This is a first time for me, >> Pho thought loudly. <<Becoming a power source for something this big. >>

<<I've never heard of Apprentices or even Adepts doing anything like this before. >> Torch replied. <<We'll be in the news-vids, to be sure. >>

Both Apprentices watched as the ship shimmered back into view on the disk. It didn't look all that solid, but the five people could be seen through the distortion now, clinging to each other tightly. To their vast surprise, they saw Topaz climb up onto the actual disk itself. He found his footing and moved towards the ship through the waves of aquamarine energy. There was a safety barrier of nearly invisible *solid-light* surrounding the ship. Topaz didn't even pause. He ran straight through it as if it weren't there.

<<OW! I hate it when he does stuff like that! >> Torch mumbled. *<<He has to be the only topaz citizen who has ever been able to shrug off solid-light like that. >>*

They saw Topaz reach the ship, and open the hatch. The waves of aquamarine energy rippled over him as he reached in and pulled two adults out of the ship. Shoving them past the safety barrier, he climbed into open hatch.

With a mighty rumble, the automated systems snapped back to normal. The ship began to fade again. It was fading so fast that no one had time to do more than gasp. The feedback of energy caught Pho and Torch by surprise and tossed them several meters.

On the disk, the ship was almost gone when there was a blinding flash of light, followed closely by a horrible shriek of metal against metal. All power in the Hub was cut off briefly then slowly lights and systems began to sputter back to life.

When Pho and Torch could see again, they saw Topaz standing in the center of a now fractured Trans-mat disk; his arms wrapped around three young girls who clung tightly to him. All four of them were surrounded by think bands of shimmering aquamarine-colored light, which faded almost immediately.

"Ok, girls," Topaz said shakily, doing his best to keep his voice from wavering. "Ride's over. Everybody out."

*

"Citran what is the meaning of this!?" bellowed Saul over the comm-screen. His face was flushed and his eyes put out yellow sparks. "What is going on over there?"

Citran was not acting when he presented a confused and flustered face to the council member. What actually worried him was the sight of his "real" superior, Pazos, standing beside Saul, taking notes. He was staying neutral faced, and only caught Citran's eyes once, with an unreadable expression.

"I have no idea, sir," Citran dithered. "I don't understand how this could have happened. The Hub systems have gone berserk!"

"What do you mean, berserk?" Saul leaned closer to the screen.

"Well, first the automated systems grabbed a passing unmanned ship out of its approach vector then the whole Trans-mat system started to behave erratically."

"And the explosion that blacked out half of the city just now?"

"No idea, sir," Again, Citran didn't have to feign confusion here. Nothing those two Apprentices could have done would have caused this amount of damage.

"You summoned assistance, I assume?" Pazos drawled, raising his eyes from his tablet. Saul glanced back then nodded.

"Y...yes sir. In fact, there are two Apprentices at the scene right now. I'm awaiting their assessment before I proceed."

The image of Saul looked down for a moment, examining something.

"My scan shows that you have three Apprentices near the Hub equipment, Citran," Saul said casually. "Are you *sure* you counted correctly?"

"Three? Impossible sir!" Citran's voice was rising slightly in pitch. What was Saul talking about? "I registered Apprentices Pho and Torch as they arrived, sir. Only two came."

"You mean you haven't recognized Apprentice Topaz," Saul's eyes were narrowing now. "He's part of the same squad as Pho and Torch. He's been working there for months now. I think that I've heard enough. Report to the Council building when you've finished cleaning up. I know that I have a few questions for you." He clicked a small case shut then rose to his feet. As an afterthought, he added: "I will make sure that the Apprentices escort you, just in case any other . . . unforeseen incidents happen en route."

Citran could feel his cover getting thinner and thinner. Fear of discovery, and a deeper fear of failing his true superiors, were gradually overcoming his senses. The image of Pazos behind Saul, shaking his head slowly, caused Citran to faint outright.

*

Pho and Torch each carried one of the little girls out of the wreckage. Topaz let the third one maintain her fierce grip around his neck with her little arms and around his waist with her legs.

"It's okay, you're safe now," he was softly murmuring into the little one's ear, wrapping one of his arms around her for his own balance. She kept her face buried in his shoulder, still in the grips of shock. He gradually made his way back to where her parents were waiting, gradually recovering their wits as well.

<*Good to see you alive, Topaz,*> Pho beamed to him. <*I'd say that you're in the focus now. You were first on scene, you called the shots, and you figured out this rescue. You're the one they will want to talk to. You up for that?*>

Nodding acknowledgment to his friend, he walked over to the couple who reached for their daughter. When the little girl he was holding felt the man's hands on her shoulders, she tentatively lifted her head and slowly climbed over to him.

"Apprentices, I can't begin to thank you," the woman said, hugging the other two girls close. "You saved us."

"You're more than welcome, ma'am," Topaz replied, using his formal voice. "Happy to help. I'm just glad that Fate had me stationed here, so that I could call my friends. It was the team that made this rescue possible." He looked over at Pho and Torch, who nodded back, grins playing across their faces.

"Well gentlemen, the Emerald Realm thanks you, especially you, Apprentice . . . er..." The man paused, searching for names.

"Topaz, sir. My name is Apprentice Topaz. My partners are Pho, representing the yellow topaz range, and Torch, representing the brown."

Reaching forward, the man clasped Topaz's hand firmly and said: "Apprentices Topaz, Pho and Torch, thank you. Without your timely aid, my family and I most certainly would have perished. I am Ambassador Vassani, of the Emerald Council." Letting go of Topaz's hand, he set his now tearful daughter down, and gathered his family around him. As a group, they bowed deeply, reverently. The Apprentices returned the bow, more than a little honored.

"The honor is ours, ambassador," Topaz replied. "That you and your family are safely here, in the Realm of Light, brightens our hearts. Once we've gotten you safely to the Emerald embassy, I'd be happy to offer our services in case you find that you need anything." A full grin blossomed on his face as he roguishly counted-off possible services on his fingers: "Tours of the Cities or the Realm itself, guides to the finest topaz eateries - local or otherwise." He eyed the girls and winked at them. "Babysitting. You just name it."

Pho and Torch, who had been standing mutely in the background, turned to each other with puzzled looks then they both turned hard stares onto Topaz. The parents both burst out laughing, then regained composure.

"I will hold you to that, young man." Vassani chortled. He shared a nod with his wife then said: "I can think of no better guardians for our children than you and your partners here, while we are busy negotiating with the topaz council. Whom should I speak to when I require your services?"

As he said this, a small line of hover-cars zoomed in, parking nearby. Saul leapt out, and moved quickly towards the scene of the accident. He looked at the ruined Trans-mat disk white-faced with horror, then he saw Pho and Torch, then he saw his nephew and the Emerald family. His face went through several conflicting expressions before settling on a welcoming grin with a sparkle in his eye.

"Uncle Saul, this is Ambassador Vassani, of the Emerald Realm and his family," Topaz intoned formally. "Ambassador, this is Council-member Saul. He is the man you would have to speak to if you ever needed me again."

Saul actually did a double-take as his nephew formally introduced him then broke into deep laughter. Seeing his nephew playing the role of the confident diplomat was happily unexpected. A new facet was surfacing here, to be sure.

"Vassani, you old stump, you can keep my nephew with you for as long as you like!" Saul said through ripples of relieved mirth. The incredulous look he gave his nephew caused Topaz to grin wildly. "He was just about to be transferred to another duty anyways. I suspect he's learned all he can from his time at the Hub."

"See, girls," the woman told her children. "The nice Apprentice is going to be our guide while we are staying here."

"Will we have to ride in another transport?" asked the little one that Topaz had been holding.

"Yes, dear. But Apprentice Topaz will be with us from now on. He'll keep us safe."

The girls looked at their mother, then at Topaz then all ran over to hug him tightly. It caught him off-guard, but he found his balance. He knelt down and returned the hug.

"I'll be right there with you, the whole time," Topaz said into the tousled red hair and freckles that were attached to him now. "I'll make sure that things go *shiny* for you."

Saul watched, and knew that the right decision had been made again . . . of course. Topaz had been in the right spot at the right time. Fate's hand acts and his nephew's secret heritage is revealed, again.

On the other hand, the side effects of Topaz's intervention looked disastrous. To an outside observer, his nephew had simply made another mess, only on a grand scale. To Saul, who knew more than most, it was clear that no topaz Apprentice could have caused this kind of damage. He was sure that his nephew had used his vast potential here, and that it showed to be more than he had ever anticipated.

"Now, all we need to do is find that bungler, Citran," Pazos said quietly.

"Quite right, quite right," Saul agreed. He turned to Pho and Torch and said: "Boys, I think that you should round up the girls and make your way together to the Control Tower. Locate Citran. He needs to come with me to answer some questions." He looked over at the control tower, to see fire and smoke billowing from the windows. Hrmm...

*

The weed you know
Is always preferable.
　　　Emerald Realm saying

Chapter 21 – Change

"Yes, councillor, I'm settled in," Pazos mumbled. The image of Saul on the vid-screen of the work desk nodded.

"Good. Are you sure that you've enough supplies? I could send another convoy. It would be able to rendezvous at the Apollonian Junction."

"No. I'm sure that this convoy has more than enough relief supplies to keep the *smokies* alive for the foreseeable future. It will give me time to ascertain how and why they've gotten themselves into a state of famine."

"Pazos, you really don't have any respect for anyone who isn't photic, do you?"

"No point, really." The little man's face took on an air of condescension. To his delight, he could see Saul's face going red with restraint again. One of these days, he would goad that man into an inappropriate outburst, then he would be able to cry foul. "I will signal you when I've arrived." And with a flourish, he shut off the screen. Ha! Take that! He really was in a fine mood.

Everything was going smoothly again. The Plan was proceeding, and it was all thanks to diligence and perseverance on his part. He had every agent and spy in this Realm working at peak efficiency, slowly weakening this powerful race of people. If he tried even harder, he might even be able to move up the date for the next Phase, and that would look very good in the eyes of Necro-command.

He sat back down into the comfortable chair and stared out the window at the passing scenery. The transport convoy was moving fast enough along its rails of hard-light to make it feel like an aircraft. He pictured what this landscape would look like once the Plan came to its inevitable conclusion. It would not be so sunny, that was certain.

His imaginings were interrupted by an insistent buzzing noise coming from his pocket. Oh! Command wanted to communicate with him! He rose to his feet to dig the small black comm-box from his pocket. It buzzed again in his hand, which made him giggle with anticipation. He set it on his desk then closed all the blinds on the windows. Once he finished switching on several more privacy-assuring devices, he tapped the top of the box, and moved back.

"Topaz Realm Control," the tiny mechanical voice chirped, identifying his position and rank. "This is Command. Inspection tour arrival immanent. Standing by for final destination point. Confirm."

With a growing excitement, Pazos turned the front of the box towards the far wall and pressed a button on the side of the device. It projected a tiny black cross-hair pattern on the surface it was aimed at.

"Target destination in motion, relaying vector. Stand by." The voice cut short with a tiny squelch.

A swirling pattern of color and shadows began to appear around the cross-hairs. Pazos recognized the pattern and came to attention. Only the highest levels of command traveled using this forbidden opal technology. He wondered who it might be: maybe one of the other Lieutenants, or a new Mission Specialist to aid him in his work. It might even be Him.

The swirling pattern of colors on wall opposite him grew till it was about two meters across, then the cross-hairs became the tiny outline of two people. It grew before his eyes until, with a liquid rippling sound, the General, the highest authority in the Fleet, the man who had devised the Plan in the first place, the most powerful user of any Gem power he chose, stepped into his cabin.

He wore the black on black uniform of the Necromancer Command. His black hair was greying at the temples, but his eyes were as terrifying as ever. To Pazos' great delight, the General's second-in-command, the dour-faced older woman who was the lieutenant from the Amethyst Realm, followed a step behind the leader. Her ice-blue eyes darted around the room, searching for any sign of intruders.

"You can relax C'Ailrem, we are secure," Pazos boasted. With a sour glance for a reply, she turned and nodded to the General.

"He speaks truth, sir," she whined, her annoyance at being anticipated showing clearly. The General nodded then faced Pazos head-on.

"General, sir!" Pazos cried in his most loyal and submissive tone. He saluted crisply. "Welcome to the Topaz Realm, sir!"

"Thank you, Pazos," he replied with perfect diction and clarity, keeping his deep voice at its minimum volume. "We are headed . . . where?"

"To a village in the heart of the Calorian Plains, our brown topaz region," Pazos answered almost before the General had finished the question. "I'm part of a traveling delegation from the Ruling Council, tasked to find out why there is a 'shortage of food' in their outlying villages." Pazos grinned at this. "Part of the Alienation Phase, sir. Of course, I'm going to make sure that the famines continue, unhindered by anyone who might try to send aid."

"Ah, good." The General spoke lightly, but his feral stare stayed locked on his topaz lieutenant's face. "I've reviewed your reports thus far, Pazos, and overall, I'm pleased with your progress. I'll be wanting a full briefing as to the state of this Realm's society, but there are a couple of items that I felt bore investigation before we begin. I'm sure that you'll be able to help me with that."

"Absolutely, sir!" Pazos nearly cheered. "Which items do you mean?"

"You reported that at the last Apprenticing ceremony that you experienced a . . ." C'Ailrem purred, as she moved to a position beside Pazos, facing him. ". . . a breakdown in the Dimensional Diverters that we integrated into the portal system that leads to the planetary Core. As a result, five graduating students got the chance to commune with the *real* Heart of Light, and thus are now fully-realized Apprentices."

Pazos kept a mild expression on his face, but her words damaged his calm. Of course, she had to start with the one incident he was still trying to understand. He took a second to compose himself then said: "Yes, that was an unfortunate and unanticipated accident. Everything was going smoothly when there was a sudden spike in energy from inside the transit wormhole. All four Diverters reset themselves to neutral d-pull. The five students were sent to the Core, and not ours."

245

"That makes no sense," she snapped. "You examined the travelers? Did any of them have any devices or prosthetics that might have caused a surge?"

Pazos found he could grin. Did she really think that he was so incompetent as to forget that? She might have been trying to rub salt on a perceived wound, but he was confident enough to enjoy her attempt.

"Yes, the travelers were the first thing I checked. They had nothing with them but the clothes they were wearing when they entered. All were in good health, and had all of their original parts."

"Show me their entry," the General ordered, his smooth, deep voice cutting the argument short. Pazos waved his hand in the air, activating the holo-projector in the ceiling. Several icons appeared hovering in the air. Pazos tapped an un-named file, and a vid of the entire Apprenticing ceremony started playing. The General and C'Ailrem moved closer to the hologram to watch. Pazos scrolled the file forward till the image of Topaz, Pho, Sollen, Torch and Ebbella entering the portal came into focus. It played all the way through till the five of them touched the Core.

"Replay this," the General ordered. Pazos complied, resetting the vid.

"Stop there." the General interjected. The image froze. The holo showed Topaz when he had just stopped in front of the disk, seemingly distracted by the portals shimmering surface. "What is that boy doing?"

"Him? Oh, that's the nephew of one of my least favorite people on the Council. He's a distracted bungler. The best I can surmise is that he was fascinated by the pretty colors like a toddler. He's like that; I have years of reports from his teachers, and from various agents that were in his classes that he's always been *focus-fuzzed*."

"Huh," the General mused, eyes locked on image locked on the screen. "Did that child produce any radiant energy before he passed the threshold?"

"No sir. Even now, he's barely able to call on the Light, despite having touched the Core. He definitely wasn't generating energy of any recognizable kind that day."

"His name?"

"Topaz, of the Rudiments Schools."

"Er, how's that again?" the General seemed to caught off-guard this. "He's named after the Realm itself?"

"Yes, sir. In our Rudiments Schools, you are called by the name of your home-world. That boy is the only native citizen to attend them. His birth name is irrelevant, for all intents and purposes. I don't even remember what it is."

The General stared at the image closely for another few moments, then turned to C'Ailrem, who nodded, then took up a position behind Pazos.

"When did we recruit you, Pazos?" he drawled slowly, his fingers tapping a pattern on the surface of the console. The Amethyst woman moved to stand beside Pazos, facing him, her shoulder crystal glowing a dark purple. Pazos had been inspected by ranking Fleet officials before, but never the General himself. The presence of the Mind-witch must be part of the general's form of inspection. He guessed the General required loyalty to such a degree that she would be used to confirm it. This thought put him back at ease - the most alert, attentive form of *ease* imaginable, of course.

"Over thirty years ago, sir," Pazos chirped helpfully. "I had just been passed over as an Apprentice candidate when you came to me, and offered me the Power of the Shadows."

"I remember now. You had been striving so hard to make that final cut that when the Committee chose that other fellow."

"I didn't take the failure well at all and had to be removed to a hospital for a bit. You met me there and offered me power equal to that of any Adept of the Spectrum. Power and the chance to work with you towards the goal of completing the Plan."

"Mm-hmmm," nodded the General. "And you've been quite useful to us, to be sure. Our first team of spies had no way of affecting anything on a broad scale. We had resigned ourselves to infiltration of their media network bit by bit. With the knowledge you possessed of your own people, we were able to tailor the Plan to this world far more effectively." The General stared out at the passing grasslands.

"Yes, sir."

"And you seem to have done well for yourself with shadow-powers we granted you."

"Yes sir! As a member of the Council here, I'm perfectly positioned to effect any change that the Plan requires, not to mention that I'm about to outrank my old rival, which has been the sweetest revenge possible."

"You mentioned the Plan, earlier. I notice that there have been some . . . *glitches* . . . happening," he began, drawing slow swirling shapes in the air with a finger as he spoke. "Not just the Apprentices, but other matters too." He started counting them off: "The Emerald Ambassador who was *not* assassinated; the shutting down of several of the solar energy collector banks; you have been losing some of your more complex shadow constructs. These are irregularities that you've yet to account for." The General swiveled his chair back towards Pazos, glancing over his shoulder at him. "We cannot afford to have irregularities, Pazos."

Pazos gulped quietly as he realized that maybe the General wasn't as pleased with him as he had expected.

"Glitches, yes sir," he chittered, sudden fear pinching his voice into an animal's squeak for a moment. "Every covert operation has unexpected occurrences that cannot be accounted for. Our progress here is not that different from any of the other realms."

The General turned the chair forward again and pulled up a holo of Pazos' reports for the past fifteen years. He enlarged the section regarding the Apprenticing ceremony.

"I guess that covers my first question, then. My second question revolves around a personal choice you made." He scrolled through forest of words till he found the passage he was looking for. "You mention here that you forced this bungler of a student into the candidate group in the first place? According to his records, he was completely unqualified, yet now he's going about life a fully powered Apprentice of the Light. What were you thinking?"

"As I said later on in that same report, sir, the boy is the nephew of Saul, our biggest stumbling block on the Council. I had hoped that the Core would reject someone so plainly unqualified. I know that he would have been destroyed had they all gone to *our* Core. It was all very carefully planned out." Pazos felt the layers and steps of his plan flash though his head. He was sure that C'Ailrem had seen them too. "With the nephew of so prominent a councillor as Saul disgraced or dead, then morale of the populace would have gone down by a significant degree. They would have gotten visible proof that their Core was 'dying'. I would have been able to use the fear and doubt that it would have created to pull us ahead even faster, sir." A tiny drop of sweat gathered together on his forehead and made its way down along his jaw-line. Pazos was so wound up now that he didn't even notice.

"True. This was a carefully thought-out idea, Pazos. And the results of success would have been wonderful, on one level." The General may have said the words lightly, but they echoed through Pazos like a warning siren. "By speeding up progress here, on Topaz, you have made it necessary for other worlds to alter their schedules before optimal, to compensate."

Pazos could only stare as he heard this. The Plan mandated that whenever he could, he should take advantage of the situations that arose, and bend them towards the final goal.

"The Fleet will not be ready to advance on this Realm for at least 3 to 4 years. If we are to drain all the power and usable resources that we need out of this rock, then we must pace ourselves and strike at the right time. Surely you see this, don't you?"

"Y-yes sir," Pazos whispered his eyes wide with all the possible ways that he *could* be punished for his impatience. Most of them were . . . not very pleasant. The best he could hope for now was the chance to show just how quickly he could learn how to be patient.

"I will be staying in this Realm for the next little while," the General declared, seemingly changing topics. "I will need all of your knowledge and experience to be available to me for the duration."

"Of course, sir!" Pazos could see a light at the end of this darkening tunnel. "I'm sure that I would be able to find you lodgings and explain your high-level clearance to anyone. I can have a private shuttle ferry you to the Capital at any time, sir."

The General lowered his eyes and shook his head, his expression almost a smile.

"No, Pazos," he purred. "That's not what I had in mind." He looked up and his eyes were swirling with every color imaginable now. His own, dark shoulder crystal was starting to glow. Beneath a haze of black and purple, all the colors of the rainbow started swirling across its smooth, rounded surface.

"I don't want you to arrange anything for me. I'll take care of that myself . . ." he continued. As he spoke, his appearance began to shift. It wasn't like a Glamour field, the General's face and body were actually changing. Within a few moments, the General was looking like a mirror-image of . . . Pazos.

". . . because, after this, I will be you." the duplicate of Pazos said, in Pazos' own voice.

With a startling swiftness, the real Pazos felt something happening to him. From his point of view, it felt as if he were being pulled by an unstoppable force, through an opening smaller than himself. He didn't even have time to react before he could feel himself pulled free and forced into a much smaller container than he had been in before. It was cold, there. He tried to say something, but had no voice . . . or mouth . . . or limbs. Then, everything went black.

*

"Is he stored?" the new Pazos inquired.

"Yes, sir," C'Ailrem said, turning the glowing purple crystal over in her hands. "The mind is in stasis, ready for storage." She opened a small case on her belt, and popped the crystal into it, wedging it between other purple crystals, some glowing, some not. "I'll take the transfer back with me. It should take my team about three hours to strip it down so that its memories can be integrated into your m.-filing system without any interference from the previous personality."

"Make it two hours," he replied. "I don't need to know his favorite color, or the name of his first pet. Just distill out the useful information, and disperse the rest."

"Yes sir."

With a wave of the General's hand, bands of aquamarine-colored energy encircled the inert and empty shell of what had once been Pazos, now crumpled on the floor. Within moments, the very molecules of the corpse disassembled themselves with a quiet whoosh of air. The General would have to make sure that the cleaning systems on this transport did a good job in here. With another wave of his hand, the far wall became swirling color again. C'Ailrem saluted then stepped through, back to her home world.

The General moved to sit down in Pazos' chair. He had to grin as he noted that the ambitious little toad even had monogramed stationary. He would have to lay it on fairly thick to get this role just right. C'Ailrem had better hurry with her task, though. He hated having to improvise without backup.

*

Saul got his confirmation call from Pazos right on time. Curse the man, he was nothing if not punctual. He tapped the comm-screen, and braced himself for the usual banter.

"Pazos reporting it," the little man said. "We've arrived. The clerks are handling food distribution now. The Adepts were sent out just a few minutes ago to see what they could learn."

"That's fine. They have my full blessing. Call back if you find anything serious."

"Absolutely. Not a problem. Pazos out."

Click. The screen went dead.

Saul had to tap it a few times to check that it had not just shorted out. No, it was still working just fine. Pazos had cut him off. He had not taken any opportunity to gloat, to hurl a veiled insult . . . nothing. He hadn't even followed comm-protocol for official Council business. Every instinct Saul possessed screamed at him now that something significant had just happened, and that things were very different now. He shuddered to think what that might mean.

*

May the Way find you.
   Opal blessing

Chapter 22 – Ascension

Every Apprentices of his generation across the whole of the Realm was excited today. They were all busily getting their finest clothes on with their most visible badges of office and decorations. For the Apprentices of the Light, a day like this was once in a lifetime.

"How do I look? How do I look?" a petite, flaxen haired Apprentice girl asked Topaz as he finished polishing his boots. The Central bunkers were crowded beyond capacity, so even Topaz was forced to share the meager dormitory that had once housed the five of them with two visiting squads from other cities. This little princess who usually ignored him was from the squad that the media was calling the Prime, since they were hailed as being among the most "gifted" of their generation. Topaz knew that this meant that they could create many pretty light-shows, and project Glam-fields better than anyone on the planet. He had to remind himself to keep from showing them up since both Dellas and Uncle Saul agreed that

253

if he and his team were to be effective in the battle to come, then they had to stay undetected. This meant that he kept his peace and tried to help this team, and the utter morons in the other group, to make themselves comfortable. They were only staying one day, so the chaos was bearable.

She had asked him a question, so he looked over at the girl from the table he was working at, examining her outfit and hair, as he suspected she wanted him to, and said:

"You look fine. Nothings out of place."

"Oh, good...good." she said, distractedly passing a brush once more through her hair. He suspected that hair-brushing must have been a source of comfort for her, since she hadn't stopped once all morning. She wandered off to gather the rest of her squad for departure.

Topaz let himself grin slightly. He was relaxed today, because the source of all the commotion was not likely to bother with him today. Today, the Gateways would open . . . the one opportunity that his generation would have to go to the Academy. No, he corrected himself . . . *Academies*. There were more than just the one, now, and the new ones were said to be just as amazing as the original. Well, that was the rumor. Most of those going to the Ascension ceremony knew that they were going to be passed over, and thus lose their chance. Topaz felt comfortable in the knowledge that he was most assuredly destined to be one of these. Odd confidence, but it was enough for him.

He re-attached the shimmering, slightly iridescent cloak that came with his specialized Apprentice uniform, and moved to join the others. They all filed into the airship and found seats. The doors hissed shut, and the graceful craft rose from the ground and sped off towards the site of the Ascension. It was an official transport, and already carried at least fifty other young Apprentices from around the Realm. Topaz's dorm was the last on the route, being closest to the

Capital. The discussion amongst the youth assembled here
was lively enough. Each had an area of expertise, and they sat
accordingly. There were no generalists like Topaz himself,
and so he sat at the front of the vehicle, staring out at the
passing landscape. It was a major population center, with all
of the industry and problems that many people living near to
each other brought.

He didn't even have the support of his four friends for
this trip. Sollen had been the first to get re-assigned. She was
now stationed back in the Blue Islands, where her Singing
talents were being used again. Pho was working with the
Security forces, assault division; Torch was in a foundry now.
Ebbella had vanished, but that was nothing new for her. If she
had been reassigned, then he would learn about her new job
when they met again. Topaz had grown quite fond of her
mannerism and more than respected her quiet wisdom. There
was always more that she could say, but usually didn't. If
there was ever someone that Topaz meant very much to visit,
it was her. He would get to the Hidden Villages eventually, of
this he was sure. They passed through the city's industrial
belt, where many of them had practiced finer control of their
powers apprenticing at the factories and assembly plants there.
Though electronics and manufacturing were not trades native
to the topaz realm, some off world companies - especially
from the sapphire or garnet Realms - still maintained a
presence here. This city was big enough that it even boasted a
Ruby Combat training center, and an arboretum maintained by
the Emeralds. Someday, Topaz mused to himself, he would
go to those establishments, just to see what they were like.

The transport slowly descended onto the road next to
an open field. Other transports were already there. The
Apprentices all debarked and scattered, joining with families
that they hadn't seen for a long time now. Since his uncle was
working on behalf of the Network, he would not be able to

attend. That was alright by Topaz. It gave him the freedom to move around as needed. To his very great surprise, there was, in fact, a small group of people waiting specifically for him. They spotted him then cheered, rushing forward to greet him. Topaz recognized them at once, grinning.

"Topaz! We're so glad you came!" cried a young copper-haired girl wearing deep green. She ran up and clamped her slender arms around his waist, in a ferocious hug. Two girls, one clearly a younger sister of the first one, and the other, a little older with pale strawberry-blond hair with a tint of green, approached and joined their sister in hugging him.

"Err...thanks," he said, blushing hotly, still grinning. He had never refused hugs like these but certainly would never get accustomed to them landing on him without any warning.

"Thank you for all you've done," said the mother, who came forward, prying her daughters off of him. The consular crest on her deep green jacket confirmed that this was ambassador Vassani's family. "We all hope that you are chosen to go on to the Academy. You deserve it," she said, kissing him on both cheeks then wiping a happy tear from her eye.

After their somewhat miraculous rescue, he and his friends had been honored guests at the Emerald Embassy for several nights. The girls had adopted him in particular, claiming their babysitter all to themselves more than once.

The middle daughter, all bright red hair, sparkling blue eyes and freckles, pulled Topaz to one side and whispered: "I saw someone get out of a black shuttle pod, right before you got here. He gave me the creeps. Be careful. I'm pretty sure he's the same guy who led the Apprentice selection committee." Topaz raised an eyebrow at her, in inquiry. "It's true!" she proclaimed. "I watched the vid of your Apprenticing ceremony a bunch of times. It's the same mean-faced man that was the announcer back then."

"Ok, ok, I believe you," Topaz said hastily. "Relax. That would be Pazos, then. I've known him all my life. He's been trying to blow me up or drive me crazy since I was a toddler. I don't think he'll be any luckier today." He put on a rakish grin and looked as much a rogue as he could. "Too many people."

The girl smiled, reassured. Nodding firmly, she declared: "Alright then. Just be careful!" She gave him one last quick hug and then ran to join her family.

With well-wishers behind him, he passed through the wrought-iron gates into wide parkland. It was very early summer, so all the trees and flowers were covered with blossoms. There were little sparkling insects buzzing everywhere. Several pathways lead off in different directions. Dead center of the area, the lights and sounds showed a gathering of many people. Topaz hurried along, merging with the throng of people there.

Standing on a podium, Pazos was decked out in his finest array today, with all of his awards and decorations in full-polished-mode. Uncle Saul was right: this little man truly was enamored with himself.

"Ladies and gentlemen!" the man said, his shrill voice ringing clear over the din of the crowds. "I am _councillor_ Pazos, and I am searching," The assembled people grew quieter as he spoke. "I am searching for the strongest, wisest, most gifted Apprentices on this world. I am here to find them and help them on their way to higher learning. I come to find our candidates for the Academies!"

Everyone cheered wildly.

"We will, this year, be choosing our representatives based on the results of several contests."

Contests? That was new. No one had mentioned anything about there being any kind of competition at this point. In fact, his uncle had said that this was a pretty straightforward ceremony. Pazos had changed things to suit his own whims, again. This meant that Topaz would have to be triple-vigilant today. It was situations like this that usually meant the Necromancers were up to something. He tried to find his four friends with his eyes, to at least let them know what he suspects.

"If you think you have the skill, the desire and the power to move on, to the Academies, step up to the podium now."

There was no ambiguity in the response of the crowd this time. All of the Apprentices of his generation stepped forward, Topaz included.

*

The contests were spectacular, to say the least. Every skill that the Apprentices had ever learned was required of them as they navigated mazes and obstacle courses, solved puzzles and riddles, constructed and used hard-light forms of all shapes and sizes. There were even a few actual foot-races and strength competitions. The winners moved on, the losers withdrew.

After two hours, Topaz still could not really tell how he was doing. He guessed that he was doing well enough, since he had reached what he thought were the finals of the competition. From a crowd of over two hundred, only thirty remained, and he was still among them. Maybe he would let himself hope just a little bit, now.

Pazos projected the final list of representatives above him. Only five people were eliminated. The group of twenty-five people left standing in the contest area looked stunned but elated. It was larger than any list of representatives had ever been. The crowds of family and well-wishers started muttering about how large the group was, until they all remembered that there was more than one Academy now. They could send up to ten representatives to each school.

Pazos had included a number from one to three beside each projected name. That guided the winners to divide into three groups. The first was clearly the most powerful. His friends, Pho and Torch, had made it there. The second group was the more subtle and clever of the Apprentices. He could see Sollen there.

Then, there was the third group, where Topaz himself was, in which all the remainders had been placed - lower powered Apprentices, skilled citizens, there were even a couple of aquamarine girls masquerading as blue topazes. This was the misfit group, clearly. It didn't bother Topaz, though. He was happy to just be here. Upon entry, he hadn't had any aspirations of succeeding, but now that he was up there, and still a contender, he felt the stirrings of hope inside of him.

Out of the corner of his eye, Topaz took a look at Pazos, and caught his breath. He could see why his little friend had warned him. After all was said and done, his uncle's greatest rival looked just a hint darker than usual. Topaz's blinked many times to make sure that he was seeing auras, and not just a trick of over-tired eyes.

"Truly the Core has chosen wisely this year, as the contests were accomplished with unusual skill, by everyone." he said, waving his hand over a control on the podium. A series of three archways materialized behind him. Two were a vibrant array of flashing lights and evident sapphire technology. The third was just an irregular, dun yellow circle of opaque mineral, no lights, and no glamour.

"It is the time, Apprentices. Now, you will be transported to one of the three greatest academies of higher learning. I can only send six of you through the first two gates." He paused to take a sip of water at this point then pointed to the first one, festooned with glittering lights and sparkling displays. "This one leads to the newest facility. It has the highest success rate of any Academy in the known galaxy. Only the strongest will find glory there. First group, GO! The first six through the gate are the ones chosen." With a wave of his hand, the first arch became a swirling portal.

Topaz tried to look more closely at the destination, as he had when he had used a portal like this to go the topaz Core, but there were too many other distractions about for him to see more that blurry shadows. One thing he did notice, though, was that as the first group ran towards their goal, a beam of pulsing shadow started to open a different destination. It was subtle, only visible if you were staring straight at it, Topaz surmised. Then the first Apprentice crossed the threshold. She passed the boundary, and her image began to fade. Topaz thought he saw her expression change from joy to one of fear, just as she faded from view. The rest of the group was entering now. Each one who passed the gate was whisked away, but their faces all became masks of fear as they started to travel. Topaz didn't understand, but his instincts told him that nothing here was as it should be. He could see Pho and Torch about to enter, and knew that his friends were in danger, though he could not say how. He called to the Core of the Realm to help him and his friend. It responded instantly to his call by charging up Pho and Torch with massive amounts of energy. The surge they were now generating shorted out the gate's systems, and the portal collapsed in a flash of bright yellow light.

"Ah well, I guess we only get four representatives at that school. The gate has closed on them." said the announcer smoothly. "Off you go, boys."

Pho's face was a grimace of frustration, but he bowed with good grace and moved away from the stage. He exchanged glances with Topaz as he passed, and sighed heavily, conveying the depths of his frustration. Strangely enough, Topaz was relieved. His friend was now safe from this nameless threat. When he looked over at Sollen, she was staring at him hard, asking the silent question: *Ok-what-just-happened?* There were residual sparks flashing in her hair. The Core had sent a pulse to her as well, it seemed. Topaz pointed to gate number 2 and shook his head, then to gate number three and shrugged. Sollen got a decidedly suspicious look in her eye, and started edging away from the group she was in, though she didn't get far.

"All remaining who wish to ascend can approach the remaining gates, and choose."

The announcer waved a hand and the second gate lit up. The third gate just stayed the same.

Topaz hung back as the faster and stronger ones in the group pelted towards their gate of choice. Most went towards the other shining gate, and vanished. A couple went to the older one. They vanished, just as the others had, but Topaz could see a beam of light exit it, instead of shadow. That was all he needed to see. He waited for the last of the groups to go - Pho, Sollen and Torch included – before moving forward. He noticed one extra ripple on the event horizon of the third gate, which he surmised was Ebbella travelling too. He hoped so. Now it was just him, so he decided to test his growing theory. He moved towards the second gate, all glitz and surely a fair dose of Glamour. He didn't go more than twenty steps before his confirmation appeared.

Pazos stepped in front of him, barring his path and shaking his head. In a quiet voice, he said "Not you, child. You don't deserve the honor of going through the second gate. A *dim-glow* like you shouldn't even be here. You will go through that gate." indicating the older one. Topaz blinked then nodded; face as impassive as he could make it. As he suspected, Pazos had prevented him from going to what was supposedly the better of the two remaining gates. Wasn't it interesting that this man had used one of his childhood nicknames, he thought to himself.

He walked over to the older gate and took a good look at it. Just as ornate as the other two, as it turned out, but it was made of what looked like one solid piece of mineral, instead of layers of mechanisms. The swirl of color and light within it clearly resembled the portal he had seen before, and so he took a chance and addressed it.

"Hello again," he said to it, quietly. The mineral in the archway seemed to glow faintly at his voice and approach.

He passed through the threshold, and he could hear a few small voices cheering for him. He turned to see the family, his friends and all the others who had graduated with him, all applauding as he faded. The last face he saw was that of Pazos, yet it wasn't. Topaz' aura sight was showing him the shadow of a different set of features. Both faces were grinning wolfishly, smug and satisfied.

As unsettling as this was, Topaz felt immense relief overwhelm his senses. Finally, he was safe. At the Academy, he would have the chance to start fresh. That dark little man could do him no harm, anymore. He was free.

As before, he could feel the pull of the destination drawing him forward. He watched the bright yellow speck that was his home pull farther and farther away from him, and he felt only a little bit nervous. A new adventure was waiting for him.

"Goodbye uncle, thank you," he murmured into the tunnel. "I'll be back as soon as I can."

*

And like that, the hidden boy made his way to the very place that he needed to be. His first trials were over, and he had passed them brilliantly. His next trials would be of a very different nature.

*

Postlude – Class

"Don't forget to close the door, boy!" the old woman barked at him from her laundry-hanging job, through her thick accent as Topaz started to leave. He nodded, turning to slide the screen door to the porch shut. He waved and descended the stairs from the backyard porch onto the pathway out to the street and started walking. He passed by many quiet little houses, all of them one or two bedrooms, most of them tidy and in good repair. The pavement was cracked and un-even enough to show that this particular neighborhood was as old as most of the residents of the houses. The deep night sky was startlingly black, scattered with strange bright stars.

In a sense, it was a good thing that he had arrived last of his group to the Academy. That meant that he had needed to find lodging outside of the main dormitories. That suited Topaz just fine, since he knew himself to be somewhat shy when meeting new people, and that it usually took him longer to learn his lessons and that others usually found that frustrating. The old woman, Blanche, who had rented a room to him, was kind enough despite having some "interesting" quirks about her. It was a different experience, to be certain.

She had taught at the Academy herself many, many years earlier. He had never before known anyone who had powers of the gem Citrine, which she had said was similar to topaz in many ways. The Residence Services Office had placed him there because of that. She had helped him settle in nicely enough, guiding him through the initial registrations and making sure that he knew what to expect. He felt her to be a little stifling, but he appreciated the time she was taking to make sure that he was able to function here. Clearly, she had billeted other students here before.

His room was at the back of her small house, across the street from a Medical center, where Amethysts, Aquamarines and Peridots learned how to administer care to the injured and infirm. He could get in through her back yard. It was a small, blank room with a raised bed, a shelf, and a closet. The back of the closet was actually the rumbling, gurgling back of the old woman's food cooler, and it churned relentlessly, trying to keep odd bits of half-eaten meals cool. It was certainly a novel experience; he had lived with his uncle his whole life, periodically staying in the dorms of residential schools. For the first time, his time was his own.

The Academy itself was mostly inside the small planet. The surface of the barren rock had been terra-formed and various invisible systems kept atmosphere in and harmful radiation from space out. There was a sun too, that rose and set. Only one, though, and it was artificial at that. He could probably set up a holo-display of the view from his uncle's cottage in the Blue Islands if it became a problem. Blanche had said most of the students who came to the Academy started out living on the surface, before moving underground for more intensive studies. There were many support staff and retired teachers on the surface as well. This made for several small communities scattered about the surface, linked by various transit services. And, of course, there were hundreds of elevators and teleport disks of various types.

Topaz flipped up the tiny 2D screen on the wrist-band that he had been given when he first stepped from the portal into the sprawling receiving center. The attendant in his metallic silver and grey body suit and cloak, waiting for the Apprentices from the Realm of Light, had handed them each one. His had shifted colors a few times before becoming a pale yellow. It hadn't taken very long for him to learn about the various things this gift could do, like act as a full sensory recording device, or a personal comm system. It was also his map of the Academy.

Scrolling the tiny image back and forth a few times, he found where he was, and where the particular elevator that he needed was to be found. The next block had several of them, so he walked at a brisk pace. It was the night cycle, the singular artificial sun on the other side of the planetoid. The deep shadows of the night sky filled with strange stars twinkling at him made him stop and just stare a few times. He was struck dumb by the immense beauty he was looking at. It was never allowed to get this dark, back home. Depending on his schedule, he knew that He would have to try to get out here as often as he could. Though he was farther from his home than He had ever conceived of, he was still too much in shock to feel any fear yet. He did feel kind of small when he stared into the vast blackness. He was not frightened of that darkness. It wasn't like the shadow worms from his home world, nor the black auras that surrounded those who his uncle knew to be spies of the "enemy". This darkness was gentle, full of secrets and treasures, light from stars that had been traveling millions of years to reach his eyes. He was seeing the history of the entire Universe by just looking into the night sky. It was humbling for him, and indescribably appealing.

He would have to file those thoughts away, though. No topaz citizen would have ever thought these kinds of things. Any "normal" person would have been frightened by the absence of illumination, and retreated into some well-lit place. One of his fervent hopes was that he would be able to learn enough about the topaz Spectrum that he would be able to understand why he was so different from everyone back home. What kind of topaz Apprentice was he? Maybe there was a teacher or a reference book that could help him understand the cryptic words the Core of Light had said to him. Many questions filled him. Maybe he would get answers here.

He finished his first voyage of discovery as he entered glass doors at the base of a tall, glass-covered tower. There were at least twenty elevators lining all visible walls. Each had a number and color code etched into the door. Some went up into the building, but most went down. He could not find door 10-22 initially. A hint of the fears that he had endured from his early childhood reared their ugly little heads in his imagination. Had someone sent him the wrong times, or the wrong elevator coding? He was far removed from all the tormentors of his childhood, but were there new ones here, waiting for him? He chalked all of these apprehensions to the newness of this experience. He was making his way on his own now. Persistence would be the key, and that was proved to him right away . . . by his finding of the right elevator door, in the farthest back corner of room.

*

The door to the left whooshed open, and Topaz stepped out into a bustling hallway. People of every age and type milled about, back and forth. All of them bore some variation of the Academy uniform that he himself wore: tunic colored to match the planet you came from, trousers of a neutral or complementary color. He remembered to look at the stylized pips on the left shoulder, which told one what year each person was in. His own solitary pip announced to all and sundry his first-year status. He watched, seeing as many and seven or eight pips on the shoulders walking by. He was taller than many, but nonetheless felt self-conscious. He tried to pick out any others who would be in his class. He spotted one, a fair skinned, brown haired girl in deep blue. She must be of the sapphire realm, then. He walked down the corridor, spotting a very large, blond fellow, in a light green jumpsuit, who was laughing infectiously at something he was being shown by a muscular brown-haired boy in bright red . . . Peridot and ruby, surely.

He could feel part of himself shrink into its protective shell as more and more people his age started walking in the same direction he was. Back home, whenever a crowd of young people his own age was going the same way he was, it meant that he was about to be beset upon by bullies. This was the same sort of situation, and he could feel himself preparing for something unpleasant to happen. After having become an Apprentice, the actual bullying had ceased, but one cannot help but keenly remember the feelings of being a victim.

To his surprise, nothing bad happened. In fact, most of the kids around him said hi, waved, smiled in some cases, but all acknowledging him in some friendly manner. He blinked, returned the waves, tried to grin. Deep inside, that tiny, untouchable core of himself that he had always kept safe from the stinging and cruel words had to pause and re-evaluate things. This was a new scene, a new place for learning. His reputation of incompetence had not followed him here, thus far. Maybe he truly had escaped his past. He told that part of himself that he would try to keep an open mind. The voices of his inner demons faded back to just a whisper again.

He made his way into the first class that his schedule had told him he needed to attend. He was one of about forty students who were making their way in from the corridor. He supposed it was an introductory course, or maybe orientation. He had been in so many different schools back home that he was somewhat familiar now with the mind-set of "teachers". It would be interesting to see how things were done here, what variations were used.

The classroom itself was very large, with a high vaulted ceiling. There was a large display on the wall at the front of room. To the side was a large workstation . . . clearly for the teacher. The student desks were similar to the teacher's desk: solid looking, more like sculpted work surfaces, with a personal display each. The seats looked comfortable, and swiveled. It looked as if they were able to be adjusted for height, too. It was surrounded on three sides by smooth surfaces. The material of the desk merged smoothly with the floor, as if it had grown out of it. A flat monitor screen faced the seat from the front of the desk, but no keyboard or other input device could be seen.

"Students, please find your seats," said a gentle voice from each of the desks. "As soon as you are all sitting, we will begin." With a quiet murmuring, the first year students all found seats. Topaz aimed himself towards the back of the room, finding the last empty station in the back right-hand corner of the room. As soon as he sat, the screen at the terminal lit up. No images presented themselves, but the voice that had spoken earlier addressed him.

"Thank you," it said, in a gentle voice. "Welcome to the Academy. The voice you are hearing is part of the Academy Central Computer's orientation program. For the first few weeks, we will be tailoring your course of study to your specific needs and abilities. All of you have come from different worlds, different schooling systems. The Academy was designed to help you develop into your fullest potential, regardless of prior experience." A few of his classmates murmured to each other but most just watched mutely. "We will begin by filling out a few information sheets about you. Please choose your preferred method of data entry." And with that, several objects appeared on the desks. There were a couple of sheets of paper and a cup holding various writing tools, a variable configuration keyboard and a microphone / headset assembly. There was a box there as well, containing many small metallic shapes in it. Finally, there were a series of bracelets and headbands.

Topaz looked at the paper, and knew right away that he would not choose it . . . his handwriting was frightful. He examined and poked at the metallic shapes in the box. These were interesting, but he had no idea what they were. The keyboard appealed to him though, so he pulled it closer to himself. It lit up when he touched it, and the other objects faded from view except for a headset/microphone that had lit up with the keyboard. Clearly the two went together, so he pulled them over his ears, and positioned the tiny microphone near to his chin.

"Now that you have all chosen your media, you may begin," the voice came over Topaz's headset. It filled his ear with sound, and it blocked out any stray sounds from the classroom. He knew that this would help him with his distractibility. The screen in front of him came to life, and a series of multiple-choice questions appeared.

He answered all of the detail questions easily enough, though the system seemed to glitch when he keyed in that his home world was the Topaz Realm. He had to enter it twice before the screen's display flashed a rapid series of symbols and then returned to normal.

Interesting as that was, the questions themselves were fascinating. One asked him if a Ruby or a Garnet would be better suited to move such and such a weight, another asked him about historical trivia from the Diamond Realm. He did his best to answer what he could, but it was clear that for some topics, he no clue.

"There is no right or wrong answer, Topaz," the voice in his headset said to him. "We just want to learn everything we can about you, so that we can work out an appropriate course of study. If you need to take a few minutes to rest, then feel free to do so. The terminal will remember where you got to when you return."

"Thank you," he said, out of habit. "Tell me, are you a computer or a person?"

"Yes," the voice said, somewhat cryptically. "The voice you are hearing is part of the Academy Computer. However, you will eventually learn that here, at the Academy, the difference between mind and machine is not as clear as you might think." With a click, Topaz could tell that his conversation was over, so he took off his headset and rose to his feet. He hadn't realized that his back was stiff. Looking up at the chronometer on the wall, he was shocked to see that several hours had passed. There were two others taking a break too. One was that ruby boy that he had seen earlier. The other was a dark skinned emerald fellow. Both looked as brain-tired as he was, so, with an astoundingly out-of-character cheerfulness, he approached them and introduced himself.

"Hi." Topaz said, his most friendly smile firmly in place.

"Hello." they answered. Rubin, in his red tinted tunic, reached out a hand in greetings. Topaz walked over and shook it. True to his gem-type, Rubin had a crushing handshake. Merald's grip was more genteel. Both were friendly enough. Topaz found himself feeling a little bit shy, speaking to boys his own age from other Realms. They did not seem too aggressive, and there was not one hint of shadow surrounding them.

"I'm Topaz," he said, introducing himself. He held up his right hand, calling forth a star-burst of greeting - after all, manners mattered. The tiny star of light lit up initially but then to Topaz's vast horror, it blurred. He blushed then looked over at fellows he was meeting. They seemed impressed, so they replied in kind: Rubin calling a gentle, steady flame into his hand, and Merald causing the image of a leaf to appear. Topaz closed his hand, and started thinking furiously.

"Nice to meet ya," Rubin piped up, banishing the flame with a wave of his hand. "So, testing, huh? Figures. It is the 'Academy', after all."

Merald nodded, adding: "Makes sense. This place teaches all, so it must have many different options available for us to use. It's a good thing that you figured out how to use the ambient heat to made flame, Rubin. Your reserve of Ruby power doesn't get depleted that way."

"Reserve?" Topaz sputtered in a distracted stutter. "We can't access the Core of our worlds here?"

Rubin shook his head. "Nope. My father tells me that when the Gates closed, all the Apprentices of the other Realms had only the energy within them to draw on when they were off-world. They had to return home after a while to re-charge, or use the ambient energy around them for any of their gem skills."

Merald was nodding along with Rubin's words, clearly having heard him say them before. Topaz added this new information to the growing list of topics that he just had to research, when he could.

"Wasn't expecting that. It changes all sorts of things, I guess," Topaz mused aloud. His new friends simply shrugged, and went back to their desks. Rubin had a larger, touch interactive display on his desk, which resumed displaying questions in the spiky flame-like font that the Ruby Realm used most. Merald waved to Topaz and returned to his own desk. A stack of papers and a stylus appeared there, which he dove into with ease.

"Heart of Light, guide me," Topaz prayed silently as he sat back down. He noticed that when he sat down, a tiny arm shot out of the back of his seat, sent a scanning beam into his shoulder crystal, then retracted immediately. The display lit up again, and the headset and keyboard materialized right where Topaz had left them. There was going to be more to learn here than he had ever suspected. And he was back at the dim end of the light-show in terms of his control over the Light, which reminded him of his childhood again. The frustration of having to start over again made him answer the questions a wee bit quicker.

*****

ABOUT THE AUTHOR

Jeffrey A. Gartshore has been a teacher for over 20 years. His has a beautiful wife, 2 remarkable children, 2 fluffy cats, and many students, both private (one of whom plays a peacock blue cello) and in school (where he works to convince them that they CAN speak French, and that they can sing.)

He is sometimes a concert cellist. Other times, he is an actor. He is the program director of the Algoma Music Camp, in Northern Ontario.

He writes in his spare time.

Manufactured by Amazon.ca
Bolton, ON